Shadows
Anderson Black Ops, Book One

Written By
Melod Anne

With
John Henley

All rights reserved. Except for use in any review, the reproduction or utilization of this work in whole or in part in any form by any electronic, mechanical or other means, now known or hereafter invented, including xerography, photocopying and recording, or in any information storage or retrieval system, is forbidden without the written permission of the author.
Copyright © 2020 Melody Anne

This is a work of fiction. Names, characters, places and incidents are either the product of the author's imagination or are used fictitiously and any resemblance to actual persons, living or dead, business establishments, events or locales is entirely coincidental. Beeville is a fictional town.

Printed and published in the United States of America.
Published by Falling Star Publications
Editing by Karen Lawson and Janet Hitchcock

Dedication

This book is dedicated to the men and women who serve, who keep us safe, and who ensure our freedom. Thank you so much from the bottom of my heart.

Note from the Author

This book has been a pleasure to work on. I, like so many others, have struggled during this odd time in 2020. We have a disease affecting all of our lives, taking people from us too soon, and scaring the entire world. We have major changes happening in our country, and we have uncertainty. So working on any project has been tough. But I sat down with great friends, and we collaborated on this book. And for a few hours a day, I got to get out of the world and work within another universe. It was a collaboration from beginning to end. We brainstormed it together, and then one of my best friends since the 9th grade worked on this book all of the way through with me, writing chapters, and outlining. I couldn't have done it without him. His knowledge of military and the rules of something like this were invaluable.

While I want realism in all of my books, we do have to step outside of our real zone and I always take liberties to make my worlds happen the way I think fits best with the book I'm working on. This book is no exception. In reality, this country does have a problem with drugs. I, personally, lost a 30-year-old cousin to a drug overdose. That should never happen. I'd like more light shed on how easy it is to get these vulnerable kids hooked on something before they know it will ruin their lives. Addiction is real, and it kills. A lot of us, me included, have had the mindset that it's their problem; it's not my fault they're hooked on drugs. While that is true, we don't know the underlying things these people are dealing with, the traumas they've suffered, and their story. I'm trying to be a more accepting person and to learn why they're on drugs. I won't change overnight. But I hope to grow and have empathy.

Thank you for the team of people who help me with all of my projects, and thank you to YOU, MY FANS!! I know this year has been tough for all of you, and still you support me. I can't thank you enough for that. Without being an author I don't know how I would've gotten through this. I've never appreciated you more for allowing me my dream career. I hope you love this new series as we have some twists and turns planned along the road. And most importantly I hope you have a team of people around you to help you through all of this social isolating. To be alone too much is traumatic. I isolate a lot when I work, but I have people in my life who don't allow it too long before they drag me out of the writing dungeon and into the light. Lately, fishing has become a passion of mine, and that's been my greatest escape in a world gone crazy. So thankful for meeting my fiancé and having him bring this amazing sport into my life. Fishing not only gives me pleasure but feeds my family too. It's a win, win. Take care of yourselves, those you love, and those most vulnerable. I truly love and appreciate you all.

        With Love,
        Melody Anne

Books by Melody Anne

Romance

BILLIONAIRE BACHELORS
*The Billionaire Wins the Game
*The Billionaire's Dance
*The Billionaire Falls
*The Billionaire's Marriage Proposal
*Blackmailing the Billionaire
*Runaway Heiress
*The Billionaire's Final Stand
*Unexpected Treasure
*Hidden Treasure
*Holiday Treasure
*Priceless Treasure
*The Ultimate Treasure

THE BILLIONAIRE ANDERSONS
*Book One – Finn
*Book Two – Noah
*Book Three – Brandon
*Book Four – **Crew Dec 2020**
*Book Five – **Hudson Feb 2021**

ANDERSONS BLACK OPS

*Book One – Shadows
*Book Two – Rising
*Book Three – **Coming Nov 2020**
*Book Four – **Coming Jan 2021**
*Book Five – **Coming March 2021**

BABY FOR THE BILLIONAIRE
+The Tycoon's Revenge
+The Tycoon's Vacation
+The Tycoon's Proposal
+The Tycoon's Secret
+The Lost Tycoon
+Rescue Me

Surrender
=Surrender – Book One
=Submit – Book Two
=Seduced – Book Three
=Scorched – Book Four

Forbidden Series
+Bound – Book One
+Broken – Book Two
+Betrayed – Book Three
+Burned – Book Four

Heroes Series
-Safe in his arms – Novella –
-*Baby it's Cold Outside* Anthology
-Her Unexpected Hero – Book One
-Who I am with you – Novella – Book Two
-Her Hometown Hero – Book Three
-Following Her – Novella – Book Four
-Her Forever Hero – Book Five

Becoming Elena
-Stolen Innocence – Book One
-Forever Lost – Book Two
-New Desires – Book Three

Finding Forever Series
*Finding Forever

Billionaire Aviators
Turbulent Intentions – Book One (Cooper)
Turbulent Desires – Book Two (Maverick)
Turbulent Waters – Book Three (Nick)
Turbulent Intrigue – Book Four (Ace)

Undercover Billionaire
Kian – Book One
Arden – Book Two
Owen – Book Three
Declan – Book Four

Torn Series
Torn – Book One
Tattered – Book Two

Series Romance

Taken By the Trillionaire
*Xander (Ruth Cardello)
*Bryan (J.S. Scott)
*Chris (Melody Anne)
* Virgin for the Trillionaire – Ruth Cardello
* Virgin for the Prince – Book Five – J.S. Scott
*Virgin to Conquer – Book Six – Melody Anne

7 Brides for 7 Brothers
#1 Luke: Barbara Freethy
#2 Gabe: Ruth Cardello
#3 Hunter: Melody Anne

Thrillers

Confessions
*Dance in the Dark; Book One
*TBA – Next Book in the Series

Fantasy/ YA

Phoenix Falling – Book One
Phoenix Ashes – Book Two
Phoenix Rising – Book Three
A New World – Book Four

Prologue
Three Years in the Past

Time: 0400
Date: November, ██, ██
Location: ████████, Korangal Valley, Afghanistan
Team: *Pilots:* Jeremy Rohns, Patrick Malone *Crew Chief:* Kevin Keller *SEALs:* Jon Eisenhart ("Eyes"), ████████ ("Morph"), Carl Schwartz ("Sleep"), ████ ("Clapper"), ████████ ("Stogie"), ████ ("Rain")
Operation: Mountain Anvil

The continually furious *thawump, thawump, thawump* of the Blackhawk's blades over the last thirty-five minutes was almost enough to make Sleep fall asleep.

Almost.

Unfortunately for everyone in the chopper, he was a high energy, mile-a-minute talking and moving team member who didn't allow a lick of rest for himself or anyone around him. When it was time for action, though, there were few better to have at your side.

"Hey, Eyes, do you think there'll be enough powder on the ground to build a snowman?" Sleep asked, finding himself amusing as the pilots flew through the Korengal Valley, which happened to be blanketed in a light layer of snow. Before Eyes could formulate an answer, more words were already coming over the com system.

"I remember a massive snowstorm we had in Philly when I was a kid," Sleep said, a smile in his voice. "I think I was eleven, maybe twelve. Anyway, around three feet dumped from Friday night to Sunday morning. We were out of school for the entire week. Hell, the whole city was shut down for a few days. My friends and I gathered a bunch of other kids from up and down Cottman Avenue, then went over to Northeast High and made about twenty snowmen on the football field, staging them so it looked like they were playing a game." They could hear the joy in his voice as Sleep got lost in old memories.

"It wasn't long before some of the kids made snowballs. One got chucked over our icy football team and hit this jackass kid from Cedar Grove smack dab in his smug face. The very well-known bully began crying, which they all do eventually, then stomped away from the field, threatening to tell his mom. We were all busting a gut at that one," Sleep continued.

"Dang, you're making me homesick," Rain said, his own memories of snowball fights as a kid being conjured.

"Me too," Sleep said with another laugh. "Of course, after the first snowball was thrown, it started a war. We were in the middle of an epic battle when the bully came back, but he wasn't alone. It was worse than his mom; it was his older brother with three of his brother's friends. These were *big* high school kids. They figured we'd cower like kicked dogs. I think it was in that moment I knew I was gonna be called to a life of making questionable decisions." He got lost in his thoughts and his team waited. They all had stories like this from their past and they knew exactly what he was thinking. It was what separated them from 99.9 percent of the rest of the world.

"The kid's brother began calling out for who had dared hit his brother. He wanted the person to step forward and take his punishment, whatever the hell that meant. I looked at my boys: Roger, John, and Jeff. They knew trouble was about to show up when I gave them my famous shit-eating grin, shrugged my shoulders, then yelled back at the bully's brother that it was me who threw it. I stepped forward, making sure they saw me, and then I winked at the bully who was cocky now that he was hiding behind his big brother. I finished up by asking what the prob was."

Clapper, one of his teammates—an overly hardened type who didn't laugh at much—had his funny bone hit hard by that and gave an actual belly laugh. Sleep, happy with that reaction, smiled because, though they were tough as nails, deep down they were also kids who enjoyed an epic adventure.

Sleep, looking back at Clapper, kept the story going "I started walking toward the teens while taking off my gloves. Nearly to them, I pretended to trip, which made the asses laugh. I was glad their defenses were down, because they were a lot bigger than me, and I knew I'd need any advantage I could get."

"The bigger they are, the better it feels when they fall," Stogie chimed in. Sleep's entire team was giving him their full attention as he continued his teenage tale of woe.

"Big brother began mocking me as he closed the gap between us. Just as he reached me, I stood, gave a look over my shoulder — not surprised to see my buddies close behind — then faced the brother and threw a super tight snowball straight into his smug face. I immediately followed that with a punch to his stomach. When he bent over, I was ready, and punched him hard in his nose, making it explode like a water balloon dropping from a ten story building," Sleep said.

Clapper started laughing loud enough they didn't need the headpieces to hear him. The story really hit Clapper deep. Sleep was trying not to laugh himself while continuing on with his reminiscing. "Big brother went down, and his friends rushed over. They were so shocked they weren't sure what to do. They weren't even looking at me as they moved to their friend. The bully was standing back gazing at me with shock and fear. Man, for a moment there, I felt as if the hand of God had reached down and touched me, making me invincible. As we all know, confidence can turn into stupidity on a dime, though," he said with a sigh.

"Hell yeah, but it gives us some crazy ass adventures and memories to talk about as we soar over barren lands," Rain said with a smile.

Nodding his head in agreement, Sleep kept going. "I lunged at the kid to my right, but he was far more ready than his buddy. He took my head in his beefcake hand and shoved, throwing me to the side, making me land face first, completely disorienting me. Before I could so much as twitch, big brother was on me, punching the back of my head. Everything was happening quick, but I still heard the baby bully egging on his brother, telling him to kill me. I was wondering if it was going to end that way. Flashes of light were sparking behind my eyes, and my ears were exploding with each slam of his meaty fists against my skull, which I thought for sure was cracking." Sleep paused for a moment, and his team knew he was back in that place as he told his story.

"This kid had at least fifty pounds on me, but my adrenaline was flowing. I got myself turned, and just as I flipped sunny side up, I took a shot to my left cheekbone. That one got my attention. Hell, it hurt bad. I wasn't even thinking anymore. It was the epicenter of fight or flight — and since I wouldn't have run even if I could, I knew I needed to get back in the fight. He was holding the front of my jacket with his left hand, so I leaned forward, and bit down hard on the bottom knuckle of his thumb. I was a pit bull on crack as I clenched skin, muscle, and bone between my teeth. It must've hurt like hell, because his eyes widened with surprise and pain as he tried pulling from me. I tasted blood but refused to let go as he screamed and thrashed his arm about like a wild banshee. I was thinking I might not die when he slammed a fist into my jaw, managing to yank his hand away. Before even a second more passed, his fist slammed down again, straight into that sweet spot at my temple. The world went black for a second, maybe two. And it could've been the end for me, but when I opened my eyes again, my friends were in the middle of a chaotic battle," Sleep said, more than a hint of pride in his voice.

"Hell yeah, for the ones you can count on," Rain said with a fist half-cocked in the air.

"Amen, Brother," Sleep said. "My friends were just a single step less crazy than I was, and they rushed forward, rabbit punching, kicking, and screaming at the top of their lungs as they connected with the high schoolers. They weren't ones to look for a fight, but they never backed down if one came at them. Their fists and feet flew in every direction along with snow and ice pelting us from all sides. If one of us went down, we all did what we could to pick them back up, even if it meant getting a busted lip or a black eye."

"Damn straight, we do," Eyes said coolly with a wicked glint in his eyes and a smile on his lips. Some might find it disconcerting the things they joked about, but those people didn't get into situations like these men did. If they didn't laugh, they couldn't do it. And the world and their families needed them doing what they did so they could all be free and safe at home.

In a grand gesture, Sleep threw his arms out, and gave air quotes at the word *might* as he continued. "As I was getting my ass whooped, I *might* have forgotten about the rest of the kids who'd been playing with us on the field that day. I was so used to my tight knit group being the only ones around. But those kids who knew me, who lived in the surrounding blocks by my house, never could've imagined what they were going to be getting themselves into that day. By the time I'd gotten to my feet, it was a revolution. The four high schoolers and the baby bully were getting pummeled by nearly every kid out there. It was beautiful, I was just starting after the—"

"Contact! Hard right!" Sleep's story was interrupted by one of the pilots as the Blackhawk made an instantaneous movement to the left and down, the G-force pulling each of them into their seats as their safety harnesses clenched at their chests.

All laughter ended for the team as they instantly shot into fight mode. They held on tight as the chopper's engine gave a hard growl, doing all it could to responded to the pilot's ace commands.

The SEAL team had gone from jovial friends to looking like marble statues in the blink of an eye as they sat straight, seat straps tight enough to impact deep breathing, and in perfect unison, their long guns etched into their torsos.

Onboard countermeasures were deployed, causing a sequence of explosions close to the chopper. The team shared a look. This wasn't small arms fire coming at them, or normal ammunition for that matter. Something big and bad enough to end everything was screaming toward them. Even knowing that, there wasn't time or energy for fear. This was all a part of the job they'd signed up for. They'd either make it . . . or, hopefully, it would end fast.

Eyes's voice came through loud and clear over the coms. "Breathe men, we might be getting out of a job a bit sooner than expected." He grinned, making the others groan. That was Eyes, making a joke even in the face of death.

The SEAL team stoically gazed at one another in case it was the last time they'd get to do just that. They each nodded, no fear seeping in, just a determination to fight until the end.

"Brace for impact!" a voice called.

That was their only warning before the engine revved, pushing itself hard for several surreal seconds. They heard an explosion far too close for comfort, and then a deadly silence fell over them for what seemed like forever, but in reality must've only been a second or two.

The chopper gave a shudder as another explosion made impact, sending a ball of heat rolling through the cabin. They lost control as their chopper began spinning, leaving them with zero idea if they were up, down or sideways. Equilibrium was gone.

Garbled screams came through the coms as they made it to the tree line, the chopper cutting into the giant masses of wood like a car plowing through toothpicks. It didn't take long for them to impact the ground hard enough to snap necks, before bouncing back up, hitting more trees, then flipping side over side for long enough to make them completely disoriented.

The chopper finally came to a halt with the windshield facing the sky. Smoke, debris, and a cloud of dust was suffocating all inside the cabin of the chopper, making it nearly impossible to breathe or see.

"Report!" Eyes commanded into the darkness.

Each of the team members did a quick body scan. They needed to know who could move, who couldn't. Seconds counted when the enemy was bearing down on them.

"Morph, good, releasing straps."

"Sleep, good, releasing straps."

"Stogie, left elbow injury, impacting hand movement. Need assist on straps. Otherwise, good," Stogie said with a deep cough.

"I've got you, Stogie," called Sleep.

"Clapper, Rain, report," Eyes called.

No response.

Eyes released himself and slid down toward his unresponsive teammates. He moved as swiftly as he could through the small chopper. "Clapper, Rain, report," he said again.

While Sleep assisted Stogie, Morph released the side door of the halo, releasing the airborne crap into the outside air, bringing them much needed oxygen. Then he moved forward, checking on the flight crew. There was no movement. He checked pulses. There were none, and blood was dripping onto his hand, covering his palm instantly. He absently wiped it on his pants. There was no time now to grieve the loss of good men. That would come later.

"Morph exiting and securing exterior. All three crew members are KIA," he said, then slid down the body of the destroyed halo.

"Morph exiting, crew down, copy," a voice replied.

Morph immediately dropped to the ground, scanning the area. No one was close — at least not yet. He knew they'd be coming soon. They wouldn't shoot down a US military chopper without plans to capture. Before they arrived, his team needed to be long gone.

Sleep made it to the door with Stogie. "Morph, I need an assist," Sleep called. Morph moved over and assisted Sleep with getting Stogie safely to the ground. Sleep slipped back inside to help Eyes with the other members.

Stogie struggled with basic tasks only having one useable hand, but finally got his night vision on, then awkwardly racked a round in his M4 and flipped the scope cover into the open position. He set the long gun back across his chest, then performed the same task of getting battle ready with his sidearm.

"Let's do a sweep," Morph said. Stogie nodded. They did a sweep around the chopper, hearing noises in the distance.

"We're pretty far up shit creek," Stogie said. His left arm was a mess, but there was too much adrenaline for him to feel pain.

"That's for sure, and damned if we don't have a paddle to navigate in the middle of this hell hole," Morph replied.

It didn't take long before they spotted the enemy. They were close. Both of them dropped out of sight before messaging their team. "You guys need to get moving. We have contact, twelve to fifteen of them, approximately eight hundred yards out, making their way up from the valley," Morph said.

"Clapper and Rain didn't make it. We'll have to come back for them," Eyes said over the coms. Pain ripped through all of them at those words.

Sleep and Eyes dropped down from the chopper, immediately getting their gear in place. Before they took more than two steps, the first shots rang through the air, coming from the forest. Sleep racked a round in his long gun, then became still. He focused on a green glow moving swiftly forward in the trees.

Eyes coordinated fast, giving his team the location to meet. They didn't hesitate. There were only four of them now, and they were determined to not lose another life.

"Okay, we're moving up this hill, then we'll look at injuries and reassess. We're going to head southeast toward JBad. It's approximately one hundred miles away as the crow flies, and we'll need to cover as much ground as possible while we have the shield of darkness."

"Copy," the other three men replied in unison.

Within minutes they'd made their way up the hill to a secure place they could take cover and still see the enemy. Eyes took the lead on triage for his team. Thankfully, Stogie was the only one who needed bandaging. The compound fracture just above his elbow needed more medical supplies than they had on hand, but as they often did, they made do.

"We have to tourniquet and compress this and get it tight to your body. You might have an artery cut, hard to tell, but you're bleeding at a good clip. Do you want your arm straight down, or chicken winged?" Then, he smiled. "No matter which you choose it's gonna hurt like hell, but don't worry, I'm not gonna feel a thing," Eyes said.

"That makes me feel *soooo* much better," Stogie said with a pained laugh and roll of his eyes. "Let's go with chicken wing. I need to be able to brace my long gun."

"Speed this up. Four insurgents broke off from the group and are heading our way," Sleep hissed. "I don't want to fire and draw all of them this way . . . though shooting a few might make me feel better about this whole clusterfuck." They all wanted revenge for their fallen soldiers, but they were disciplined enough to do the job without compromising their mission.

"Two minutes," Eyes said. He moved quickly, and Stogie, breaking into a sweat as his arm was bandaged, didn't utter a sound as Eyes worked. He finished in record time, thanks to Stogie's pain threshold and training.

"Let's go," Sleep said, and Stogie stood, moving slow and a bit uneven, but at least he was moving.

In a flash, the entire forest lit up brighter than a nightclub with a dozen strobe lights going off at once. Gunfire rang out from multiple directions. Eyes was on it in less than a heartbeat.

"Back over the hill, now — Go! Make contact with those four insurgents and do it quiet and fast," Eyes barked over the blasts ripping up the ground and trees near them.

Morph and Sleep made quick work of the four men who'd been on their way toward their team. Stogie had his sidearm out, firing shots, but he was in the wrong place at the wrong time. He turned, and that's when Eyes watched blood explode from the left side of his chest as a bullet ripped straight through him. Shock registered on Stogie's features as he looked down for a brief moment, looked back at Eyes with a look of disappointment and then dropped to his knees and fell face forward to the ground, his body jerking once before going still.

Eyes rushed to him, checked his pulse to be absolutely sure, then closed Stogie's eyes. He wouldn't allow his brain to open the door to even think about grieving. He grabbed Stogie's ammo, incapacitated the fallen soldier's long gun, then followed his other team members over the crest of the hill, down the way they'd just come from.

Morph took the lead while Sleep and Eyes flanked each side of him, approximately six feet separating them, moving as swiftly as they could in unfamiliar territory. They took out several insurgents as they made their way through the forest, not once breaking their stride.

Eyes kept an eye on their back, making sure the enemy wasn't coming up from behind. The good and the bad of the situation was that the enemy was spread out, not united, and unable to coordinate within their own ranks, making it all but impossible to call out the location of the SEALs. However, it gave Eyes and his team no sure route to take since the enemy could turn on a moment's notice, blocking a new path.

As they took a new direction, they noted the enemies' voices were growing fainter. Morph turned the team down an old animal game trail and heard what sounded like rushing water. Thirty yards down the path, their trail opened to a rock outcrop with a waterfall to the right, dropping into what seemed an endless black abyss. They weren't in a good position. Their options were quickly dwindling.

"Any ideas, boys?" Morph asked, not admitting how pissed he was that he'd led them to this location, even though none of them knew where they were. They'd landed at least a couple of hundred miles from their original drop-off point. "We can double back and peel hard right where this damned goat trail started," Morph added through a tight jaw.

Before they could form a new plan, shots rang out again. Morph dropped, a shot ripping through his right leg, just above his knee. Without hesitation, he turned his body toward the forest and gave instantaneous return fire in rapid three round succession. Eyes and Sleep each took a knee and fired a barrage of 5.56 rounds, aiming at random green objects that were placed at sporadic yardages. This enemy had little strategy, but endless numbers, which seemed to keep growing.

"How in the hell are this many of them converging?" Morph snapped as he fired several more rounds.

"I don't know. Maybe from the pits of hell," Sleep thundered, his own rifle only ceasing to find a new enemy to target and stamp out.

Eyes looked at the situation and knew if they didn't change something real quick none of them were making it out of this. Half of his team was gone, plus the crew that had been transporting them. They might die that night, but they wouldn't do it without one hell of a fight, and certainly not without taking down a whole lot of these savages. He made a quick decision.

"Sleep, pull Morph down the edge of this damn mountain, and cease fire. I'm going to take these guys on a magic carpet ride, and if the fates are with me I'll create a flank," Eyes said. He grinned and gave his brothers a wink.

"Eyes, you realize you're not funny, right? Not in the best of times, but definitely not in the worst." Morph huffed at him, though his own lips twitched, even with the amount of pain he had to be feeling.

"I just have a tough crowd," Eyes replied. He then nodded to Sleep and Morph. Nothing else needed to be said. Sleep would follow his command.

He turned and ran directly up the trail — straight toward the fire coming at them. He barely missed a shot straight at his head before he dropped behind a downed tree then fired a couple of shots.

Sleep watched Eyes leave, hoping it wasn't the last time he'd see the man he considered his brother-in-arms and, more importantly, his best friend. He was glad they'd managed to give each other a smile. Neither fear nor defeat was the last thing they'd see on each other's faces.

He wasn't able to turn away until seeing the green outline of Eyes popping back up from the fallen tree, dropping two insurgents, then sprinting again to another tree. He stopped for only seconds to fire rounds before moving again. Soon he was swallowed up by the dense woods.

"Let's go," Sleep said, sliding Morph over the edge. "It looks like there's enough of a grade we should be able to support ourselves. I'll get your leg wrapped and we'll get these sons of bitches put down."

"I don't think this is getting wrapped," Morph said. "I'm cold, and getting lightheaded. I'm losing too much blood. I can feel it pooled in my boot." His voice was fading.

"Get your ass over this ledge and we'll bandage you up. It's just a spot of blood," Sleep's voice hammered down.

Morph gave it all he could, leaning heavily on Sleep as they moved to the ledge. They were just about over when a heavy, thick, metal pinging sound bounced toward them.

They turned in unison, adrenaline coursing through their bodies, as they decided they needed to change directions fast. They both knew what that sound meant and knew how little time they had.

"Get out of here alive and tell my family my last breath was filled with love for them," Morph said.

"No!" Sleep screamed, but it was too late. With the last strength Morph had, he wrapped his thick hands over Sleep's shoulders and twisted their bodies just as the grenade exploded.

The explosion instantly killed Morph, miniature pieces of shrapnel piercing his entire body. Morph's shock-waved momentum sent Sleep flying over the edge of the cliff, screaming Morph's name as pain ripped through him.

Sleep couldn't control his movements as he rolled down the jagged mountain, his limbs and torso repeatedly slamming against objects. His head cracked against a tree, then his ribs felt as if something had pierced straight into them. He was hit and twisted in so many ways, he wasn't sure how he was still conscious.

After what seemed like an endless amount of time, he finally stopped, lying on the ground. He wasn't sure if he passed out or not, wasn't sure how much time passed, wasn't even sure if it was day or night anymore as he tried shaking cobwebs from his head and gain his breath.

As consciousness came to him, he had no doubt that he had at least one rib completely broken, making it nearly impossible to breathe. He also was very aware that Morph was dead, and he had no idea where his remaining team member was. Sleep couldn't breathe fully, couldn't see, and could barely move. It was either down to him alone, or him and Eyes.

As much as Sleep wanted to close his eyes and rest he knew if he did, they mostly likely wouldn't open again. He willed his body to do what he commanded of it and sat up, instantly coughing blood. He understood things weren't looking good. But he wasn't a quitter and he sure as hell wasn't going to die sitting around doing nothing about it.

Fumbling in his pack with shaking fingers, he found his med kit, opened it, and took out what he needed. The pain was excruciating, but he pushed it down. He ripped open his jacket, felt his rib cage, then took the needle from the kit and pushed it in with enough force to puncture his lung.

Instant relief washed through him as oxygen flowed inside his damaged body. As he took slow breaths and secured the needle so it wouldn't fall out, he formulated a plan. He wouldn't lie there and die. He wouldn't dishonor his friends, his team, or himself by giving up.

Sleep quickly spread out everything he had on him, and then gathered the most critical items, knowing it wasn't possible to haul all of his gear with how beat up his body was. He got to his feet and had to lean against a tree as his head spun and blood dripped freely from his mouth. Pain was everywhere, but he pushed it down. Slowly, he began moving to the edge of the river. It was a well-known truth that all waterways eventually led to civilization.

He took one step, then another, and then another. He didn't think, didn't focus on the pain. He simply moved one step at a time. He had no idea how much time passed, no idea how far he was traveling. He just focused on one foot in front of the other. Daylight began to break over the horizon and he still trudged forward . . .

If he made it one hour, he might just make it long enough to get to where he needed to go.

Chapter One

She was seventy-nine years old, and though she might be moving a little slower and definitely had a few more marks on her skin that showed the joy and sorrow throughout her wonderful time on earth, she felt as if her life was in its prime.

Katherine Anderson was married to a legend of a man, and not once had that made her feel like less of a woman. The entire world knew of their epic love story, knew of the countless lives that had been impacted because of their journey. Katherine was proud of their legacy — and even more proud of her husband — Joseph Anderson.

Their love story had begun so many years ago that she couldn't imagine a time she hadn't had him in her life. It was rare indeed she had time to herself. Joseph had only become more attentive and protective as they'd entered their rocking chair years. She didn't mind his attention one bit. There was absolute security in knowing another living being on this earth truly would die for her.

Katherine's vehicle drove through the gate of the veterans center she'd been a part of creating and she sat for several moments as she thought about her life. Yes, it was good, wonderful even, and yes, there were times she felt smothered. But a person couldn't know joy in life if they didn't have hardships. A smile flitted across her pink lips as she thought of her crazy, beautiful, loving family. She was more blessed than so many.

"Where would you like to go first, Mrs. Anderson?" her driver asked.

"Over by the trail," she said.

"Yes, ma'am," he replied and quickly navigated to where she wanted. He stopped the car and she undid her belt.

She stepped from the luxury town car and gazed out at the Anderson's latest project. It was certainly awe inspiring — a giant veterans center consisting of nearly one hundred fifty acres. There was a huge building in the middle of it all, called the Medal of Honor House, horseshoed by a multitude of other facilities all aimed at helping the United States veterans when they returned home from duty. Her favorite spot on the enormous campus was the manmade lake surrounded by Japanese cherry trees and home to fish, frogs, ducks, and other critters. This beautiful oasis was in the middle of the property, giving the residents who came and went from the spectacular campus a sense of being in a small town that had been built just for them.

The vets could come to the campus to heal, to grow, to feel safe, and to learn. The facility was for those who'd been abandoned, for those who were unsure where they belonged now that their lifelong career was over and they felt lost, and for those who were heroes to all of America.

The project had begun when she and Joseph had discovered some long lost relatives. Just when they thought their hearts couldn't grow any fuller, they discovered a lost triplet Joseph's mother's doctor had stolen at birth, bringing new nieces and nephews into their life. And then as if that hadn't been enough, a few years ago, they'd located the children of Joseph's terrible uncle Neilson, adding even more family.

The discovery of those family members had prompted the veterans facility project. It had helped them bond as a family, and it was bringing so much joy to an entire community. Of course she and Joseph had welcomed their new relatives. And she was so pleased that all of them had embraced her vision for this campus.

Their relatives, and the entire community where they'd built the center, had rallied together to make it happen. They weren't quite finished, but it came closer to completion each day. It was finished enough to operate. She couldn't wait for the day it was working at full capacity.

She'd been standing by the car for several minutes, staring out at the vast campus, when her driver Jeffrey drew her attention.

"Let me park the car and I'll walk with you," Jeffrey said.

"No. It's a beautiful evening and I want to take a moment to myself and watch the sun set over the other side of the pond."

"You know Joseph will have my head if I don't go with you," Jeffrey warned. Katherine gave him a coy smile and chuckled.

"Then we just won't tell him, will we?" She turned and walked away.

She knew Jeffrey would respect her even if he didn't like what she was doing. This facility had cameras everywhere and security personnel she fully trusted. She was perfectly safe to walk the grounds alone. Besides that, she wasn't quite ready to go inside — knowing the second she did, she'd have people demanding her attention. She normally loved that, but not on this night — not when she was dealing with how to tell her husband the truth about something she'd been hiding for the past few months.

How did you break such terrifying news to the man you loved? She wasn't quite sure. She knew beyond a shadow of a doubt she'd been utterly lost when Joseph had been in a coma several years ago. She also knew that if something were to happen to her, her beautiful husband would be even more lost.

While making her way to the north side of the campus, a shiver ran through her as she clutched her cardigan tightly around her. She gave a deep, exasperated sigh, thinking about the difficult conversation she had to have with Joseph. He'd go straight to the worst case scenario.

Katherine continued to move along, growing farther away from people. Along the way she passed numerous gazebos strategically placed along the lake. Lots of those who came to this facility needed isolation while also knowing people were close by. These gazebos gave them enough privacy and space for just that. The Anderson family had tried to make this a safe place for all levels of trauma.

This was the preferred route she took when coming to the campus. She enjoyed the absolute stillness of their private campus. She was no longer able to go into the city alone. The population had grown too much over the years and grew in violence. Add to that the fact some weren't as fond of the Anderson empire as others, and it caused her to need security wherever she went.

There were many out there who'd love fame — she wasn't one of them. She missed the time she'd been able to go to a carnival, eat a corndog, and enjoy a thrilling ride. Of course, her old bones wouldn't be able to do that anymore anyway, she mused to herself.

She passed one of the beautiful cherry trees on the campus — another bookended the other side of the bench she was almost to. One of Joseph's good friends had gifted all of the trees to the center. They'd known each other since they were kids, and Joseph had helped Lee create an empire of growing and selling his specialty trees all around the world. She loved that they lived in a world where many nations' cultural items could be seen in one place. Each country might have its own laws and customs, but at the end of the day, they truly were all one people. If more humans understood that, there wouldn't be so much chaos on this beautiful planet.

Katherine reached her favorite bench that overlooked a magical lake with an incredibly beautiful fountain that shot up water, creating a prism of rainbows when the light was just right. And with the ambers, pinks, and deep purples of the sun starting to rest on the horizon, it was spellbinding.

A few of the vibrant cherry blossom petals were scattered along the path around the pond, their pale pink petals beginning to wither. They wouldn't be there the next day because the veterans who spent time at the center were responsible for jobs on the grounds. They weren't charged for using the facility, not to live there, not for full medical or physical therapy, and not for education or career transitions. That was important for their healing. Instead, they were made whole through a lot of hard work and a sense of pride in helping to build and keep this place pristine.

Katherine leaned against the railing of the pond, basking in the final rays of sunshine for the day. She could curl up in this place with a good audio book and get lost forever.

Too soon, Katherine's quiet was broken by the sound of voices. She was getting ready to turn and move away, not wanting to visit right then, but also knowing the people wouldn't be aware she was there and might be discussing something urgent from the sounds of their muffled conversation.

She moved toward the center of the campus, but instead of fading, the voices grew louder — and angrier. She shivered as she picked up her pace. She knew this place was safe, but she didn't want to get into the middle of an argument — not tonight of all nights, not when she was dealing with personal demons.

Turning a corner, Katherine stumbled into two men, one who was handing something to the other. She tried to turn and exit the way she'd come. But before she could, they both looked up, not appearing to be happy at the interruption. One of the men she recognized, but barely. He'd only been on the campus a couple of weeks, and he'd been very quiet in his time there, which wasn't unusual. He wore a look of anger, possibly fear, and what appeared as raw need on his face.

The other man gave her the creeps. He wore a worn baseball cap pulled low on his brow with dark, greasy hair hanging down his shoulders. There was nothing at all kind in his expression.

To make matters worse, he smiled at Katherine, a predator's expression if she'd ever seen one, showing only a couple of rotted teeth in his open mouth. This was wrong — she knew she was in a dangerous situation. She was trying to remember what she was supposed to do. It hit her like a ton of bricks when she realized she was most likely witnessing a drug deal.

Everything in her wanted to challenge these men. How dare they taint this sacred campus? But Katherine wasn't stupid, and she knew this wasn't the place nor time to challenge anybody, especially being alone. A person on drugs was unpredictable. She needed to get to security and ask how this had happened. Were there flaws in the state-of-the-art security system?

"I'm so sorry to interrupt," she told them. Personalize it, she thought. "You're Vince, right?" she questioned, not daring to step closer. "I won't keep you guys. I'm just taking a walk. Joseph will be here any second." Her voice was pleasant. She'd learned years before how to smile when it was the last thing she felt like doing.

"I haven't heard about Joseph coming today," the greasy haired man said as he moved a step closer. Everything in her wanted to retreat, but she knew that would give away her fear, and she absolutely couldn't show it. She had to pretend as if she was simply a clueless old woman out for a stroll.

"Yeah, he always comes on Fridays, but never on Tuesdays," Vince said, no longer looking in her eyes. He appeared ashamed. She wanted to comfort him, to tell him not to do this, to not be near this man. He'd never make progress if he went back to hanging around a lowlife like the man he was currently with.

"Yeah, we know Joseph's schedule *real* well," greasy hair said.

"I wanted a special visit today," she said, as if they were having a normal conversation. "They just finished up the game room, and I love beating my husband at a good game of pool."

"I wish you would've walked a different path," Vince mumbled, seeming on the verge of tears.

"Oh, don't worry, I walk all of them," Katherine told him as she felt a chill travel down her spine. "I'll be on my way now." She didn't give them a chance to say anything further as she turned down a path and swiftly walked away.

She wasn't sure if she believed they'd let her escape. But she didn't make it far when she felt a blinding flash of pain in her temple and stars exploded before her eyes. She barely had time to realize she'd been hit before she crumpled to the ground.

* * *

She heard voices before she realized she was gaining consciousness. Pain radiated in her head, shoulder, neck and jaw. A disgusting copper taste filled her mouth, and she tried to move, making the world spin around her.

"Katherine! It's okay. I'm here. It's okay," a voice said as she felt her shoulders gripped. "Don't try to talk. You're safe. It's Brooke. I'm with you, and more help is on the way."

Katherine felt relief as she realized Brooke Anderson was there. Not only was she the lead nurse practitioner of the facility, but she was a combat-trained veteran. There was no chance those men would get the jump on Brooke.

"I need to sit up," Katherine croaked.

"I don't know if that's a good idea. I have no idea what's happened to you," Brooke said. "I just heard a cry and came running. I saw two men over you and shouted, and they took off. I think they were going to seriously harm you, Katherine," Brooke finished.

"Yes, yes, I think you're right," Katherine told her. The spinning was lessening, and she finally managed to open her eyes. "I can sit up now."

Brooke only hesitated a second longer before helping her, using her own body for Katherine to lean on. She was grateful her nephew, Finn, had married this woman.

"I need Joseph," Katherine said. "He needs to know something is wrong on this campus."

"Do you know what happened? If we call and say you've been attacked without telling him why, he might deploy the Army," Brooke said, only somewhat jokingly.

Katherine gave her a hint of a smile. "Yes, I fear you're right. But if we tell him the truth over the phone, it might be the entire state of Washington he deploys," she said. She was quiet a moment before she spoke again. "I witnessed a drug deal. I was simply in the wrong place at the wrong time. Please call Joseph and tell him I'm fine, but I need him."

Brooke nodded, then picked up her phone. She kept it short, and to the point, when Joseph answered.

"Yes, my love?" he answered, his voice filled with adoration. She'd called from Katherine's phone.

"Joseph, it's Brooke," she said. He tried to speak and she talked over him, not an easy task. "Katherine witnessed something at the center. She was attacked by the pond and knocked unconscious. She's alert, and speaking, but she's going to need to go to the hospital."

There were a few heartbeats of stunned silence before Joseph's voice thundered over the line. "I'm on my way. Let me speak to my wife."

There was no possible way Brooke was going to argue with her uncle-in-law. She handed the phone over. Katherine's voice was weak. "I'm okay, darling, but I don't want to talk on the phone. You just keep calm and come to me."

"I love you," he said, tears in his voice.

"You're my world," she replied. "I'll see you soon." She hung up, knowing her energy was waning and not wanting her devoted husband to hear the pain and weakness in her voice. He'd go out of his mind without being able to be at her side.

"That man is the love of my life. I hate putting him through the stress of this," she told Brooke.

"Can you imagine the heads that would roll if he wasn't called until you were at the hospital?" Brooke asked.

Katherine smiled. "I wouldn't put anyone through that temper tantrum," she said. Her head was throbbing and the nausea was growing worse. "I'd better lie back. Call the ambulance."

"They've already been called," Brooke assured her.

Katherine faded in and out, giving her no sense of time as she lay in Brooke's arms, grateful her niece was with her. She heard voices gathering as more people found out what was happening. Then, much to her relief, she heard the thump, thump, thump sound of helicopter blades splitting the air. She had no doubt it was her husband. Katherine smiled a weak smile as she looked at the sky.

She was sure Joseph had already called out the full scope of the military —FBI, CIA, and every other alphabet soup agency in the book — as he'd rushed to get to her. The scary thing was she could see many of those people responding, willing to do what it took for Joseph, for the man who'd done so much for the country they loved.

The chopper drew closer, and Katherine knew her husband was on it. He wouldn't have waited for traffic to get to his wife. He'd have the thing hover as he took a rope down, just to get to her. It truly was humbling to be loved that much. Even in pain she let herself smile, just a thin one though, as the fire in her jaw and head amplified when she moved even the slightest muscle in her face.

She felt stars behind her eyes again as her vision began to fade. No! She didn't want to pass out. She wanted to see her husband rushing to her side.

"Katherine, you stay with me. I don't like your color. I know you want to rest, but I want you to stay alert. The chopper is only minutes out," Brooke said sternly, but with gentleness. Though Brooke had been talking to her the entire time they'd waited, her voice now sounded as if it was coming to Katherine through a tunnel. She tried to answer, tried to smile, but she wasn't sure if she managed either. She heard Jeffrey yelling for her to open her eyes, and she thought to herself "when did he get here?" but she couldn't answer or do what was being asked of her.

Darkness surrounded her again as the pain faded and the world went quiet.

Chapter Two

You could've heard a pin drop in the utterly silent courtroom. That didn't happen often in a place known for outbreaks of sound, gasps of pleasure, and cries of pain. The sound of a gavel hitting wood over and over again was another familiar noise. And the lies, oh, there were so many lies spoken in this room where people swore to tell the truth, the whole truth, and nothing but the truth.

Avery Klum sat at her table, her face unreadable, her back perfectly straight, her hands clasped in front of her, and her eyes facing forward, as her client walked to the witness stand. Though her insides were twisted into a thousand knots, not a drop of sweat would dare drip down her perfectly composed features.

Avery was twenty-nine years old, five feet one inch tall, petite, dark haired, olive toned, and had nearly black eyes. She was the youngest highest-paid junior defense attorney in San Francisco. She took a lot of pride in that. She also paid for it with a lack of sleep, absolutely zero social life, and the destruction of her morals.

Why was that?

Because she defended the undefendable.

In the beginning of her career, which had started at the tender age of twenty-two since she'd graduated from college early and aced law school, she'd thrived on winning. She'd been unstoppable. She still was. But back then, she hadn't cared if her clients were guilty or not. She'd just wanted to win, and she hadn't looked back, or quite frankly had chosen to not look forward at the possible destruction they'd later create in the world. She knew there was a chance they'd already committed the crimes they were accused of, giving a high chance they might do it again.

She'd lost one case in her seven years as a lawyer, and that had been in her second year. She still hadn't gotten over that one. She couldn't stand losing at anything. But to her credit, the monster who'd gone to prison *had* killed his mother, father, wife, and two children. She'd told herself she was fighting her best for him, but she knew deep, *deep* down, she'd been as disgusted with the man on trial as the jurors had been. That case had made her practice for months on end how to blank her expression, how to give the look the jury needed to see to judge whether she believed what she was saying or not. She was incredible at poker because she couldn't be broken when she set her mind to it.

"Do you swear to tell the truth, the whole truth, and nothing but the truth?"

"I do."

Not! She was screaming that word in her head as her client held up his left hand, his right resting on a Bible. She was somewhat shocked the man didn't go up in flames for blasphemy. No one spoke the truth anymore. *Everyone* lied. The level of the lie depended on the situation.

Oh, I've lost ten pounds when you'd actually gained five.

That dress looks amazing on you. I can't see the fat at all as rolls ripple down their back.

I didn't even look at the waitress as he leans over to get a better view.

I don't mind doing that. I love nature when in reality you're allergic to the pollen in the woods, but you want to please him.

We all lie.

We lie to make people admire us, to like ourself more, to spare someone's feelings. Or we lie to manipulate, to get out of trouble, to break the law. Some lies aren't a bad thing, but some are detrimental. Avery's current client didn't fit into the white lie kind of category.

He was an *absolute* monster.

She stood, walking with confidence in her two-thousand-dollar, three-inch deep blue Valentino heels, and her four-thousand-dollar black Armani suit with a crisp baby blue blouse beneath to highlight those heels. She looked like the epitome of success because she absolutely was.

There wasn't a hair out of place in the perfect bun on the back of her neck. Her slim gold necklace sat exactly where it was supposed to with the clasp lined up on the back of her neck and a blue sapphire drop dangling just above her modest neckline. Her simple gold hoops were the only other jewelry touching her skin. Her philosophy had always been that less was more.

She stepped closer to her client who was leaning back in the witness stand as if he didn't have a care in the world, his cocky attitude clear on his face, his clothes rumpled, and his hair in need of a trim. She gave him one sharp look and he shifted, his back going straight and his head bowing. When he looked back at her, he was a new man, still rumpled, but now his expression showed humility and fright. It really did boggle her mind at how easy it was to manipulate people, especially a jury of your peers.

While he looked like the rumpled kid next door, she looked as immaculate as a statue. Her olive skin was nearly flawless, allowing her to put nothing more than lotion on it. She added a touch of light pink lipstick, a swab of blush, and a swipe of mascara to highlight her already outrageously thick, long lashes.

This trial was nearly over. She just had to bring it home. She loved calling her witnesses to the stand. A lot of lawyers didn't, as they weren't confident their clients would do what they wanted them to do, and they didn't know what the other side would ask, so they couldn't prepare ahead.

Avery was the opposite. She studied her opposing council before a trial ever began, watched them in the courtroom, reviewed their cases, and got to know as much about them as humanly possible without violating their rights. She might push that to the edge though.

She then watched them during her trial, saw how they examined witnesses, studied up on the experts they chose, and was rarely surprised or wrong about how they'd cross-examine her people. That meant she could have them fully prepared, solidifying her case.

"Are you comfortable, Mr. Sputfield?" she asked, the first words spoken in at least five minutes.

"Not really," he said, his voice coming out slightly choked, his eyes downcast.

"Can I get you anything?" she asked, showing just the right amount of concern.

"I just want to go home," he said, looking younger than his twenty-four years.

"I know. These trials can be so hard on you *and* your family," she said as she turned and pointedly looked over at his mother who let out a wail, drawing the jury's attention. Beautifully timed like her very own puppets, her client's father wrapped an arm around his wife to console her.

Perfection.

She snuck a glance at the jurors, a couple of which were holding their hands against their hearts. Yep. Nothing got to a mother like seeing the pain of another mother worried about her child.

"Objection, Your Honor, this is all a dog and pony show," opposing counsel said as she knew he would.

Before the judge could interject, Avery looked toward the jury. "I apologize if this seems like a show. I assure you, it's not. The kind of pain this family is going through is *very* real, but the district attorney wouldn't know that as he's not a father."

The gavel slammed down. "Council, to the bench, *now*," the judge thundered. She had to fight a smile as the other lawyer practically stomped to the judge's bench while she glided over.

"I've seen your work before, Ms. Klum, and I'm unimpressed. If you try that crap one more time in *my* courtroom I'll have you found in contempt of court, and I think a few days in jail alongside some of these men and women you keep getting freed would do you a world of good."

It wasn't often Avery was shocked inside the courtroom, but as the judge spoke, she found herself in all new territory. This judge wasn't playing around. Her brain worked quickly, though, as she revised her methods in an instant. She did all of this without showing a single emotion to the judge or the DA.

"I apologize, Your Honor," she said, looking properly chastised. "I care about all of my clients, and sometimes I let that get in the way of my more reasonable brain."

The attorney next to her snorted as fire sparked from the judge's eyes. "You're so full of bullshit," the attorney spat beneath his breath.

"That's hurtful," she said, hoping she was properly remorseful.

"I don't think you can be hurt, you freaking robot," the attorney spouted. Oh, yes, he was riled. That benefited her a whole lot.

"I get called for speaking of family, and you aren't going to say a word to him about his personal attacks?" she asked the judge, trying to widen her eyes and look close to tears. That was one thing she couldn't do — fake tears. She was too disgusted by people who did it.

"That'll be enough, Mr. Satch. Let's get back to the trial. And *don't* forget my warning," he said, barely glancing at the DA before he focused on her again.

She should've been ticked the other attorney had so blatantly gotten away with what he had, but she knew the case was hers. She'd ticked off the judge *and* rattled her opponent. Now she just had to drive it home.

She made a show of walking back to her table and grabbing her notepad, looking down at it. She didn't need a refresher. She knew exactly what this case was about and what she needed to say and do. She simply wanted to give the jury time to stare at the opposing council who looked as if a lighter would ignite the short fuse he was sporting.

The rest of her questioning went exactly how she wanted it to. The cross examination didn't go well for her opponent, who was known for unraveling once he became unsettled. He looked weak, unstable, and as if he was ready to jump across the barrier and attack her client. She had a feeling a new DA was going to be assigned very, *very* soon.

She had no more witnesses, and court was dismissed for lunch. All that was left for her was her closing argument, and then it was in the jurors' hands. That was the one area of law she hated the most. She didn't like to leave anything to chance, and she could study all she wanted, but at the end of the day, humans were known to be unpredictable. Well, most humans were. Someone like her was as easy to predict as any day having a dusk and a dawn.

Avery walked from the courtroom, not moving too slow or too fast, thinking she was virtually invisible. Yes, she wore expensive clothes and carried a five-thousand-dollar briefcase. But all she wore and carried was of the best quality and fiber, fitting her to perfection, and helping her to blend in, to hopefully remain unseen. Nothing about her stood out — that was the way she wanted it.

What she didn't notice was the man in the back of the courtroom who rose as she walked by. The man who had eyes for her — and her alone. The man who didn't like at all what she was doing, or who she was getting freed to terrorize more people in a country he valued and loved.

Chapter Three

There were times in life that seemed to fly by in a flash. You were twenty, then forty, and then three quarters of a century old. But the clock didn't stop turning, and life didn't stop progressing. If Joseph Anderson could bottle time, and slow it down, that's exactly what he'd do . . . on most days.

Today, however, time was dragging. Today he received a call he'd never wanted to receive. Today, he was in a panic, and the clock kept on ticking in slow, agonizing motion, making him agitated, frustrated, and more than anything else — scared.

Thankfully, if that word could be used in this situation, he had access to the fastest transportation in Seattle. He'd been sitting in his den at home when the call had come through — the call that his beautiful Katherine had been attacked.

He couldn't tell you how long it had taken to get into the air, or how long it had taken to fly to her, but it seemed to have been hours before he was hovering over the roof of the main building of the veterans facility.

A light shone from down below with Joseph craning his neck to find his beloved Katherine. There was a man waving his arms frantically, letting them know that's where they were. There was a helipad at the far end of the facility, but that put him too far from Katherine.

"Here! Lower this chopper right here," Joseph shouted.

"Sir, this is super tight. I'm not sure we'll fit," the pilot responded.

"Just get close then and I'll jump," Joseph said in the voice no one dared to argue with.

He unbuckled and slid open the side door, making the co-pilot turn and glare. "I'll get on the ground, but if we crash . . ." He stopped and faced forward before muttering into Joseph's earpiece. "You won't be any good to your wife if you are injured."

"I won't be good to anyone if I don't get to her right now," Joseph said, not willing to compromise even a little.

He loved to hear people's opinions and loved to make business deals. He didn't, however, compromise when it came to his family. A tornado could rip through the area and he wouldn't care. He was getting to his wife no matter what.

The lower they came to the ground, the clearer the scene became. Joseph's eyes filled with tears as he saw Katherine lying in Brooke's arms with Jeffrey standing beside them waving his arms. In the distance Joseph could see the muted lights from a medic chopper that wasn't more than a few minutes behind Joseph's. An ambulance would take too long. He wanted a chopper transporting his wife, and he wanted one with all of the best medical equipment on it. That's why he'd called it in the second he'd hung up with Brooke. They hadn't argued with the man who donated hundreds of millions to their hospital.

They were about twenty feet from the ground when Joseph held the grip and stepped onto the railing. He wanted to get to Katherine yesterday.

"Dammit!" the pilot called out, saying a few choice words into his mic before Joseph ripped off his earphones. The chopper lowered a little faster, which he wanted. It barely touched down when he leapt off the edge. He didn't bother to look back at the men who'd gotten him there so quickly. He had eyes for only his wife.

He stumbled when hitting the ground, but it didn't slow him. He was sure he'd feel the aches later, but he'd take on any amount of pain if it helped Katherine. People wondered why he was so set on his family finding love. Well, it was *this* reason right here. He loved this woman more than he loved life itself.

Joseph felt the wind at his back as the chopper rose back into the air. The chopper couldn't safely stay where it had dropped Joseph so the pilots would take it to the helipad in case they were needed again. Joseph wanted a backup in case the other chopper didn't land, didn't get to his wife fast enough.

Joseph reached his wife just as the helicopter banked away from them, making the trees shake with the wind in its wake. Petals from the trees blew in every direction, some landing on his beautiful Katherine as he dropped to his knees and reached for her. His heart shattered when he saw blood dripping from the corner of her mouth.

"Wake up, Katherine. I'm here, my love. Please don't leave me. Please don't go. I'm here. I'm sorry it took so long. I'm sorry I didn't insist on coming with you. Please don't leave me," he said, his voice choked with tears.

He pulled her from Brooke's arms into his own as he rose in one smooth motion.

"Sir, she shouldn't be moved. The medic flight is coming. I see it in the sky, and they will bring a stretcher," Brooke said as she rose beside him.

"I'll take her to them," Joseph said. "There's no way for them to land here safely. They'll go to the helipad, and I'm not waiting. Seconds can mean everything," he said as he began his way to the southwest side of the facility.

"Katherine, I have news to share, so you just hang in there," Joseph said, telling her over and over again how much he loved her as he made his way to the helipad.

"Joseph, what's the update?" a guard asked as Joseph reached the helipad. The medic chopper was lowering to the ground.

"She will be fine, "Joseph said. He refused to think any other way.

"Yes, she'll be fine," the guard finally said after a few seconds, his expression saying something else entirely. Joseph couldn't even look at him.

"Yes, she's going to be just fine," Joseph said, panic and sorrow coming through loud and clear in his voice. He stood back as the medic chopper landed. The rotors shut off as people merged onto the helipad.

"They're bringing out a stretcher for Katherine," Brooke said. Joseph nodded his appreciation as two paramedics rushed forward.

"I can get her on the stretcher," a paramedic said, offering his arms.

"No! I have this," Joseph said, unwilling to let go of Katherine.

The paramedics stood before Joseph with patience. They'd obviously dealt with many traumatized spouses and knew there was a chance Joseph might snap. They were treating him with kid gloves.

"I understand you're afraid right now, sir, but we want nothing more than to help your wife. Let's get her on this stretcher, so we can examine her and get her to the hospital. All we want to do is help her," the paramedic assured Joseph, his hand held out.

Joseph shook off his stupor as he stepped up to the stretcher and gently laid his wife down. "Brooke, I want you here with her as well," Joseph commanded, not trusting strangers with the full care of his wife.

"Sir, we can't have unauthorized personnel inside the chopper," the paramedic said.

"Brooke and I come with my wife," Joseph said, steel in his voice.

The paramedics looked at each other, then shrugged. They knew it would do no good to argue with Joseph Anderson. And they didn't want to delay this process any longer. They nodded.

"Let's go," one of the paramedics said as they began rolling the stretcher to the chopper. Katherine was loaded in seconds with Brooke and Joseph climbing in after. The blades began spinning again as the paramedics hooked her up to IVs and monitors, speaking in a language Joseph didn't understand. Brooke sat beside him, holding his hand as she monitored the progress.

"Why won't she wake up, Brooke? What is happening to her?" Joseph asked. "She was speaking to me just fine a few minutes ago on the phone. Why did she pass out? Why won't she wake?"

"She's alive, Joseph. Focus on that. I've seen a lot of miracles in my time. I don't know exactly what happened, but I don't like her stats right now. Her breathing is shallow, and her blood pressure is down. We needed to get her into the hospital ten minutes ago," Brooke said as her eyes remained glued to the monitor that beeped beside his wife.

Joseph appreciated that Brooke wasn't lying to him, but her words scared him more than ever. He reached over and took Katherine's hand, her fingers far too cold. Another tear slipped from his eyes. Joseph Anderson didn't cry, not ever. But he felt so powerless, so utterly helpless in this moment. It was too much for him to bear.

And that was saying a lot for a man who'd conquered the world and didn't know the meaning of the word failure. But right now, he felt completely helpless. If they made it through this, he vowed nothing would ever happen again to put him in this place.

Suddenly he felt the world start to grow fuzzy as his head began spinning, and he couldn't catch his own breath. He swayed backward, and fought panic as he lost control of his emotions, his body, his mind.

Before he could figure out what was happening, there was a stinging sensation against his cheek. The shock of it made his eyes flash open as he found himself focusing on Brooke's worried gaze.

"Sorry, Joseph. I think you were having a panic attack. I had to slap you back into reality," Brooke said as she lifted her hand and gently rubbed his cheek.

"Thank you," he said.

She gave him a watery smile. "I never thought I'd get a thank you from a man I just slapped, but I'll take it," she said. She then gave him a quick hug before sitting back and holding his arm while she looked at the monitor. "She *will* be okay, Joseph. I know she will."

"Don, I need assistance," the medic, Max, who was closest to Katherine, called in an urgent voice.

"Hook this line to the monitor and take a new set of vitals," Max told Don. He did as his partner said. "I'm starting another IV."

Don looked at Brooke as he continued working. "How long has she been unresponsive?" he asked.

"It's been at least fifteen minutes. We know she was hit on the head. We don't know how many times. She was conscious when I arrived, but she was fading in and out. She finally passed out for a final time and hasn't responded since," Brooke said, making sure Joseph could hear her words. He appreciated that.

The two paramedics worked together like choreographed dancers, speaking in direct, rapid-fire sentences as Brooke told him all she knew. Joseph wanted to do more, but knew the best thing he could do for his wife was sit back and allow the experts to administer to her. Katherine's beautiful face was beginning to bruise, and she was so white. But she *would* make it.

"We have a code three, and she's seizing," Don called into his mic. Brooke looked over at Joseph, their eyes connecting. She didn't have to say a word for him to understand what was happening — they were losing his wife.

The paramedics said a few more things into the mic, and then Brooke turned to him, gripping his hand once more. She was his link to reality. She knew what they were saying and how to interpret it.

"Joseph, they are taking us to Mercy Medical. Let your kids know," Brooke finally said. He stared at her without comprehension. He was having a hard time clearing the fog in his head, getting past the fear of what was happening. "Don't focus on the medical or the fear, Joseph, focus on your kids. Call your family. Call Lucas, and he'll get the phone tree rolling. Let them know to meet us," Brooke continued calmly.

Her words finally registered, and he nodded. He knew she was trying to distract him from the needles and the mask on his wife. He knew she was trying to keep him focused so the capable paramedics in the chopper could help Katherine.

He picked up his phone, feeling dead inside.

He couldn't talk to anyone in his current state so instead sent a group text in a family thread that had been created long ago. His children and their spouses used it to share photos of the grandkids, work out schedules and calendars for get-togethers, and send funny memes to each other.

How sad that this text was for a family emergency. Maybe he was blessed because they hadn't had much loss in their lives. But that didn't mean they hadn't been scared many times. The message was short. *Meet me at Mercy Medical. Mom's hurt. Do not call. Phone is off. Just come. Brooke will send more information soon.* He hit send, then turned his phone off.

He gazed at Katherine again, her body seeming more lifeless by the minute. She was now breathing with the help of a machine while the paramedics kept administering drugs through her IV. Katherine didn't make a sound. He so wanted to hear her lovely voice. He wanted to wake up from this nightmare and find out none of it was real.

The paramedic grabbed the mic again. "Mercy, this is medic twenty-one with a trauma alert. We have an elderly female, trauma to the head from an unknown object. Suffered a ground level fall with positive loss of consciousness lasting for approximately twenty minutes. She just had a thirty-second seizure, and her airway became compromised. Current GCS is three. She's intubated, and vitals are BP 103/78, HR 112. Sinus rhythm on the monitor, Sp02 98% and is currently being bagged at a rate of 16 breaths per minute with 100 percent oxygen. FSBG 98. Her pupils are sluggish but equal and reactive. We have two large-bore IVs in place. Our ETA is five minutes on the helipad."

The next five minutes might as well have taken five hours. Joseph stared at the tube in his wife's throat and felt his own closing. These men didn't hesitate as they kept working on his wife. Joseph thought for a moment how lucky he was to have people care about her this much.

They arrived at Mercy Medical where a team of doctors were on the roof waiting. It didn't take long for them to be taken to an elevator and then briskly escorted into a large room with a sign reading Trauma 1. A paramedic once again gave his report to the men he was handing Katherine off to as Joseph stood like a zombie, not knowing what to do next.

"Move her on the count of three," a man said. They lifted in unison and smoothly transferred Katherine from the chopper stretcher to a hospital bed. Then a doctor, who Joseph instantly recognized, took over her care, pushing the others aside. Brooke moved to Joseph, wrapping an arm around his back while he placed his arm over her shoulder and gazed at his wife looking so pale in that big bed.

"She *will* make it, Joseph. You know the best of the best work here," Brooke told him.

"We'll save her, Joseph," Dr. Spence Whitman said. Joseph couldn't even smile at this man he'd admired since the first time they met many years ago.

"Don't let her die," Joseph managed to croaked from his tight throat.

"You know I won't let that happen," the doctor said. But there was fear in the doctor's eyes that he was trying to hide. Doctor's never told family they could keep someone alive. But in this case, they'd keep that promise no matter what it took.

Joseph nodded, and then in a flash, the team of doctors and other medical staff were gone . . . along with his wife.

Just like that, his Katherine was taken away from him. He took a hesitant step to follow, but Brooke gently grabbed under his arm and stopped him, letting go once there was no resistance.

"Let them do their job," she said solemnly. "Let's go look for the rest of the family."

Joseph wanted to argue, but he knew deep down she was right. These men and women might have to cut Katherine open, they might have to do things that Joseph couldn't possibly watch.

One thing was sure, though, Joseph wanted Katherine to have the best possible care. He wanted them to care for her to the best of their ability. And he knew if he was there glaring and barking out orders, he could mess them up.

He hung his head as his body slumped at the weight of not knowing what was happening. He absently allowed Brooke to comfort him as best she could. The only person who could give him real comfort was Katherine.

"I can't lose her," he said, panic and sorrow clear in his broken whisper.

"I know, Joseph, I know," Brooke said.

Once again, she gently wrapped her hand under his arm and started moving forward, leading both of them to the waiting room. He wasn't sure what would come next. If it wasn't good, he didn't want to know because he wouldn't live without Katherine.

She was his world.
She was the center of his universe.
She was his everything.
The sun would no longer rise without her, and the stars wouldn't shine.

"Save her," he whispered as he looked upward. Brooke didn't respond. She knew he wasn't talking to her right then . . . he was saying a heartfelt prayer. He gazed upward for several moments, and then he bowed his head. He uttered a long, needful, sincere prayer for the first time in a long, long while.

Chapter Four

"Not guilty."

For just a second, the entire courtroom went completely silent. But that was bound to break — and break it did.

Throughout this commotion Avery's face didn't change — not even a tick of the eyes or a slight twitch of her lips. She didn't smile or frown. She was steady, calm, and facing forward as cameras zoomed in on her.

Carl Schwartz, formally known by his call sign, Sleep, had been unable to look away from this woman for weeks as this trial had dragged on. At first, he'd only made an appearance to make sure the absolute piece of garbage who was responsible for the death of a highly decorated veteran paid the ultimate price. Carl had planned to attend one or two days of the trial. But after his first visit, he hadn't been able to stay away.

At first he'd been impressed with the young lawyer, not at all worried about the outcome. The man she was defending was absolute scum. There was no way anyone would let him off for his crimes. But then he'd listened to the woman speak. She might be petite and look as if she wasn't even old enough to drive let alone practice law, but she might be the most intelligent person he'd ever run across. And that was saying a lot, as he was surrounded daily by brilliant minds. He wasn't too far down the rungs on the genius level IQ test himself.

But this woman was brilliant.

She was beyond capable, and she was fighting for the wrong side. He'd witnessed her falter only once, and he was sure not a single other person had noticed the moment. He'd only caught it because he couldn't keep his eyes off of her.

Her client had been walking into the courtroom early in the morning, the reporters talking amongst themselves, not paying him or anyone else any attention as the trial was nearing its end, and they'd watched the man walk in dozens of times now. Avery had been leaning against the wall at the back of the room looking forward as the client entered.

He'd noticed she liked to arrive early and observe the room. She was good at watching everything around her. Their eyes had connected once. He'd made sure it hadn't happened again. He wanted to be a ghost to her, to be someone she could pass on the street and not recognize. That helped him to be as invisible as she tried to be outside this room.

He'd made sure to not sit in the same seat twice, to move about the entire room, to get different perspectives, to make himself not only invisible, but to be able to see different faces, to judge the temperament of the room. He'd also changed what he wore daily, the way his hair was combed, and even his posture as he sat. Because he was sure this woman took note of all of that and categorized the people in the audience as much as she did the legal players and the jurors.

But on that morning, he was in a back corner, slouched down and looking at her with hooded eyes. Her client had entered the courtroom between two officers, then passed by the young, pretty court recorder and flicked his fingers across his boner as he'd licked his lips. With his hands cuffed in front of him, it would've been hard for anyone to notice. But Carl wasn't the average person, and he was even more observant than Ms. Klum.

For the briefest of moments, Avery had narrowed her eyes, utter disgust showing in them as she'd looked at her client. It had come and gone so quickly, even if the reporters had been focused on her they never would've captured the image on film. But he was sure she wouldn't have made that expression if the cameras were turned her way. She was far too professional for that. In that moment he'd known she hated this man she was defending. What Carl didn't understand was how she could hate him and still defend him.

Her client, Jeremy Sputfield, was a major drug dealer. He was a rapist, a thief, and an embezzler. It didn't get more evil than that.

He obviously had zero conscience. He was also *very* good at covering his tracks. No witness had ever been identified, at least no one who'd been left alive. But Jeremy was smarter than he let on, because even suspected cases of his left zero evidence — *until* this trial.

A hooker who was currently in witness protection had been one of two of his last victims, and after a night of drugs and violent sex, she'd been left for dead, her throat slashed, her body bruised, and her heart barely beating. She'd told the police he'd kneeled on top of her as he'd slid his blade across her throat, doing it several times, each slash a bit deeper as she'd been able to do nothing but stare into his cold, dark eyes.

He'd laughed as he'd said he loved watching a life slowly ebb from a whore. He'd told her how much fun he'd had with her that night. She'd thought for sure she was dead. She believed the only thing that had saved her was that as he was slashing her throat for the fourth time, a phone call had interrupted him. He'd paused and answered, then smiled at whoever had called. She'd gone dead still, her eyes closed, her chest unmoving, as it was difficult to take in air anyway. She'd felt his weight leave her, then heard him chatting with someone as his voice faded.

She hadn't moved and must have passed out, because the next thing she remembered was being in a hospital room, armed guards at her door. She'd been afraid to tell her story, knowing this man was a huge player in San Francisco, knowing there was nowhere far enough she could run. But when another attempt to take her life had happened in her room, from a nurse who had barely been caught in time, she'd known she had little choice but to take their offer of witness protection.

There had been another victim with her that night. He hadn't survived. He'd happened to stumble onto the scene, a homeless veteran who'd served his country — and whose country had failed him upon returning from a war he'd never wanted to be in, but had done what he'd believed he'd had to do. Living with those memories had all but destroyed him. His next few decades on earth had left him drifting and unable to come back to societal norms, desolate, body broken, mind shattered, and all alone. In his last act on earth, though, he'd tried to save the woman — and he'd died for her. If he hadn't, she'd surely be dead too.

And somehow, even with eye-witness testimony, this piece of scum was still walking away. Carl was seething. He wanted to blame the entire system. It was so messed up. But he couldn't blame these jurors. They only had the information that was presented to them. The DA was an incompetent idiot who shouldn't be in his position and, unfortunately, Avery Klum was damn good at her job.

Carl watched as she walked away from her client, not saying anything to the man she'd set free to enact more deaths in the world. He watched as she passed reporters while uttering no comment, and then left the room.

He'd followed.

He was beginning to learn Avery's routine. He should simply walk away. But there was something about her that wasn't allowing him to do that. He wasn't sure what it was. Maybe it was because he knew she didn't like doing what she was doing. She should be fighting evil, not helping it. Or maybe he was wrong. He shook his head as he smirked. That was laughable — he was *never* wrong.

But then he was surprised again.

Avery changed her routine that night as she walked about ten city blocks, turning away from the main drag. It was pretty impressive considering the heels she wore. They must have some damn fine insoles. But after a while she stepped into a bar — and not a snobby business district, rubbing elbows, kind of establishment as he'd expect a woman like her to enter. He waited a minute, then followed her inside.

It was a Friday evening but still early. There were about a dozen people in the room, a band setting up in the back corner, and a few drunk guys sitting at the bar, talking about who caught the biggest fish, who'd been in the most fights, and who'd been wrongly arrested. It was typical bar talk. There were only a few females present and Avery's entrance hadn't gone unnoticed. But she wasn't making eye contact. She'd found an empty table in the back corner, and her body language screamed *do not touch, talk, or come near*.

He never had been good at following directions. He made his way toward her when he stopped just out of sight as an older, female bartender approached Avery.

"Hi, baby girl, rough day?" the woman asked as she set down some fruity looking drink.

"Yeah, not my best," Avery said with a sigh.

"Do you want to talk about it? I have a few minutes," the woman said.

"You know I can't talk in here, Mom. But you can tell me about your day," Avery said. "I could use the distraction."

"You know nothing exciting goes on in my life. I have to live vicariously through you," her mother said.

Carl was nearly speechless as he listened in on this interaction. From how cool and collected Avery was, he'd have expected her parents to be as icy cold as she appeared to be. But he knew appearances could be deceptive. Hell, people judged him all of the time — and they were always wrong.

Carl was a former SEAL, though he never talked about that time in his life. The last mission had been far too painful. When the dust had settled on that mission and he'd been forced into a medical discharge, he'd been lost. He hadn't allowed himself to wallow too long though.

SEALs didn't wallow.

He stood six feet tall, kept his body shredded, and took as much care with the insides as he did the outside. He was thirty-three, but had already lived enough lifetimes that there were days he felt ninety-three. He was originally from Philadelphia, his father a blue-collar construction worker, who'd taken his kids to church every Sunday and expected the rules to be followed.

His dad had believed in God, country, and discipline. His children had been raised with a firm, but loving hand, and though they might not have appreciated it as they were growing up, they sure as hell did later on in life. It had made them who they were.

His mother had emigrated from Germany, and from the moment his parents had met, it was love at first sight. While his dad was the authoritarian, his mother was the homemaker . . . and the comedian. She'd make them laugh when they wanted to yell or cry.

She'd held them when it felt as if the world was ending. He'd truly had the best of both worlds, and he missed them every single day.

Carl shook himself from his thoughts and focused again on Avery, wondering if she'd had a good childhood. What had shaped her into this controlling, super-composed woman he'd been watching for the past few weeks? What had made her seem so unflappable, and what above anything else, had made her defend the guilty?

"I won't get out of here until three so we might have to wait until Sunday to talk about it," her mother said.

"I know, Mom. The weekends are busy. How's Uncle Tom doing?"

"He's feeling a little better but hasn't been able to work for nearly a month now."

"I bet it's killing him, leaving the running of his bar to his baby sister and what he calls his hoodlum staff," she said with a genuine smile that completely transformed her face.

"Haha, it's almost as if you know him," her mother said.

"Well, he was the only father figure I had, so I know him a bit," Avery said.

"I know, baby girl. You've had a rough life. But look how well you're doing now," her mother said, apology in her tone.

"I didn't have it any rougher than a lot of kids, Mom. You did the best you could. I wish you'd come live with me, I have more than enough room for you. We could even get a different place that you could make feel like your own."

"I've told you a thousand times, a mother shouldn't be imposing on her grown child. I take care of myself just fine, and it's your turn to shine. I want you settling down and maybe even giving me grandbabies before I take my eternal rest," the woman said. Carl smiled, because this was a damn fine guilt trip. How many times had he heard that same speech during his life? Too many to count.

"I know I haven't been keen on getting into relationships. Of course, I saw the worst of the worst in my lifetime, but that's not the reason I don't get involved. I need to buckle down now more than ever before if I'm going to start my own law firm in the next few years," Avery said.

Ignoring the big career news, and instead focusing on the lack of interest in a relationship, her mother told her, "Don't ruin your life because of mistakes I made, Avery. I screwed up so many times. You don't have to do the same. You're beautiful, talented, and independent. You'll attract like-minded men if you'd simply open your heart to it. I wasn't anything. I didn't finish high school, and I was gullible. I regret that now. Yes, a career matters. But that won't hold you on a cold, lonely night.

You can look at certificates on your wall, but those honors can't comfort you when nothing goes right. A family will give you peace, and trauma, but it will always be there for you, and ensure you have help to get through the hardest times in life."

"I get what you're saying, but you have to stop blaming yourself, Mom, for everything that happened in your lifetime and mine. You did the best you could under extreme circumstances. I don't want to hear you blaming yourself for things that were beyond your control."

"I try real hard not to, but when I see you miserable, I can't help myself," her mother said.

"Well then, I guess I'm just going to have to show you how truly happy I am," Avery said, reaching across the table and squeezing her mother's hand.

"I love you, darling," her mom said as she stood, regaining her composure after allowing herself to wallow for a minute. Avery stood as well and gave her mom a hug before the woman walked back to the bar. Avery sat back down, and that's when Carl moved in, taking a seat across from her without asking for permission.

If looks could kill, Carl had no doubt he'd be toast right then and there. Avery didn't say a word as she lifted her fruity drink and took a sip from the straw, her eyes like daggers, her body language anything but welcoming.

He leaned back and grinned, glad he'd decided to speak to this woman. He had a feeling it was going to be one hell of a conversation. He'd been ticked at her for weeks — but also, strangely drawn in. The plot had thickened tonight, and he wanted answers. Maybe he was making it a new mission. He wasn't exactly sure what the heck he was doing, but he was excited, whatever it was.

When he didn't say anything, he saw surprise in her eyes. He could tell other men had tried to pick her up in bars before, and he was pretty sure all she had to do was give them the death glare and they went scampering away. She obviously hadn't met a real man yet.

Before their silence was broken, her mother was back, a huge grin on her face as she looked from her daughter to Carl. Carl broke eye contact to look at Avery's mom.

"What can I get you to drink, sugar?" she asked. He finally was able to read the letters on her name badge — Bobbi.

"Hi, Bobbi, my name's Carl. How are you?" he asked with his most charming smile. Women had told him all he had to do was smile and it made them want to drop their panties.

He loved women — all women. They were beautiful, fun, soft and sleek, and great to speak to . . . and very easily interchangeable.

Why wouldn't he love women of all ages, races, and bodies? Life would be boring if he stuck to one type. Having a new woman as often as most people cleaned their floors was like taking a new adventure multiple times a year.

Before she replied to his question, he answered her original inquiry, noting the glare coming from across the table, "I'll take a double rum and coke on ice, please. I'll trust your decision on the rum," he added while giving the woman a flirtatious wink.

"Are you going to be eating?" she asked. Carl heard the exasperated sigh from Avery across the table. He could practically feel the heat coming off of her as anger built. She was feeling betrayed by her mother for not kicking this strange man from her booth, and ticked that this man was at her table. But not only was Bobbi not escorting Carl away, she was befriending him. Carl instantly liked Bobbi, and Bobbi obviously liked Carl — a big advantage in his mission to break this woman into talking to him.

"I'm starving, and there's nothing better than some good bar food," Carl said.

This time Avery huffed outloud, drawing the attention of both Carl and Bobbi.

"Are you hungry too, dear?" her mother sweetly asked.

"He's *not* with me," Avery said through gritted teeth. "I've never met him before. I don't know why he's sitting at my table, and I *really* don't know why you're catering to him!" Her voice rose in the middle but then tapered back down. Carl learned another weakness of Avery's. She obviously didn't like creating scenes. He, on the other hand, didn't mind doing that one little bit.

"Well, that wasn't very neighborly." Bobbi scolded her daughter, and Carl had to fight not to laugh. He could see himself coming to this bar again. He was enjoying Bobbi's wit and company.

"I'm not *trying* to be friendly, Mother. I'm trying to decompress after a long day of work," Avery said, her cheeks having a physical reaction as they pinkened.

"Well, sometimes we do both at the same time," Bobbi told her daughter. She then turned back to Carl. "What's your full name, sugar?"

"Carl Schwartz," he said, standing to show her respect as he shook her hand. "It's very nice to meet you."

"I'm Bobbi Klum, and the pleasure's all mine," she said with the slightest giggle that made his grin grow.

"Are you *flirting*, Mother?" Avery gasped. "He's *half* your age."

Bobbi didn't even blink as she smiled at Carl, then turned and winked at her daughter. "Oh, baby girl, that just means he's more fun," she said with a laugh. "I'll get those menus." She turned and sashayed away, her hips swinging. Carl let out a whistle, making her turn and send him a kiss through the air.

When he turned back to look at Avery, he laughed. Her mouth was hanging open as her eyes whipped back and forth from him to her mother. She wasn't doing so well at keeping that steel composure she was so damn good at in the courtroom.

"What are you eating?" he asked as if they were two ordinary people having a normal conversation. He decided right then and there he wasn't bringing up the case — not yet. He wanted to figure this woman out first. Then he was going to pounce.

"I'm not eating! At least not with you. And what in the hell was that? If you're some gigolo, just know that my mother doesn't have money."

His grin never faltered. Setting up his words specifically to get a reaction, Carl said, "Oh, I'm no gigolo. I have my own money, little girl. I look for quality in my partners."

"I'm not a little girl," she said, her voice agitated. "I'm a successful businesswoman." She lifted her chin in a haughty expression as she seemed to remember who she was. It was fascinating to watch how instantly she pulled herself together.

"Oh, really, what do you do?"

She opened her mouth, shut it again, then shifted. "It's none of your business. I have zero desire to get to know you or tell you about myself."

Her mother returned with menus, which Carl didn't glance at. He enjoyed switching his gaze between mother and daughter much more than gazing at a menu that was nearly the same in every bar. "I'll have a bacon cheeseburger, cheese fries, and another double rum and coke."

"You have good taste," Bobbi said. "And you, dear?" she asked her daughter.

Carl felt as if he'd won a gold medal when she sighed, giving up, at least for now. "I'll have the fish and chips," she mumbled. "Extra tartar *and* cocktail sauce, and thousand island for my fries, and another drink please."

"Sure thing, darlings. I'll put you at the front of the line since this is a family place," Bobbi said. "And since you're so dang edible," she added to Carl.

"I do like to nibble," Carl said with a bite in the air that led to another disgusted sigh out of Avery. Both Bobbi and Carl laughed. Then Bobbi sashayed away again. She truly was a gem.

"Are you just kidding around, or are you *really* trying to pick up my mother?" Avery asked.

Damn, Carl was enjoying his night. He'd been so angry with this woman for weeks, and now he was finding himself truly enjoying her company. Something was wrong with that — but he wasn't a man to fight his instincts, and right now, they were telling him to find out all he could about this woman.

"I like your mom. She's pretty fantastic," he said, meaning it.

"That didn't answer my question."

"Then I guess there are some things you just don't get to know," he told her, leaning back again, making himself comfortable.

"Why did you sit with me?" she asked.

"Because I wanted to," he told her.

"Do you always sit with random strangers without an invite?"

He thought for a moment. "Not always, but when I feel the need, I go where I want," he answered honestly.

"And what if you're not wanted?" He could see why she was such a great attorney. She wasn't one to back down, nor ask a question in a multitude of ways. He liked it.

"I can tell when I'm truly not wanted. That doesn't happen very often," he said with a shrug.

"Here you two go. Enjoy," Bobbi said as she placed their drinks in front of them. "Be right back with the food."

She was gone and back again in a flash. Carl didn't ask how the food had been made so quickly but figured his cheeseburger was lifted from another order, and Avery probably ordered the same thing each time she came in, so it was started as soon as she stepped inside. His mouth watered at the sight and smell of the food Bobbi sat in front of them. He picked up a fry that wasn't covered in cheese, reached over, dipped it in her large container of thousand island, then took a bite. She gawked at his audacity.

"Delicious," he said, licking his lips. Her hooded eyes gazing at his mouth didn't go unnoticed. That made him realize he hadn't been with a woman in a while. He wondered why. It wasn't as if he didn't have options. When he felt the need, he satisfied it. He realized he just hadn't felt the need in a while. Apparently he was feeling it now — with *this* woman.

"You are so . . . so . . . so . . . rude," she said, scooting her dipping sauce closer to her.

He reached over and dipped another fry, then laughed after he swallowed. "I have much longer arms than you, dear," he said. "And you have plenty there for the two of us. I think the cook likes you, cause he or she went way overboard here." They each had enough food on their plates for four people.

"This is a lot more than they normally serve," she noted. "Maybe it's because Julianne looked out, saw the size of you, and decided a buffet probably couldn't fill you." He didn't think she'd meant the words as a compliment, but he still smiled.

"Thanks, I like to take care of myself." He lifted his burger and took a bite, the flavors bursting on his tongue. "Hot damn!" he exclaimed, making her jump as she nibbled on a fry. "I've just found my new favorite place. I might have to wear sweats the next time I come in here though so there's room to expand."

She stared at him, trying to keep her features composed, but then a laugh spilled out. She was beginning to loosen up. He liked that — he liked it a hell of a lot.

"It's shockingly good here. And as greasy and terrible as it looks for you, my uncle actually buys quality oils and ingredients so you get all of the bar flavor, with a little less of the heart attack risk."

"You're obviously proud of your uncle," he pointed out.

She smiled again. "He's a really good man — one of the few good men out there," she said. She seemed to realize she was interacting with him and tried to stop by taking a big bite of her fish that was smothered in tartar and cocktail sauce. A bit was left on her lip, and he had to fight himself not to reach across the table and wipe it away. This woman was growing sexier by the second.

"I always find off-the-wall places to dine, knowing I'll get better food. And I love supporting small business owners since I grew up in a very blue-collar family. Pops worked the same job for thirty-eight years," he told her.

His words seemed to make her thaw a bit more. He noted that the alpha routine worked slightly, which was good as he couldn't change his nature, but she did seem to respond to honesty even more. He could give her only so much of that, enough to draw her in without going overboard, which would make him vulnerable — a place he never allowed himself to be. After losing a lot of brothers-in-arms, and then a couple of years later his paretns, and then his sister, he really locked that part of himself up tight.

He also knew he needed to bait the hook and draw her in without tugging so hard she slipped away again. There was a delicate balance with a woman like Avery. If he wanted a one-night stand, which he wasn't knocking, he could have that. But if he wanted a bit more, there was a dance that had to be performed. He was confused at wanting to spend more time getting to know her. Where did that come from?

He'd been wanting information, wanting to grill her. He was finding he wanted more than that. He wasn't sure what that *more* was yet.

For the next hour he kept the conversation light, managing to draw a few things from her, without giving too much of himself away. He also noticed she stopped herself at three drinks, leaving her with a slight buzz, without sending her into the drunk zone. She had a lot of control. Everything about her impressed him.

He drank his rum and cokes and barely felt them. He had an iron gut, and it took a lot to inebriate him. When it came time to pay, he refused the family discount and overrode Avery as he paid the tab, leaving a hell of a tip for her mother.

"I'm thinking we'll continue tomorrow," Carl said as he stepped outside the increasingly loud bar, taking in the fresh night sea air, a welcome relief after being inside for so long.

"Not a chance," she said with finality, or what she supposed was a hard no. She obviously hadn't been paying attention to what he was saying with both words and body language if she thought he was so easily pushed away. She kept on talking as she moved toward the street. "This was a one-time deal."

"I don't think so," Carl told her, confidence radiating off of him. "I tend to get what I want."

She stopped and looked at him, her arm in the air as she waited for a cab. She looked absolutely adorable — and utterly out of place in her expensive suit and shoes. She gave him a confident smile, a smile he was sure she aimed toward her opponents in court.

"You better prepare for disappointment, Mr. Schwartz, because I don't do what I don't want to do." A victorious smile shaped her lips as a cab pulled up.

Before she could reach for the door, he stepped up to the car, opening it for her. She gave him a roll of her eyes before she slipped inside, and then he leaned down, way down, getting his face very close, their breaths heating each other's lips. He was utterly satisfied when her breath hitched and her eyes widened.

"I've been disappointed in life. I won't be where you're concerned," he promised.

He didn't allow her to reply. He simply shut the door, gave a couple of knocks on top of the vehicle, and the cab drove away. He smiled, knowing she had to be seething that he hadn't allowed her the last word.

A smile was resting on his lips as he watched the cab speed away. He was interrupted from his smug thoughts as a familiar voice spoke. "I haven't seen a man hold my daughter's attention for that long in . . . well, forever."

Carl turned to find Bobbi leaning against the side of the building, puffing on a cigarette as she smiled. She seemed to be stunned and impressed at the same time. He tended to have that effect on people.

"That's because she hadn't met me yet," he said as he moved to stand next to her. "Do you have any advice for me?"

She laughed, then inhaled and sighed before releasing a large puff of smoke. "I keep trying to quit these damn things, and I do great at home, but then I come to work and smell them, and it's all over," she said with a laugh.

He nodded. He knew all about addictions. He'd watched many of his brothers and sisters suffer with them after all they saw on the battlefield. It had broken his heart to the core when his sister had overdosed. He struggled with the flash of that memory until Bobbi's voice started up again.

"The best advice I can give is that her bark is so much worse than her bite," she said as she put the cigarette out in the ashtray and walked back inside without saying anything more.

Carl walked away, his place a couple of miles from the bar. It was a beautiful night, and he was up for the walk. It would give him time to think. He wasn't sure what was drawing him toward this woman, or where that was leading him, but he *was* sure she'd be at that bar the next night — and he was going to be there.

This had become about more than just one court case. This was a woman he needed to know more. He didn't know why, but he *had* to know her. Hopefully that ebbed pretty dang quick. He shrugged internally. It always ebbed. The voice in the back of his mind was telling him the draw had never been this strong before though.

    He ignored that voice. This would pass just as life continued to pass every single day no matter how much a person tried to stop it.

Chapter Five

The hospital waiting room was utter chaos, which was nothing new. In downtown Seattle there was always something happening, whether it was illness, accidents, or uprisings. The bottom line was the hospitals were filled to capacity a lot more than anyone would like.

Brooke Anderson led Joseph to a large waiting area where they managed to find a few empty seats. He was running on autopilot, allowing Brooke to take the lead. He was so panicked at losing his wife he could barely stand, let alone walk and think about where he was going.

"Sit, Joseph. We'll know something soon," Brooke gently told him.

He glanced down, the seats blurring before him, then he turned and sat, hoping his depth perception was okay, otherwise he'd end up in a room next to his wife. Maybe that wasn't such a bad thing.

Brooke took the seat beside him, and reached over and took his hand, squeezing it, causing his eyes to water. There were so many unanswered questions. How had this happened? Why? Who had done it? And would Katherine be okay?

Maybe a few seconds passed, and maybe minutes. But finally Joseph found his voice. "Brooke?" he uttered, his voice croaking. He cleared his throat and found he couldn't get the words out. She squeezed his hand, letting him know she'd wait, that he could take all the time he needed. It was odd to be on the receiving end of such comfort when he was normally the person administering it.

"What is it, Joseph?" she finally asked when the silence stretched on for too long. He wondered if that was the voice Brooke used with her patients. It was calm, and kind, and did have a way of soothing him.

He cleared his throat and tried again. "What happened? What do you know? How? Please . . . tell me . . ." He paused again as he fought tears. "Please tell me anything you can. You might find it small, but it could be the break in the case."

Brooke looked beaten as she maintained eye contact. She then exhaled as he saw her thinking over the past hour. It had been one of the longest of his life, but he was sure it had been just as bad for her as she'd been with his Katherine, feeling utterly helpless.

He sat up straighter as he tried getting stronger. His wife needed him to be the man he'd always been. She needed him to not fall apart. He had to work on that and stay in the here and now, not letting his mind take him to the worst-case scenario. He couldn't go anywhere; he had to be with his wife.

"I don't know who or why besides what Katherine told me about a possible drug deal," she finally said. "I saw Katherine walking away from her favorite place near the lake. I was excited to see her since she'd called me the night before, but I hadn't been able to talk as Finn and I were walking from the house to go on a date. She told me she wanted to hear all about it before ending the call. Finn and I had such a beautiful night and I couldn't wait to share with her." She stopped as tears choked her voice.

"I was lost in my thoughts when I moved down the trail, then lost sight of Katherine. I stopped for a few minutes when I saw a mother raccoon with her babies stumbling after her. If I hadn't stopped I would've been there sooner . . ." She gasped as tears fell down her cheeks.

"Do not blame yourself," Joseph said, this time squeezing *her* hand, comforting her. He knew how guilt could eat away at a person's soul, and this was in no way Brooke's fault.

"I know that logically, but I was excited to talk to her, and then to get distracted by something that silly. I don't think it was so much the animals as it was that I also know Katherine truly enjoys alone time by that lake. I was giving her a few extra minutes before I bombarded her. Of course, as much as she enjoys her alone time, she also loves speaking to each of us about our romantic life. I know I'm babbling here, but I just wish I would've been there sooner."

"Go on, Brooke. I want to hear it all," he told her. "And I'm grateful you were there. If you hadn't seen her, if you hadn't gotten to her, I don't know what would've happened." A shudder passed through him.

"When I turned the final corner, I saw two men standing over Katherine," Brooke finally said, barely able to talk through her tears. "I couldn't see their faces. But one of the men had shoulder length dark hair. The other was slightly taller and far skinnier. I yelled at them while pulling out my phone and dialing nine one one. They fled as I drew near."

She stopped again and caught her breath. "I called you next and then tried to help, but I didn't know what they'd done to her and I didn't know how long they'd been there. It couldn't have been more than two minutes, but a lot of damage can be done in that amount of time and she wasn't sure what had happened. I'm so sorry, Joseph, I'm so sorry I stopped to look at those stupid raccoons!"

He had to fight tears as he gripped her hand. "Do not apologize again. This wasn't your fault," he repeated.

Joseph took in all of her words as he thought about the situation, his forehead curving in an angry scowl, his eyes becoming slivers. He needed to get his hands on someone. He needed the men who'd been standing over his wife to pay. There'd be a reckoning, that was set in stone.

Joseph didn't enjoy feeling this way. He was a man who preferred to smile and laugh, and maybe even cry once in a while. He was a man who loved big and took kindness and compassion as the real strength of a man's character over revenge and victory. But all of that was overridden with the need for justice. He wasn't often pushed, but when he was, he didn't back down. In his honest opinion, he was simply a man who knew the difference between right and wrong.

"I'll find out who did this," Joseph said, unaware he was going to speak until the words came out. His voice sounded deadly.

"Let's get through tonight, and then we'll figure this out, Joseph," Brooke told him.

He knew she was being wise, but it wasn't what he wanted to hear. He was a man of action, and to sit there doing nothing wasn't a good place for him. He leaned back, getting lost in his thoughts as he put together a few actionable plans inside his jumbled mind.

Anything could be solved if you looked at it long enough. Life was like a game of chess. Each move you made dictated the next play. If a person moved wisely, they'd ultimately win. If they messed up just once, their game became much more difficult.

Time stopped having meaning as the two of them sat there. He was pulled from his ever-evolving thoughts as a familiar voice broke through his reverie.

"Dad." The voice was urgent and loud as his eldest son, Lucas, walked through the large waiting area.

Joseph looked up, along with all of the other patrons in the room, as his frantic son moved forward. Only a step behind Lucas was Alex, his middle son. Joseph could instantly see the best of his wife in his two sons. Mark, the youngest of the three boys, resembled Katherine the most in features and personality. While his two eldest were more like him, Mark was a softer soul like his beautiful mother.

"Dad," Alex said. Joseph stood as they neared. The doors opened again and two women stepped through. Of course they were there. Not only did they love and support their husbands, but they loved Joseph and Katherine. Joseph was a blessed man indeed. Before the sliding doors could begin closing, a young woman walked in, and Joseph felt his heart flow with love.

His eldest granddaughter, Jasmine, came through, looking up, immediately making eye contact with Joseph. Her face was red and swollen, yet it didn't alter her looks. She truly was beautiful, inside and out. He stepped forward, meeting his family halfway, tears flowing down his cheeks. He didn't care that his raw pain had manifested into tears.

"What happened? Do you know anything?" Lucas asked, his voice choked. Joseph hugged him hard.

"I'm scared," Alex admitted, something Joseph realized he'd never heard Alex say before.

"We're all scared and so very sorry," Amy, Lucas's wife, said, before grabbing Joseph next, and holding on tight with her small arms.

Questions were fired at him without giving him a chance to answer. That was okay because he wasn't sure he'd be able to speak for a few moments as the love of his family flowed over him.

"Grandpa, please tell me she's okay," Jasmine said. Amy stepped back, allowing her daughter to reach her grandpa, and Joseph clung onto Jasmine, the two of them shaking in their mutual pain.

Every family said there was never a favorite, but each family also knew that was a white lie said to make sure no one felt hurt. Jasmine was his first grandchild, his first realization that his family would go on forever. From the first moment he'd held her in his trembling arms, there had been a bond between them that nothing in this world, or the next, could ever break. Holding her right then was exactly what he'd needed to keep his feet solidly on the ground.

"Your grandmother is so strong, baby girl. She *will* pull through this. It's just a bump in a very long and very beautiful road," he told her, stepping back only far enough to look into her glassy eyes.

A moment of happiness ran through him — he was pleased that up to this point his granddaughter had never experienced anything but joy in her short eighteen years. Her words brought him back to attention.

"How do you know that, Grandpa? On the ride here Mom and Dad said she . . ." She stopped, not able to repeat what had happened in the chopper. Her parents had been told she'd flatlined, but none of them could say the word outloud, not when it was in regards to Katherine.

"I have faith, Jasmine. We all *need* to have faith," Joseph said as he took her hand and placed it on his heart. "Feel this?" he choked. "It's too full of love to lose her. And I know yours is just as full. Our love will keep her with us." He had to stop or he was going to completely fall apart.

Jasmine didn't even attempt to stop her tears as she cradled her head against her grandpa's heart, allowing the gentle beat to soothe her. He rubbed her satin hair as she shook in his arms. Needing to be strong for her was helping him more than anything else could have at that moment.

"Do you have more information?" Alex asked. Their voices had all quieted as they stood in a circle. Joseph knew that Jasmine being there with them was keeping the panic down, was keeping them from shouting. None of them were used to waiting for anyone. Situations like this were foreign to them. They were leaders, they were warriors. They didn't like their lives being in someone else's hands.

Joseph didn't know what to say to Alex, but he was saved from answering when the doors to the room opened again and more family stepped inside. Now the already crowded room was growing to alarming numbers. Mark and Emily pushed their way through. They gave Joseph half hugs as Jasmine wasn't leaving his side, both giving their niece a gentle kiss on the top of her head as they backed away to the rest of the family.

Jasmine was the only grandchild there. Some of the kids were too young, or staying at camps, and some were watching the younger children at home. The hospital wasn't the place for the kids right now. They wouldn't be able to see their grandmother yet, and it would only cause them panic. It was better to gather at the mansion when the initial scare was over. Joseph had no doubt it *would* be over and he *would* be taking his wife home first thing in the morning. He'd never let her out of his sight again.

"We have a room for your family," a nurse said as she stepped forward with Brooke. "Brooke's let me know there will be many more people showing up, and we thought we'd give you privacy."

Joseph could barely focus on the young redheaded nurse. He wasn't able to process her words. His mind just couldn't focus on anything.

"This way, Dad," Lucas said as he gripped Joseph's free elbow and smiled at his daughter, who was still clinging tightly to her grandfather.

"Okay," Joseph answered, finding himself walking forward, surrounded by a circle of his family.

They moved down a hallway and entered a room with dim lighting, a lot of seats, a few tables, and other items that were meant to occupy a waiting family. Joseph didn't care about any of it. He just cared that his family was there.

"What do we know?" Alex asked, trying again to get information.

"We should wait for the rest of the family. We know more are coming," Brooke said. The look she got from Joseph's kids was incredulous. They didn't care if the story had to be repeated five hundred times. They wanted answers.

Just as Brooke began to tell the story again, the door opened and in walked George and Richard, Joseph's brothers.

"Oh, Joseph," George said as he rushed forward, his wife, Esther, at his side. "Please tell me she's okay." It was a command, and Joseph knew how his brother felt. He wanted to command she be okay too.

"We're still waiting," Joseph said. Richard stepped up and hugged him.

"She *will* be okay. There's no doubt in my mind. She's too strong not to be," Richard assured him.

"Yes, she's a strong, stubborn, and kind woman. Nothing can take her from us. She's a fighter, and some criminal thugs won't get the best of her," Joseph said, his eyes flashing in anger at the end of his words.

"Tell us what in the hell happened," Lucas said, his patience ending as he waited to hear what was going on with his mother.

"I'm sorry, Lucas," Brooke said. "Let me give you the quick version before the door opens again," she said, touching his arm, instantly calming the man who was normally so kind.

Brooke gave a shortened version of how she'd seen Katherine, then the men standing over her, then their ride in the chopper.

When she finished they were all silent, not knowing how to respond or what to say. They were in utter shock that someone had dared attack Katherine. What sort of monsters did that to a frail woman?

"I need answers, updates, *anything* on how Katherine is doing," Joseph said when there was a lull in the conversation.

"On it," Brooke said. She didn't work at the hospital, but she had connections, and she was well aware that the Anderson name carried power in this place they had practically built. She stepped from the room, and Joseph knew it wouldn't be long before they got an update.

She came back a few minutes later with a semblance of a smile. "I requested Dr. Spence Whitman." At her words, Joseph felt relief rush through him.

His family and the Whitman family had been friends for years. As a matter of fact, Joseph might not say it out loud, but he'd had a hand in matchmaking with Spence's father and a few ladies in Montana, to find Spence's wife, Sage. Spence was so sought after as a surgeon he spent several days a month in Seattle. He was sought after nationwide for his phenomenal emergency room skills.

Spence was there in minutes, and his relaxed gait as he moved forward had more of a calming effect on Joseph than any words that could've been said. Spence didn't stop, just pushed forward and gave Joseph a hug.

"I should've been in here sooner, but I was with someone more important," Spence said.

"Damn straight you were," Joseph said. He wanted to demand answers, but he knew this honorable man well, and he knew if there was something horrible, he wouldn't beat around the bush.

"I'm sure as hell glad you're here, Spence," Lucas said.

"We all are," Mark said. They all shook Spence's hand.

"Tell me what's happening with my wife, Doc," Joseph said.

Spence smiled. "Doc? Really?" he replied.

"Here, in this realm, you are *Dr. Whitman*," Joseph insisted, emphasizing the word *doctor* as he gave a quick glare at his sons for their lack of respect. Even in the hardest of times, you had to have respect, or what was left in the world? "You're keeping my wife safe and you're one hell of a doctor and that's what you'll be called."

"Alrighty then," Spence said. There was so much admiration between the two of them. "I can respect that."

"We had scans done. The CT results are being reviewed by the neuro team. I've also had

X-rays and MRIs worked up to ensure there are no broken bones. She's on a ventilator, but before you panic, don't. This is to keep her safe. We have her in an induced coma while we wait for all of these tests to be reviewed. The top neuro doctors in the hospital, and a couple in our sister facility, are on this, and we aren't panicking because we *are* keeping her stable."

Placing a hand on Joseph's shoulder and looking at him like he was the only person in the room, he said, "Trust me when I say this, she isn't in pain. I don't make promises, Joseph, but I can promise you that I don't believe there's anything right now to cause me to believe she won't come out of this just fine. I would tell you to worry if I believed you needed to. As I get more information I won't make you wait," he promised, slowly dropping his hand.

"You can't say words like ventilator and coma and not expect me to panic," Joseph said, his throat tight and his heart thumping.

"I know it seems scary, and none of us like to see anyone in this situation, but I'm assuring you we're being overly cautious. We know what Katherine means to all of you and to my family too. She means the world to this entire hospital. She won't be alone for a second, and like I said, the best of the best are working on *and* for her."

"I'm scared," Joseph admitted.

"I know, Joseph. Keep your family with you, remind yourself you've been through hell, and come out the other side. You're strong, and your wife is stronger, even if she hides her strength in kindness and compassion. She's also healthy and so much better off than most at her age," Spence said.

"Age is just a number," Joseph said.

"I believe we're going to find nothing more than a severe concussion causing all of the issues. We can get control of that," Spence said.

"My poor Katherine," Joseph said with a sigh. He was going to kill those men who'd put her in this hospital.

The rest of the family asked several questions that Spence happily answered. After twenty more minutes, they finally gave the doctor a reprieve from the multiple voices raining down on him.

"I'll keep you updated," Spence promised before shaking hands all around, then walking from the room.

Joseph leaned against a chair and took a deep breath. Katherine was stable for now. And he was more than ready to get answers. He looked at Lucas, and his son seemed to understand without any words being spoken.

"What do you need, Dad?"

"I need to split this group up for a few," Joseph said. "Would you ladies mind if I speak with my brothers and the boys for a few minutes?"

"Of course not," Amy said. "We'll hunt down some coffee and snacks. This might be a long night and day, and we'll be prepared for it."

With that the women left the room. He loved how in sync his family was. No one had their feelings hurt, and they all worked together as a team. He looked at his brothers and his sons, and then he began to speak . . .

Chapter Six

Avery paced back and forth in her apartment as she told herself repeatedly she wasn't going to the bar. She didn't want to see the obnoxious man from the night before. She *hadn't* been intrigued by him — not one little bit. She was going to stay in the house tonight and review files. Work was her life.

She sighed as she moved to her window and looked outside at the city skyline. Work *had* always been her life. But lately she'd been disillusioned. She couldn't help but feel bad for helping free some of the people she had. She could tell herself all day that she was doing the right thing, and she knew, more than anyone else, that innocent people *did* get convicted. It's what had made her enter the justice system in the first place.

But her last client had given her the creeps. A shudder ran through her as she thought about that man. He'd done some truly evil things. There was no doubt about it. And still, she'd fought hard for him, and because she had, he was now a free man. Would he hurt someone else? Would that be on her shoulders?

She shook her head, trying to assure herself he'd never actually admitted to her that he was guilty, *claiming* his innocence the entire time she'd defended him. She thought back to that day in court where he'd groped himself while walking by the court recorder. She'd been utterly disgusted by his action.

Her clock chimed and she looked at the wall, seeing it was eight. That might be early for a Saturday night in the Bay Area, but it was late for her. She liked to be in bed by ten so she could wake up at dawn, take a nice jog, and then start her workday while the rest of the city was just rising from the comfort of their beds. She liked to be better than everyone else. The more competitive she was, the further she'd make it in life. Wasn't there a saying that you could sleep when you were dead? That was the plan. She'd work hard her entire life, and then have eternal rest. Her stomach growled, reminding her she hadn't eaten since having a banana that morning after her run.

"I could go get a bite to eat. I'm sure he won't be there," she said aloud, feeling foolish that she was now talking to herself, and hating that a part of her was hoping he *would* be there.

It was absurd.

She knew nothing about this man. Yes, he'd been charming and said he was going to see her again. But he'd spent half the evening flirting with her mother. What in the heck did that mean? Yes, she knew it had been a joke with her mom, after her initial shock of it all, but still, she found herself slightly jealous. She wished she was able to be as confident and as at ease as her mother. Her mom had often told her she was far too serious.

But Avery had always needed to be serious. She'd seen the consequences of thinking life was nothing more than a game. It didn't go well. Sure, people had fun for a while, but then they found themselves broke, alone, hungry, and homeless, and often addicted to drugs and alcohol.

"The heck with it," Avery muttered as she grabbed her purse and headed for the door. "It's not to see him. I want to check on my mom, I'm hungry, and I don't feel like cooking." She shut and locked her door.

"What was that, dear?"

Avery jumped at the question, then felt her cheeks flush as she looked at her neighbor, Greta, who was obviously returning from walking her sweet little dog, Bella, who Avery had dogsat and walked a few times when Greta hadn't been feeling well.

"I guess I got caught talking to myself," Avery said with a sheepish smile.

"Oh, that's nothing," Greta said with a laugh. "I not only talk to myself on a daily basis, I also talk to my sweet Bella, who thinks I'm a genius." Avery laughed.

"That's because you are," Avery confirmed as she bent down and gave Bella a scratch behind the ears. The dog quickly flopped down and exposed her belly for a nice scratch.

"You are spoiled, little girl," she told the dog who grinned up at her with half hooded eyes while Avery kept scratching her. She reluctantly stopped and stood, the dog giving her a pouty look. "I'm going to see Mom. Is there anything you need from town?"

"You're always such a sweetheart, but Bella and I are headed to bed. Maybe next time I'll have you bring me back some onion rings," Greta said.

"I'll make sure I go earlier next time and do just that," Avery said. She loved her neighbor. She was quiet and kind . . . and definitely nosy.

If any stranger entered this hallway, Greta was on it in an instant. Not that Avery ever had visitors. It was impossible to have friendships when a person worked as much as she did. Well, her mother and uncle came over on occasion, but Greta knew them. She'd have cookies waiting for her uncle when he showed up. Greta made cookies for a lot of the people in the building.

The two women said their goodbyes, and then Avery was on her way. She always took the stairs, knowing she was too sedentary about 70 percent of the time with the job she had, so she was active as much as possible when she wasn't locked to a desk.

She made it to the curb, then hailed a cab. It didn't take her long to reach her uncle's bar, and as she stepped from the cab, she could hear music blaring. It was loud and bound to get even worse as the night wore on. She'd probably have a hard time getting a table, let alone her favorite one in the back corner. And she didn't want to seem as if she *wanted* to see Carl if he did happen to be there.

The second she was out of the cab, though, another person climbed in, and it pulled away. She stood on the curb, hesitating. She could always hail another and make a quick retreat. That didn't sit too well with her as she didn't like living in fear or being indecisive. She began walking away from the bar, though, needing to think for a few moments. Why was this man she'd met the night before even entering her thoughts? Why did he have any affect on her at all? She'd talked with him for a couple of hours. He was nothing to her. He certainly shouldn't be influencing where she went.

Avery was never indecisive. It wasn't in her nature. Why was she was acting that way all of a sudden? Maybe it was her last case, or maybe it was a lack of sleep, or maybe it was a six-foot man who'd made her feel something she didn't want to feel — hormones.

By the time she looked up she was about a block away from the bar. At least it was quieter. But this wasn't her favorite neighborhood when the sun went down. Her uncle was fine anywhere as he looked scarier than most criminals with his six-foot-plus height and three hundred pounds of mostly muscle. When you added in the long beard, tattoos, and eyes of steel, he was downright intimidating. To her, he was a big teddy bear though.

She turned to head back to the bar, her steps determined as she decided she wasn't going to live in fear of a man who'd been on her thoughts for twenty-four hours straight. However, she didn't make it more than a few steps when fingers clamped around her arm and she was being pulled into a dark alley.

"Stop!" she yelled as she frantically tried pulling away from the person who'd grabbed her. She knew better than to be wandering, especially when she wasn't paying attention to where she was going and wasn't carrying her pepper spray. Her mother was going to kill her if this person didn't do it first.

"I heard you come here. I was hoping to get you alone," the voice said, sending chills down her spine. She opened her mouth to scream, but her throat had constricted in fear and realization.

No matter how she tugged against him, he kept on pulling her with little effort, his fingers tightening around her arm. She tried kicking him, but her foot barely grazed his massive leg.

Then she felt a sharp stab of pain on her skull as something solid impacted her head. The world began spinning as stars flashed in front of her eyes, and she tried desperately to stay conscious. What had he hit her with? His fist? A gun? A bat?

"Why?" she asked weakly, her vision fading as he dragged her deeper inside the alley.

"Because I've been wanting to have a taste of you from the moment you stepped into that tiny room inside the jail," he told her. "I haven't ever had a woman as fine as you, and your ice-cold exterior makes me want you that much more. I'm sure there's a lot of repression tucked deep down inside, and I'm gonna bring it *all* out." He paused as he laughed. "Thanks for setting me free." He then leaned in and ran his tongue along her cheek and to the corner of her mouth, swiping it across, before his teeth nipped her bottom lip, making her stomach turn.

It was her client. It was the miserable dirtbag she'd defended with everything she had. It was the man she'd just set free the day before. She truly was a fool.

There was zero question now if he was guilty or not. The only bright light she could see at this moment, was that at least *she* was the victim, and it wasn't someone else. But even as she was telling herself that, she knew she wouldn't be his last. He'd never stop killing. It was who he was. He thrived on the power of taking what wasn't his, of bending whom he deemed weaker, to his own will.

As the dizziness slowed, making her able to focus again, she could finally see his face in the pale light from the streetlamp that cast more shadows than light in the narrow alley. There was nothing but evil in the man's expression. She'd seen it flash in his eyes in their time together over the past couple of months, but he'd managed to tamp it down. He wasn't even trying now.

"I messed up," she said. Her voice was stronger. She'd fight him with all she had, even knowing he'd easily out power her. She wouldn't cower though, wouldn't give him the satisfaction of begging. A man like him truly enjoyed the dominance of making someone submit.

"You *definitely* messed up. But I love how professional you were the entire time. Because for me, all of my time in that courtroom and inside that disgusting jail, whenever I was sitting next to you, I was fucking you in every way imaginable in my head, just waiting for the day I could make my fantasies a reality," he told her as he slammed her body against a solid brick wall.

The alley smelled stale and moldy. She could hear scurrying from behind a dumpster, and there were no voices to be heard, not even in the distance. She could scream, but she knew it wasn't going to do her a whole lot of good.

He reached up and cupped her breast, and that's when she knew she had to fight or die. She acted as if she was defeated as he ground his body against hers, burying his face in her neck and biting her skin before his grotesque tongue swiped out. He moaned against her as he pressed in closer, and she choked back the bile rising in her throat.

"You smell so damn good," he said before biting her again. She had to fight not to cry out. He was hurting her and getting off on it. The more she cried, the worse he'd be. She waited for a split second longer, and when he pulled back the slightest bit, she made her move.

Her knee lifted with all the strength she had as she aimed for his most vulnerable part. She connected, but he turned the slightest bit at the moment of contact, and though she'd glanced his parts, the majority of the impact was on his thigh. He yelped, but didn't let go of her as his fingers tightened even more, one hand squeezing her breast so hard she wondered if it would be disfigured, the other digging into her arm, his nails cutting the skin.

"You'll pay for that, bitch," he hissed, pain laced in his voice.

She struggled against him, trying to pull away before he made a full recovery. But his hands were vices, and his body was blocking hers. She was trapped between him and the wall, and neither force was giving. She finally managed to scream with everything she had, but she'd barely gotten any sound out when he punched her straight in the jaw. Blood filled her mouth as she crumpled against him, the pain excruciating. Her stomach heaved and she almost threw up at his feet.

He stepped back, then threw her to the ground with the force of a wrecking ball. She landed on her hands and knees on the dirty, hard asphalt, barely managing to stop her face from connecting. And then she did vomit as his foot connected with her abs, jerking her body up, before she flew sideways, landing on her back, this time her skull connecting with the pavement, making her see stars.

Her head was spinning out of control as she tried spitting excess vomit and blood from her mouth. She couldn't stop the spinning, couldn't focus her eyes. She couldn't fight if she couldn't see her enemy.

"I wanted to take my time with you, but now you've pissed me off," he said as he dropped down on top of her, sitting on her stomach while pinning her arms beneath his knees, her body unable to move beneath the massive weight.

He pulled out a wicked looking blade, and she felt tears come to her eyes. She wouldn't shed them. There was no way she was going to let him see her defeat. With all of the energy she had left, she glared. Her poor mother was going to be devastated when she was found.

He dropped the knife toward her chest and she stared into his face, unwilling to close her eyes and give him the satisfaction of her terror. She attempted to smile, to mock him into ending this fast, but her lips wouldn't cooperate. She might not be telling him she was scared, but she *was* terrified. The things he'd done to that prostitute had been so horrific it had been unthinkable one human could do that to another.

She felt stinging pain as the tip of the blade cut her chest. But he hadn't been trying to slice her open yet. He'd simply cut through her shirt, exposing her breasts.

"You're disgusting," she said as he grabbed her breast again, squeezing so hard she couldn't keep the cry of pain back this time.

"You have no idea," he told her as he began to bend toward her chest. The thought of his mouth on her again made her try to struggle, but it was no use. He'd won. She couldn't watch this any longer. She closed her eyes and turned her head, hoping she could take herself somewhere else in her mind.

But his mouth never made contact. There was a grunt of pain, and then his weight was off of her. She was afraid to open her eyes, afraid he was poised above her, waiting for her to open her eyes before he did his next sadistic thing.

A crunching sound was followed by a cry of pain a few feet away. Her eyes flashed open and she saw him on the ground, blood dripping from his nose and mouth. She only saw that face for a millisecond before a fist slammed into it again, crushing what was left of his nose. His head rolled back as his body jerked, and then he was still, his body lying at an unnatural angle on the ground.

The man who'd hit him turned, a ferocious, dark look in his eyes. He took a step toward her, and she flinched away, not sure who to be more afraid of.

It was Carl — or at least it *looked* like Carl.

But the friendly, joking man of the night before was nowhere to be seen. This man slowly moving toward her was a warrior. He was fierce and powerful, and he looked as if he could win a war with only his bare hands. The pure rage in his eyes was enough to make anyone back down.

"Sorry," he said as he turned away from her as she slowly scooted her beaten body a few inches away. She wasn't moving quickly. When he stopped coming forward, she managed to pull out some strength and sit up, crossing her arms against her chest, her breathing heavy, her entire body aching.

It took a few nerve-wracking seconds before he turned back around. This time his face was much more composed. It wasn't back to the easygoing look of the man he'd been the night before, but it wasn't so murderous — so terrifying.

"I'm going to give you my coat," he told her. She was having a hard time processing his words. Her head was fuzzy and she wasn't sure what had just occurred.

Even as she thought that, she watched as he pulled his jacket off, leaving him in nothing more than a tight black T-shirt as he handed over his coat. She gingerly took it, wanting to cover herself. She pulled it tight, inhaling the scent of leather and spice, finding a bit of comfort in the warm material draped across her. She couldn't find her voice to thank him, so just sat there gazing at him.

"I'm sorry," he said again. "I heard you scream. I don't know how, as it was barely echoing through the night, fading quickly. But I *knew* it was you. I ran as fast as I could. When I saw what he was doing, I lost it."

He didn't touch her as he moved closer, letting her know he was there if she needed him, but not pushing it. She appreciated that he was taking his time. When he was about a foot away, he slowly lowered himself, kneeling in front of her.

"I'm sorry I didn't get here sooner. How badly are you hurt?" he asked. He reached toward her, but still didn't make contact, as if he knew she was on the verge of a panic attack. She had to speak. He waited. How could he go from the fierce warrior of moments before, to this understandingly compassionate man in a single heartbeat?

Who was he?

She took a deep breath, her chest hurting, then she finally spoke. "He hit me a few times, kicked me in my abs hard enough to send me into the air, and then he was beginning to use the knife, but I'm lucky you got here when you did," she said, her voice scratchy and weak, her body beginning to shake.

"Can I check for injuries?" he asked.

"Are you a doctor?" she replied.

"I'm trained for emergency field medicine."

"I don't think I have any serious injuries. You got here in the knick of time," she said, the shaking growing worse.

"Let me at least check your torso," he insisted. "If that bastard kicked you hard enough, he could've done some serious damage. I'm also going to check your arms, neck, and face. The shock you're in might not be registering the true extent of possible injuries."

She didn't respond, but she also didn't stop him as he slowly moved forward, placing one hand on her back to steady her, then bringing the other to feel her stomach. It was tender, but not excruciating as he gently pushed in multiple areas.

He then pulled an arm out from under the coat she'd pulled tightly to her chest, ran his fingers along the entire length, a low growl escaping as he felt the cuts and swelling. Lastly he cupped his hands around the base of her neck, slowly swiveled her head, leaning in close to look at the broken skin on her face. The gentleness of his touch, the compassion she felt as he took care of her in that moment, was too much. She tried to stop herself but couldn't, and even though she held her eyes shut as tight as possible, tears started to form and slide down her cheeks.

Carl paused as he dialed 911. She was silent as he gave a quick rundown on what had occurred and their location. When he said the man was currently subdued, but had been attempting murder, the operator said there was personnel in the area, and they'd get there ASAP. He hung up, then sat next to her, slowly giving her time to stop him if she truly wanted to. She didn't. Then he reached over and gently pulled her onto his lap. Her crying grew worse.

"It'll be okay. He's going to prison this time. I'll make sure he confesses *all* of his sins. The only thing keeping me from killing him right this instant is you sitting here. You don't need to see that," he said as he gently ran his hand through her long hair while cradling her against his solid, warm body.

"Don't tell my mom. I don't want to upset her."

"There's *no* way I'm keeping this from your mother. For one thing, she'd come after me if she found out I was here and didn't tell her, and for another, *she* scares me far more than you do," he said. She *almost* smiled at his words.

In the end, it didn't matter though. The sirens pulling into the alley were enough to draw the attention of everyone at the bar, *including* her mother. She came out to investigate what was happening. And her mother, being nosy, came too close. When she saw it was Avery who was injured, all hell broke loose.

Avery was pulled away from Carl's arms, instantly making her feel cold and scared again. She hadn't wanted to be taken away from him.

Jeremy, the monster she'd freed the night before, was handcuffed and hauled away in a police car, the female medic saying he didn't need a hospital, that he could sleep it off in a county jail. She gave him a quick check, was pretty sure his nose and eye socket were broken, with a possible crack in his jaw, but there weren't any cops or paramedics there who had much love for the man. He'd caused pain and chaos in their city for a very long time.

Avery was lucky they were helping her. Maybe they didn't realize she was the one who'd gotten him off the last time. Or maybe they still had compassion for victims, even if that victim had helped the perp. Whatever the reason, she was thankful they were taking care of her.

There were too many people there, all of them blocking her view of Carl as he was questioned and she was assessed. Before she knew it, she was loaded into an ambulance she insisted she didn't need. Her mother climbed in with her, and the doors shut with Carl on the outside. She hadn't gotten a chance to thank him or tell him goodbye.

As the ambulance pulled away, she wondered if that was the last time she'd ever see the man who'd been her hero. She didn't know where he lived, didn't know his phone number, and had no idea how to contact him. The man had saved her life, and she literally knew nothing about him.

She was sad at the thought that it was done before it had begun. She should feel relief. She'd been telling herself for twenty-four hours she didn't want to see him again. And now wasn't the time to see anyone. *Especially* now. After this day, she wasn't sure she still wanted to be an attorney. If she mentally looked back through all of her cases, it made her wonder how many evil men she'd helped free. How many of them had turned around and attacked more people. What had she done? And how many more victims were out there because of her? Tears cascaded down her face.

"It'll be okay, sweetie. I promise it'll be okay," her mother whispered.

"I don't know if it will, Mama," she said, using a term she never used. She was so raw and broken. Her entire life was in crisis.

Carl's fierce face flashed in her mind again, making her yearn for him, but she pushed the thought aside. She *definitely* didn't have time to delve into these strange feelings for a man she knew nothing about. She forced her body to relax as she leaned her head against the hard pillow on the stretcher and let her mother's soothing words comfort her as they made their way to the hospital.

Tomorrow, she'd be able to think more clearly. Tomorrow, she'd try to figure out what was going to come next in her life. Tomorrow, she'd forget about Carl. Tomorrow she'd forget about this monster. Tomorrow she'd have all of the answers. Tomorrow . . .

Chapter Seven

Joseph felt his strength returning as he stood before his brothers, and his sons. He took a moment to look each one of them in the eyes. With a purpose in mind, and a mission before him, he wasn't left feeling helpless. Each person in the room with him met his eyes with determination. They needed action as much as he needed a plan in motion.

"Someone dared to lay hands on my wife," he said. "That's your mother he touched," he told them, looking at each of his sons. "And your sister-in-law and friend," he added, looking at his brothers. Each person had a visible reaction to his words. Lucas's hands clenched into fists, Alex's eyes turn to slits, and Mark's body entire body tensed.

"I want to know who did it, and I'm not waiting idly by for answers. I can't leave this hospital, but I'm asking you to do what I can't. First, Sheriff McCormack needs to be called. Tell him *exactly* what happened, and that I want him here ASAP. Then the local police need to be called so a team of investigators get to the veterans center before the crime scene is destroyed. One of you need to be there to keep track of it," Joseph said.

"Of course," George responded. "I'll do that." Joseph nodded at his brother.

"Second, I need one more at the veterans center to go over every single security tape at the facility. We have the best equipment and the best security team working there, and I want to know how in the hell this could happen on *our* grounds. It's unacceptable."

"I'll supervise it all," Alex jumped in next.

Continuing on to the men in attendance, Joseph said, "Make sure the security team works with the police without territorial wars. But we also don't give away anything. We will *share*, we will provide copies of anything requested, no hesitation, but ensure no originals are given out. I want to personally look at every . . . single . . . piece of video, which means I need a laptop and access to the cloud-based server the files are stored on. I won't be leaving this hospital without my wife, and we don't know how long that will take, and I can't sit around feeling helpless so I need to do what I can."

"I'm on that, Dad," Lucas said. "I'll get the laptop and appropriate accesses and we'll watch those videos a hundred times if we need to."

"Yes, we will," Joseph said. He was confident they'd get to the bottom of this.

"Finally, the rest of the family needs to be kept updated, so a tree needs to start. As much as everyone wants to be here, we can't overwhelm the fine men and women also waiting to hear how their loved ones are doing. Other families are hurting as much as we are, and we need to have respect for them and the pain they're going through."

"Of course," Richard said. "Why don't I do that so all three of your boys can go to the center? I think they'll work much better as a team. The sooner we get a handle on this, the better we're all going to be. I believe I have all the needed contacts but will review with Amy before sending any information out."

"I couldn't agree with you more," Mark said. He'd been oddly quiet through this entire meeting, but Joseph knew that was how his youngest son processed. He might be silent, but he was in no way complacent. He'd been thinking and planning from the moment he'd received the message that his mother was in need of help.

"Good. I feel better knowing we're all on the same page. I can't sit still. I have to have a plan or I won't make it through another minute, let alone days, or possibly weeks, of uncertainty," Joseph said.

"I feel the same, Dad. Not having answers and being unable to move forward will cause me to start yelling, and I don't like getting crazy," Lucas said.

"No one likes that, brother," Alex said. "But Mom will be fine. There's simply not any solution to this other than that. And we'll find the men who hurt her. They *will* pay, and they won't do this to another person."

"Amen to that," Mark said.

"Let's plan on a video conference with the entire family once we have something worth sharing. Don't make me wait too long. I know all of this takes a while, but speed it up as much as you can while still doing a thorough job."

"You know we all want this done rapidly. It will happen," George assured his brother.

Joseph had worked hard his entire life, then taught that same work ethic to his children, and he'd never been easy on them. He'd wanted them to be assets to society and never have anything handed to them. Raising them that way, he knew he could turn anything over to them with complete confidence the task would be accomplished.

He also knew his brothers had the same work ethic. They'd have this solved with or without police help. He had the utmost respect for the men and women in blue. But he was also very aware of what could be accomplished without hands being tied behind backs, and unfortunately, all government entities had their hands tied behind their backs at some stage or another. Sometimes painting outside the lines was the best solution for everyone involved. Joseph was *very* good at finding his own path, and he answered to no one, so no one could ever tie his hands.

"Keep us updated and let our wives know we'll return," Lucas said.

"Of course," Joseph assured his sons.

They all hugged then parted ways. Joseph's heart was heavy as he made his way to a bathroom and splashed his face with cool water. When he looked in the mirror he barely recognized the man staring back at him. He seemed haggard and old . . . and broken. But the light he normally saw shining in his eyes was trying to break through. He wasn't shattered, would never be as long as he had Katherine.

When he got back to the waiting area, his daughters-in-law were there with Jasmine. He moved over to them and sat, giving them a quick explantion of the boys departure. He normally wasn't a man who could sit around for hours on end. But for now he had little choice.

He leaned back, closed his eyes, and felt a moment of peace as Jasmine's fingers wound through his. No one said a word. They all just sat together saying silent prayers and they waited . . . and waited . . . and waited . . .

Chapter Eight

Avery had always despised hospitals. It wasn't that she didn't appreciate them, it was just that she felt a person could heal more fully at home where they were comfortable. No one she knew had ever said they liked the constant monitoring a hospital was so good at.

As she shifted in her bed for the hundredth time, Avery turned and glanced over at her mother who was napping in a chair in the corner of the room. She'd lasted for hours, but deep exhaustion had finally forced her to rest. Avery wished she could get some sleep herself. She glanced at a clock with a sigh. It was three in the morning.

The doctors had been concerned about the knot on the back of her head and the bruising on her temple. Thankfully, there hadn't been any internal damage. But with any head wound they insisted on at least one full nights stay. Her mother was refusing to leave her side.

She truly did love and respect her mom. Their life had certainly been less than easy as Avery had grown up, but it had been far from awful. Her mother had made some poor choices early in life, mainly about men. But, she'd always been fierce in her protection of her only daughter. Avery truly appreciated that now that she was an adult and saw the dangers of the world, especially since she'd never known her father.

He'd taken off before Avery had been born. There'd been times she'd wondered about him, who he was, and if he ever thought about her. Did he have other children? Did it even matter? As the years had gone by, she'd wondered about him less and less. Now, it was rare that he crossed her mind.

Maybe she was thinking of her father now because her mother had always been there for her when she'd needed her the most. And looking at her as she slept with her head against the back of the chair, seeming at ease, made her realize just how much her mother had sacrificed while Avery had been growing up.

While there had never been enough money in her youth, her mother had tried to make up for it by taking her to lakes and rivers and letting her fish and catch crawdads and frogs. She'd take her to the woods to pick flowers, and the two of them would make beautiful bouquets to decorate their small, dilapidated homes. They'd make art with sidewalk chalk, play catch in the park, and jump rope on the street. It hadn't been until she was a teenager that she'd realized how poor they actually were.

The absolute best gift her mother had given her as a child was school. Her mother hadn't graduated, and she'd had deep regrets about that. So she'd pushed Avery from a young age to read, to study, and to do reports on all of it. She'd worked on math, science, and geography with her, telling Avery she was learning with her. She'd given her assignments in the summer, and she'd pushed and encouraged, never giving up.

It had worked. Avery had looked at school as a gift rather than a punishment, and she'd graduated early then was awarded a full scholarship for college. And she'd never looked back. She should've become a teacher since she knew the importance of a good education, but she'd wanted so much more.

As those thoughts flitted through her mind, her eyelids grew heavy. She sighed with relief as she grew sleepy. Some might say her childhood had been deprived, but she was grateful for it. Without the advantage of money, she'd been forced to use her imagination and skills. It had made her who she was later in life.

That was a gift a lot of kids never received. If they were handed everything they thought they wanted, then they didn't have to work for what mattered most. Avery felt sorry for those kids she'd once envied. They'd never learned how to fight for what mattered most.

She closed her eyes and drifted off . . .

***

When Avery woke, light was streaming in through the windows, and her mother was sitting up, her eyes blurry, her hair a mess. She looked over and grinned.

"Good morning. I obviously fell asleep which is good as I didn't think I'd ever sleep again after seeing you in that alley," Bobbi said before letting out a big yawn and stretching in all directions.

"The one good thing about our bodies is they will force a shut down even when we don't want to stop," Avery said, feeling a lot better after a few hours of sleep. "As you used to always tell me when I was little, we need sleep to heal our bodies, our souls, and our minds."

"I believe that more now than ever before," Bobbi said with a smile. She glanced over Avery's battered face. "You look better this morning. You're pretty bruised, but there's color in your cheeks and you look confident again instead of scared." She stood and walked to the bed, running her hand through Avery's hair just as she'd done a million times when Avery was growing up.

"I do feel better. I'm glad you're with me, Mom."

Her mother leaned down and kissed her cheek, then stood back and looked around the room, obviously searching for something. It wasn't long before Avery knew what it was. Her mother was trying to stay upbeat, but she was one of those women who didn't normally wake up in a good mood, especially after a terrible night's sleep.

"I need coffee."

"I don't think it's going to magically appear in this room," Avery told her with a smile. Bobbi gave her a frown and looked around again as if she could prove Avery wrong and see a cup appear. Before her mom could respond, another voice broke in on their conversation — a *very* sexy male voice.

"Well then, I guess it's a good thing I'm here."

They both turned to find Carl leaning in the doorway, a coffee carrier in one hand with three large cups sitting in it. In the other hand he carried a bag that was bound to have something good inside.

"Oh, see, this is why I still believe in magic," Bobbi said, her eyes lighting. "Gimme, Gimme," she added as she fled Avery's side, swiftly moving toward Carl with a look of lust in her eyes — and it wasn't for the sexy man in the doorway — it was definitely for what he'd brought.

He laughed as he met her halfway, Bobbi's eyes on nothing but the coffee.

"I wasn't sure what you both drank so I got three kinds and figured we could fight over them," Carl said. "This one's a white mocha, this one's a caramel latte, and this is strong brew with cream."

"Caramel latte is all mine," Bobbi said, taking the cup and immediately pressing it against her lips. She took a long swallow before stepping back with a beaming smile. "Heaven, pure heaven. You're my favorite person on this planet right now. Thank you. Thank you. Thank you."

"You are very welcome," he said. "They wouldn't let me come in earlier because of visiting hours, so I thought I'd bring goodies with me since it drove me crazy that I couldn't check on you last night." He moved over to Avery as he spoke.

She wasn't sure what looked more delicious, the coffee or the man holding it. He might just be more appealing than the coffee, and that was saying something since she was a serious coffee lover.

"I'd love the white mocha if you don't want it," she said, feeling unusually shy. She didn't normally drink sugary coffees, but she figured she'd earned it. The night before had truly sucked.

"I was hoping you'd say that," he said with a chuckle. "I got so used to drinking black coffee in the military that it feels decadent just putting cream in it."

"I know what you mean. I'm always on a diet, so I normally drink my coffee with a little shot of sugar free cream. I tried the black thing and can't stand it. That's far too bitter for me," Avery said.

He handed her the cup and she wondered if she looked just as enchanted with the brew as her mother had. She didn't even care. It was truly *that* good.

"I have more," he said, a twinkle in his eyes that made him appear far more approachable than the hard glint he'd worn the night before.

He pulled out a box from the bag he was carrying and set it on the large tray next to her bed. He slid the tray over her, then opened the box, making her mouth instantly water. Her mother moved to the other side of the bed and gazed into the box as if she was looking at precious gemstones.

"I don't know which to pick," Bobbi said.

"I know the problem," Avery said, her eyes looking over the dozen pastries.

Bobbi reached in first and took a cream filled lemon bar. She stepped back, took a bite, and let out a moan. "Oh, hell yes," she said, chewing fast, then taking another bite.

Carl laughed. "If I'd known I'd get this kind of reaction I would've carried pastries with me everywhere I went from the time I was young. Maybe I'll have to start doing that now."

Avery reached in and decided on the heavily iced cinnamon roll. She took a bite, and her own moan escaped. It was soft, warm and gooey and filled with cinnamon, nutmeg, and allspice. Yum.

She was about to take a second bite when Carl reached out and rubbed his thumb across her bottom lip. Her stomach clenched as she stared at his thumb that had some frosting on it. She then about melted through the bed when he lifted his hand . . . and licked the frosting away.

She found herself unable to move as their eyes connected. His smile faltered as his eyes bored into hers. The heat of his gaze scorched her. She forgot her mother was even in the room until she spoke, laughter in her tone.

"Well, the coffee is amazing, and the pastries are just about as good, but I think I'm going to take a walk and stretch this old body. Sleeping in a chair was a lot easier when I was younger." She reached into the box and picked up a maple bar.

"You're leaving me?" Avery asked, almost panicked at the thought of being left alone with this man who made her feel so . . . so . . . heck, so tingly and warm.

"You're a big girl. I think you'll be just fine," Bobbi said, walking away laughing.

Avery was alone with Carl. For a moment, she didn't know what to do. But her mother's words before leaving had broken the spell that had been surrounding them for several tense seconds.

"You have a great mother," he told her as he reached into the box and picked up a cinnamon twist. He grabbed a chair, bringing it close to her bed and taking a seat, before he kicked back, shocking her when he pushed off his shoes, then put a foot on the edge of her bed.

She was unsure what to do or say. But she realized she liked having him there so she decided to go with it. After all, the man had brought them coffee and pastries. That was definitely worthy of respect.

She took a sip of her coffee before biting into her cinnamon roll again. "I really do appreciate you bringing this to us. I have a feeling it's much better than what the hospital will be serving."

"That's for sure, though I've had some pretty good hospital food," Carl told her as he finished off his donut in about three bites. He looked at the box as if he was going to grab another, but must've decided it was too far from his reach so he sipped on his coffee instead.

They chatted about food and hospitals, the good and the bad, for a few moments before a nurse came in, checking her vitals, saying the doctor would be there within a couple of hours, and she should be getting discharged that day. The aide came next with her tray of food —

yep, the pastries were far better. But she laughed when Carl reached over and snagged her pudding.

"Are you really going to eat that?" she asked. He peeled back the top.

"I don't know why, but I seriously *love* hospital pudding. I know it's the same brand you get in the store, but it's just not the same," he told her with a shrug. She couldn't help it. She laughed. The man was unpredictable.

When Carl's face turned serious, Avery felt a tug in her gut. She didn't want the conversation to take a different direction. She didn't want to think about what had happened the night before. It was too soon and too painful. She was at a crossroads and she didn't want to talk about it.

On the other hand, it wasn't as if she had friends to bounce ideas off of. She could certainly talk to her mother, but her mom always told her to do what she felt was right. She could shave her head and run around naked, and her mother would say okay, as long as it made her happy.

Maybe talking to a virtual stranger wasn't such a bad thing. He wasn't biased about her situation and didn't really know much about her. He'd been attracted to her, had forced a conversation, felt a connection, and now they were here in her hospital room.

"How are you feeling?" he asked. Before she could answer, he gave her a smile as he slowly ate his pudding. "I wasn't sure if I should bring it up or not, but as I see the yellowing on the side of your forehead, it's staring me in the face."

She lifted a hand, touching her tender face. She hadn't had a chance to look in a mirror yet. She was afraid to. She wasn't vain by any means, but she didn't want a constant reminder of what had happened every time she passed a mirror. At least the bruising and cuts would eventually heal — hopefully her mind would too.

"I honestly don't know how I feel," she admitted.

"I can understand that. I've been in some situations that have taken me weeks, or even months, to work through. Some of the things I've done, I'll never fully work out. That's the life of a military man."

"Ah, a military man. My little attack is nothing compared to what I'm sure you've faced," she said, almost embarrassed she'd been so upset over one little assault when this man had probably been through much, *much* worse.

"Never undervalue what you've experienced, good or bad. Each person has their own path they walk, and it affects each of us in different ways. It doesn't make you weak to be afraid or sorrowful for what's happened to you," he assured her as he set down his empty pudding cup and reached for her hand.

"I don't think I want to be an attorney anymore," she blurted, her voice filled with shame.

"Why?" he asked. If there had been judgment in his eyes, she would've stopped right then. But all she saw was compassion and understanding.

Still, she felt her throat close as she thought about her reply. How much did she want to tell? Was he going to look at her differently? With that thought, it made her wonder how the rest of the world viewed her. Did they think she was a monster? It was a humbling thought.

"That man who attacked me," she began, her voice choked. She pushed it down. She was a lawyer for goodness sake. She didn't allow emotion to clog her voice. She was known for being able to turn it all off. She began again.

"The man who attacked me was my client. We'd just won our case the night before."

"Your client?" he asked when she took too long to continue.

"Yes, I'm a defense attorney, and I'm a damn good one. I've only lost one case and that was at the beginning of my career. I work hard, and I know how to read people, so I know when my strategy needs to change." She stopped.

Even saying that made her feel like a monster. She couldn't imagine what he was thinking.

"Why do you want to defend criminals?" he asked. Again, if there'd been judgment in his tone she would've stopped speaking. If he'd looked at her with disgust she'd have stopped. But he was simply asking her, looking more curious than anything.

She sighed. "I can tell you the answer I give my mother," she said with a derisive laugh. "I believe they're innocent. I don't ask if they aren't, and they always tell me they're being framed."

He looked at her for several heartbeats before asking his next question.

"And what's the real reason?" he asked.

She looked into his soulful eyes and it felt as if he could see straight through her. She'd never had someone look at her that way. It was eerie. It was as if he could cut through all of the crap she normally spouted and get straight to the heart of her.

"There are two reasons," she admitted. "The second one is that I'm competitive. I love to win at any cost. I've worked hard my entire life, and I take pride in it. If I'm going to do a job, I'm going to do it to the best of my ability and I won't back down until I'm so far past the finish line, you can't even see the winners circle anymore. If I'm not better than everyone else, I'm not satisfied with the job."

There was a look of admiration in his eyes that made her feel better. "And what's the first reason?"

She had to tamp down her emotions once more. "I became an attorney because of my uncle, the one who owns the bar, the one who was more a father to me than most fathers are to their own children. He was wrongfully accused of a crime. He spent ten years in prison before the truth came out. His record was expunged, but even that was done reluctantly, and he lost his wife, his daughter, and ten years of his life for a crime he didn't commit because he'd pissed off the wrong politician. I haven't seen my cousin since my uncle was convicted. Her mother took her away and refused to let my mother or me have any further contact."

She could see the shock on Carl's face. She'd never told anyone the story before this moment. She'd been interviewed many times after she'd won cases, and not once had she brought up her uncle. First of all, she hadn't because he wanted that period of his life forgotten. Second, it was no one's business what her family's life had been before, or what it was now.

"I'm sorry," Carl said after a few minutes. "I don't know what to say."

"Nobody knows what to say in a situation like this. People avoid personal situations. Don't get me wrong. I'm all about law and order. I believe a lawless country would be disasterous. However, people have no clue how many are falsely charged. We need changes in our system. It needs to be better."

"That's something I've never thought about," he honestly told her. "I guess when you've always been a law-abiding citizen you don't have to think about it. The law is as natural to me as breathing."

She threw her hands in the air and let out a frustrated sigh. "That's the attitude that infuriates me," she told him. "I bet you grew up with money." She let her words hang there as he shifted in his seat.

"I didn't grow up wealthy by any means, but I guess you could say I grew up middle class."

"In a nice neighborhood?" she pushed.

"It was a decent neighborhood in Philadelphia."

"That's my point. I didn't grow up in a neighborhood like that. I grew up in a low-income area where crime and poverty went hand in hand. I understand a lot of people think only minorities or only huge cities have problems with money and equality. The fact is that the highest poverty rate is that of single mothers of all races and backgrounds. Out of the eleven and a half percent of poverty-stricken US residents, twenty-five percent are single-parent households with no husband present. I fell into that class even though my mother worked hard."

Carl stared at her for several moments before speaking again. He was obviously being careful with his words. She appreciated it. That was another discussion she didn't have too often. No one would take her seriously anyway when she was wearing two-thousand-dollar shoes or carrying a five-thousand-dollar briefcase. They'd call her privileged and think she had no idea what she was talking about. They wouldn't take the time to look at her past, to see how hard she'd had to work to get to where she was now.

"How did you get out of it?" he asked.

Now she smiled for real. "I had a mother who wouldn't allow me to settle. She pushed me hard to read, and not just for fun, but to read to actually absorb the material, to do extra schoolwork and educate myself out of the slums. And then I pushed myself. I took extra classes and I received scholarships. I worked real jobs from the time I was old enough, and I didn't spend money on frivolous items. I saved every dime I made for when I went to college. I gave up pretty dresses and the latest gadgets and phones. I saved and saved and saved, and then I went to college. Instead of going to parties or taking classes like trampoline and bowling, I took extra science and math courses. I studied and I pushed myself. I wasn't going to be a victim of circumstance."

"Most people don't have that drive," he told her.

"I agree. But I also don't respect those who cry about what they don't have when they aren't willing to work hard to get it," she said a bit more sharply than she wanted.

"What about those who are disabled?" he asked.

She sighed. "If there is anyone out there who thinks we shouldn't take care of the elderly, disabled, or young, they aren't worth having a conversation with. But those who want more in life can't just hope for a magic fairy to wave a wand; they have to work hard. That means an education, a job, and making sacrifices. In the long run, giving up something like the latest pair of Miss Me jeans is worth it because later you can have a career and buy a two-thousand-dollar pair of shoes," she said with a smile. She really did have a thing for shoes.

"That we can both agree on," he said with a chuckle. "Except the shoes. I think spending that much on shoes is simply insane."

"I bet you spend money on other things I'd find frivolous. We all have our things."

He shrugged. "I do have a thing for cars," he admitted.

"Most men do." She sighed again, getting off her soapbox. "I know everyone has their own story. I know some have had a much rougher life than others. But I believe anyone can do anything if they want it bad enough to work hard for it. I also believe the poor are generally treated badly. My uncle was convicted when he shouldn't have been. If he'd come from a fancy neighborhood and hadn't had a bunch of tattoos, he'd have been looked at differently. I get so sick of people making judgments based on people's appearance, status in life, or color of skin. Why don't we judge people by their actions instead?"

"I agree fully with that," he said. "I'm sorry about your uncle."

"Me too. That's what led me to defense law. But I can't excuse it anymore. I can't justify it. I can say I believed in my last client the entire time I defended him, but I'd be lying. I *knew* he was a monster. I *knew* he'd do it again . . . and I *still* fought to free him. This time it nearly cost me my life. But I deserved that because I'm sure some of the other people I've helped free have committed heinous crimes again. I have to live with that now."

He reached over and took her hand again, squeezing. "That's on them, not you. But I do agree that you shouldn't be a defense attorney. I'm sure there are those who truly need you. But with your passion and conviction, you should be on the other side. You have an eye for justice. You don't care about color or status. You only see people. You should be a prosecutor and go after the bad guys, fight for justice, fight for victims, and put the evil men and women in this world away so people can be safer, so people can rise up just like you did. Maybe you can even become a DA."

His speech stopped what she'd been about to say.

"That's something I've never really thought of doing," she said, shocked she hadn't.

"Why not?"

"Because of my uncle. I was so ticked off at the system, it never crossed my mind."

"Just as you can't judge all by the actions of one, you can't judge the system of law and order by a few bad politicians. There are always going to be those who are power-hungry and use their position to hurt others. But if you're one of the good guys, and you're doing your job right, you can go after the bad DAs and the bad politicians. You can fight corruption on every single level."

Those words lit a fire beneath her. "I can't believe I've never thought of doing that," she said with wonder.

"Well, now you have something to think about."

She felt like a new woman. She hadn't wanted to talk to this man; now she realized this could be one of the most important conversations of her life. If she were able to leap from her bed, she might've launched herself from it and kissed him.

"Thank you. I'm really glad we've talked about this," she said, wonder and excitement in her voice.

"Me too," he told her.

He leaned back and they went silent for several moments, as both of them got lost in their thoughts. Avery realized she might just be moving forward on a whole new path in life . . . and it was all because of a random meeting with a stranger after a really bad day. It truly was funny how life had a way of steering you in a direction you hadn't known you wanted to go in the first place until you finally reached the right destination.

Chapter Nine

Joseph wanted time to move quickly, but when a person wanted that, it never managed to work out that way. His family stayed with him while his sons investigated, but there was so much data and so much property to go over.

Lucas had come back, giving him tapes, and then he'd sent his daughters-in-law, and his granddaughter, home as morning light crept over the hospital. His wife was stable, but they were keeping her in the induced coma, and they'd keep him updated throughout the day. He'd needed time alone to think. He fell asleep in the waiting room while watching security footage, hating he couldn't be with his wife.

It was early evening, nearly twenty-four hours after they'd originally arrived at the hospital, when his sons returned with their wives and Jasmine, who moved over to her grandpa and gave him a hug. They had law officials in tow. Joseph was instantly alert as he waited to hear what his friend, Sheriff McCormack, had to say. Two of his deputies were behind him, but Joseph only trusted the words of the sheriff.

"I'm sorry this happened, Joseph," Sheriff McCormack said, coming over and shaking Joseph's hand. "We *will* get this solved."

Lucas stepped up beside the sheriff. "We do have reports, but first and foremost, are there any updates on Mom?"

"Nothing yet," Joseph answered with a sigh. "They come in every few hours, and she's stable but still in a coma. Nothing has changed."

Everyone in the room frowned before Mark spoke up. "Stable is good," he said, and Joseph gave him an appreciative look.

"Thank you, son. I'm trying to tell myself that, but it gets harder with each passing hour. I need to focus on something else right now." He turned back to the sheriff with an expectant look. "What news do you have for me?"

"We got a break," Alex said before Sheriff McCormack could speak. They all huddled closer, everyone exhausted but determined.

"We reviewed the crime scene then looked through the security camera footage for the entire facility. We also spoke to a couple dozen people, anyone who could've possibly been in the area where the assault occurred," Mark said.

"Your boys have a guaranteed job if they ever want to come to the blue side," one of the deputies said, respect in his eyes.

"No one at the center saw anything. But we did get a break from some mechanics at the helipad garage. They'd been alerted to keep their eyes out and one of them saw a man attempting to hide behind the trash receptacles near the landing zone."

"And?" Joseph practically shouted.

"The mechanic managed to sneak up on the guy before he knew what was happening," Lucas said, excitement clear in his tone.

"So what happened?" Joseph asked.

"The mechanic threw him against the wall, got in the guy's face, and questioned what he was doing, where he'd been, who'd seen him, and who he'd been with. The man clammed up, and that was answer enough for our mechanic. He marched the scumbag to the hordes of onsite security, cops, and others looking to assist."

"I need you to get to the end of this story," Joseph said.

"It didn't take long for this piece of scum to break," McCormack said. "He admitted he was there when your wife was attacked, but he swore he didn't touch her, that he'd wanted nothing to do with it, and had begged his accomplice to leave. He knows exactly who you are and knew the hounds of hell would soon be nipping at their feet."

"I don't care if he laid his hands on her or not. He was there! He *will* pay," Joseph said.

The sheriff nodded in agreement and continued talking, "Yes, he'll pay. He's more than willing to cooperate. He knows he's in a world of hurt right now, so he's spilling his guts. His name is Lenny. The man who was with him is called Travis, at least that's the name the dealer gave him. Our perp doesn't know Travis's last name. Travis is a local drug dealer. Katherine simply ended up in the wrong place at the wrong time. Lenny has been staying at the center, and this Travis has been coming in for a couple of weeks. Lenny said he's bought meth from Travis three times in the past two weeks. Lenny told us he simply texted the guy when he needed a fix."

"So did you guys text him?" Joseph asked.

Joseph had no doubt Sheriff McCormack was fair, but also tough as nails. No one would give him a bullshit story and get away with it. He was impatient for the end of the story though.

"We took him to the interrogation room where he's being questioned to see if his story holds, but I believe him. He had a cousin he said he got Travis's number from, but his cousin died from an overdose last week. We confirmed the OD story. Unfortunately, we've seen a huge uptick in overdoses the past few months. There are some new strains of drugs out there that are killing people. We did try the number for Travis but there was no pick up or response, even using Lenny's phone. We're assuming this man knows our perp would get caught and sell him out fast. The number was a burner that's already been burned," the sheriff shared.

"I want him found," Joseph said, his normally boisterous voice, scarily quiet.

"These thugs aren't the best or the brightest, but they know how to keep hidden when a deal has gone south. But eventually they make mistakes," McCormack said.

"I don't have time for *eventually*," Joseph said.

"Look, Joseph, we've known each other a long time so I'm not going to lie to you," McCormack said. "We're going to head back to the center in the morning, and we won't give up on this, but it's not hopeful. This lowlife, along with many of his colleagues, are real good at ghosting. And this Lenny, the one we have in custody, is so spun out there's no way he'd be able to give a positive ID even if we do find someone we think is the attacker. That causes reasonable doubt, and it would be hard as hell to hold him."

Joseph was stunned. This wasn't what he'd been expecting. Why wasn't the law working? He wanted to blame someone, but he also knew in his heart these men were doing the best they could. They didn't have the manpower or the resources to do what had to be done to get these killers off the streets. So what did that mean?

"Was Brooke a witness?" McCormack asked.

"Yes, but I didn't see much," Brooke said, hanging her head in frustration.

"You might've seen more than you realize. Why don't you come to the station with me and see if you can identify this man. It might spark something you've forgotten."

"Yes, I'm willing to do anything I can," she said.

"Good," McCormack said before turning back to Joseph. "Don't give up. We won't stop forging ahead."

"Thank you," Joseph said. They shook hands, and the sheriff exited along with the two deputies who'd come with him.

"We were hopeful when we found him. This feels like failure," Lucas said, his shoulders slumping.

"How do we find the other man?" Jasmine asked in a broken voice, making Joseph's heart shatter into a million pieces.

Joseph took a deep breath. "This man was dealing drugs at the very place we built to help the men and women get away from them, then he laid his hands on my wife. He *will* be found," Joseph said, his voice steel.

The group waited for Joseph to speak, knowing now wasn't the time to interrupt. They could see the wheels turning. Joseph walked over to the door and firmly shut it, then faced his family. They calmly waited.

Joseph made eye contact with each member of his family, took a deep breath, then spoke. "I'm only going to say this once. Someone attacked my wife, your mother, and the person who conceived the idea of that facility to help those needing help. The criminals need to pay. The law is bound by rules, regulations, financial roadblocks, and political hurdles; the law can only do so much." He paused.

"I don't have patience for a system that might never find the scum who did this. Sometimes a man has to take matters into his own hands, not leave justice in the hands of a system that can be tripped up at any point. I have respect for the men and women working inside the system, and have always believed in them, but I also have faith in our family, and faith in the power of love. We're motivated to solve this where a person with two thousand cases on their desk can't make it a priority."

He looked skyward, then focused on each person again. "I'm not willing to wait. I'm not willing to let this case grow cold. Tell me now who in this room is in . . . and who'd rather not know what's going to happen next."

Everyone looked at him with a bit of shock, but not one of his family members turned away. Fire lit up their eyes as they faced him, each person standing a little taller, each one's shoulders going back. They were with him all the way — just as he knew they would be.

Each of them nodded without uttering a word. Then Mark stepped forward. "I'm not going to lie and say whatever this is doesn't scare me. But we do everything together. We also need to realize when we need help, and we need help right now. What we are discussing needs people who know how to work in a world we know next to nothing about. We need to call Chad."

There was a collective sigh of relief at Mark's words. "Why didn't I think of that?" Joseph finally asked.

"We're in this together and that's how we'll stay," Lucas said.

"Yes, together," Alex and Mark said.

"Always," Amy added. "And we also know the fewer people who know the details, the better." She kissed Joseph on the cheek, then kissed her husband. "I think it's time your wives go on another coffee run."

Joseph grabbed her for a hug. "I love you. I'm so grateful my son was smart enough not to lose you," he said.

"Oh, Joseph, I'm the one who will be forever grateful. Go get this man," she said, lightning flashing in her eyes.

"We will," Joseph said.

Each wife kissed Joseph's cheek, hugged him, then moved from the room. Jasmine stepped in front of him and glared.

"I'll go for now," she said. "But I'm no longer a little girl, and you're going to find that out real soon. This is *my* grandma, and I *will* be a part of bringing her justice."

Joseph couldn't be prouder of his granddaughter. He gave her a hug so tight she practically broke in half. Then he released her and watched as she stiffly walked to the door. Right before she left, he called her name. She turned back and looked at him.

"You *are* growing up fast, Jasmine, and trust me, I have no doubt you'll be a fierce warrior through all of this." It was the truth, she would become fierce during this trying time, but there was no way on earth she was going to be allowed to even dip a toe in the waves that were about to crash over all of those involved in harming Katherine. He wouldn't risk her or any of his grandchildren.

Some of the defiance fell from her shoulders as she gazed at her grandfather with love in her eyes. Then she nodded and walked away. Joseph looked at Mark, a look few had

ever seen from the man. A look carrying a weight that would crumple most men.
"Make the call . . ."

Chapter Ten

Avery wasn't thrilled as she grabbed her purse and walked from the fourth floor corridor at the hospital. She'd been there for nearly forty-eight hours. They'd said the day before she'd be released, and then a new doctor had come in, and that had all went out the window. They'd wanted to monitor her head injury because she'd exhibited signs of a concussion and they knew she lived alone.

She'd assured them her mother could come stay with her, but her mom, ever the worried one, had told them she couldn't be there twenty-four/seven because she had to work. And Avery couldn't afford to leave against medical advice since her insurance wouldn't pay for the stay if she did.

She'd been poutier than a three-year-old child who'd been refused ice cream, but she'd stayed. They'd finally released her at nearly six in the evening the next day, and she wanted nothing more than a stiff drink to drown her sorrows until she figured out what she was going to do next.

She'd decided to leave her job, had an intense connection with a man, and been nearly killed by a client all in the span of twenty-four hours. Life could only happen this way in a book, right?

Right, she decided.

She finally made it down the elevator and out the front doors, but was stopped in her tracks right there. Sitting in the loading zone was a sleek black SUV — and next to it, looking far too sexy in a pair of black fitted slacks and a white button-down shirt with the top button undone, was Carl.

He was seriously better looking each time she saw him. As she drew closer, he looked up and smiled, a heart-melting, core tingling smile that had her insides doing all sorts of flips and flops. He stepped forward and leaned down, his lips grazing her cheek for a brief moment before he pulled his hand from behind his back and presented her with a huge bouquet of roses, lilacs, and baby's breath. She didn't know what to say.

He smelled unbelievable, intoxicatingly incredible. It was spice and leather, sugar and cinnamon, and cool and dark all at the same time. Those flips in her stomach became Olympic-winning cartwheels with a few spins through the air added on top.

Her last few days had been hell, but it all seemed to change in an instant. It was a damp, warm California evening with a hint of rain in the air and, with the heat her body was letting off at the sight of this man, she was wondering why steam wasn't rising from the ground.

"Your chariot awaits," he said smoothly, his deep voice better than an Icee on a hot summer afternoon. He moved over to the back door of the SUV and opened it. She didn't move. "How are you feeling?" He seemed as if he didn't mind waiting all night for her to get in.

"What are you doing here?" she asked, ignoring his question. She was seriously sick of people asking how she was doing. Not much had changed, and she wasn't sure *how* she was feeling. She hadn't had time to process all that had happened in the last week.

"You need to get home, and I wanted to be the one to take you there," he told her.

That's when she noticed a driver in the front. She knew he had a vehicle, but she didn't question him about his ride choice. She was feeling quite tingly and warm that he'd thought to pick her up. Her mother must've told him what time she was being released, because she hadn't. He'd texted her quite a bit the entire day — fun, flirty, core-wetting texts — but neither of them had said anything about what came next. He was rapidly breaking down her walls, and she wasn't sure how he was managing to do so.

It wasn't that Avery was completely against dating, it just seemed nearly impossible to get to know a man with the limited amount of free time she allowed herself. Work was her life.

As she had that thought, she realized that wasn't the case right now. If ever there was a time to have a fling, not that she knew how to go about that, it would be now. Should she go for it? This man was different from anyone she'd ever met before. The chances of it lasting were slim to none, but wasn't it time she had a bit of fun without worrying about the future?

She decided it definitely was.

"I don't want to go home. I've been cooped up inside for forty-eight hours. I want to be around people, and I want a stiff drink," she told him.

His smile grew. "Well then, your chariot still awaits. I know the perfect place."

"Okay then," she said. She sat down and he leaned in once more, this time giving her a kiss on the lips. Before she could utter a word, he pulled back and closed the door. Her breath hitched as she lifted her hand, letting her fingers trail across her mouth where her lips were tingling. She jerked her hand away as he opened the other door and climbed in next to her.

"I'm glad you showed up. It's a nightmare getting a taxi or Uber at this time of night in Francisco," she said, feeling a bit shy and awkward all of a sudden. She didn't have much experience in the dating arena, so she wasn't sure if this was a date.

Could a lift from the hospital be considered a date? She thought about that, her brain conjuring scenarios in her head all in the matter of nanoseconds. She'd always been brilliantly smart, and her mind never stopped spinning. Maybe that was another reason she rarely dated.

She was easily distracted, and grew bored in minutes if she didn't feel stimulated. Most men didn't find it attractive to have a woman look at them with glazed-over expressions as they spoke. Some didn't even notice. She wasn't sure which type was worse.

"I wanted to be here," he told her. "It'll take about an hour to get to our destination with the heavy traffic tonight. But on a positive note, this will be our third date."

She gave him a quizzical look. "Third date? When did we have our first two?"

"First date was at the bar," he said, holding up a finger. "Second was at the hospital when I brought coffee and donuts," he added, holding up the second finger. "And now, here we are."

As the vehicle pulled out of the hospital campus, she decided to go with the flow. That was very unusual for her, but it was all part of the fun. She grinned. "I can't count this as a date. Even though you *did* bring me flowers, which are incredibly lovely by the way, I don't have a drink in my hand, and this is a long car ride to be thirsty."

Carl laughed, his eyes sparkling. He had a beautiful, infectious laugh that made her lips twitch upward as she got lost in his gaze for several heart-accelerating moments. Then he leaned forward and told the driver to stop at the corner market two blocks ahead.

They arrived and walked in the store together. They moved to the back and Avery looked at the huge liquor selection, having no clue what she wanted. She normally was a vodka girl and didn't drink much else. She had zero taste for beer. She didn't understand people's obsession with it when it tasted like dirty socks.

"From the scowl on your face, I take it you don't like beer," he said with another award winning grin.

"No, not my favorite," she told him, deciding to leave the sock analogy out of it. A lot of men liked the fowl tasting stuff, and since she was giving this a go, she didn't want to be too rude. She'd already covered rudeness on their night at the bar.

"Do you like wine more or those fruity drinks you were having the other night?"

"The fruity drinks," she told him.

"Ah, then this shall hold you over until we reach our destination," he said, pulling out a six-pack of Mango White Claw. She didn't have a lot of faith in his selection as it was in cans.

Her uncle had been trying to make her a beer connoisseur for years. It hadn't worked.

They walked to the counter, and he didn't give her a chance to pull out her wallet. She wanted to argue, but with one look she knew it was pointless. She didn't like to argue unless she knew she'd win. She had a feeling she wouldn't win too often with this man. Was that bad or good? She honestly didn't know.

"Thank you," she said as they slid back into the car. Carl had already given the address, so now all they had to do was sit back, relax, talk, and ride. Would she make it the entire hour? The back seat suddenly felt more intimate than it had when she'd first climbed inside.

He cracked open a can of White Claw and handed it to her. She smelled the top and wasn't instantly turned off, so she gingerly lifted it to her lips and took a sip. It was surprisingly good, tangy with a hint of sweetness and a bit of fizz.

"Thank you, this is actually tasty," she told him before taking a longer sip. "And it's exactly what I need."

She leaned her head back with a sigh.

"It's been a rough few days," he said as he cracked his own can and turned his body so he was giving her his full attention. Being with this man was odd. Most people only felt half listened to. With him, it was the opposite, it was as if he was reading her mind, body, and soul, paying attention to even the smallest details.

"Yeah, this hasn't been my best week. But, I don't let things get me down. I think people who wallow will become what they are upset about in the first place. If we always look at the bad, then we're far more likely to miss the good," she told him, surprised when her can was empty after only a few minutes.

He took it from her and handed over another. She gladly accepted.

"I've always believed the same thing, but sometimes it's easy to get lost in everyday life; it's easy to complain or feel sorry for yourself if everything isn't going perfectly. Like you, though, I've never allowed negative to creep in for long."

"I think the world in general would be a much better place if everyone felt the same," she said, then giggled. He lifted a brow. "I was thinking if everyone expressed themselves correctly, and looked at the brighter side of life, I probably wouldn't have a job because there wouldn't be any need for lawyers."

Carl laughed. "You might be right. But don't worry, there are plenty of miserable people out there; your career is safe."

As they continued to weave through busy traffic, Avery realized she was having a wonderful time. The two of them didn't get into a deep conversation, but they did talk and laugh, drink and verbally spar, and most surprisingly of all, everything worrying her seemed to disappear.

By the time they arrived at the Marriot Marquis hotel in downtown San Francisco, Avery had a new worry. She liked this man — liked him a lot actually, but she was worried about him taking her to a hotel. Did he think something was going to happen?

He exited the car and came around, opening her door. Her concerns must've been written on her face because he grinned again as he placed one hand on the back of her seat, and the other on the back of the passenger seat, caging her in. He leaned close so his face was next to hers. She felt all tingly and warm as his lips moved within inches of hers.

"This place has an incredible rooftop bar with great drinks and food. That's why we're here. I'd never pick you up and take you to a hotel expecting anything. I don't have a room here, and I don't plan on getting one. This is just a date."

His words at once offered comfort and surprisingly . . . disappointment. She was so turned on by this man, she was a bit upset he didn't want to seduce her. What in the hell was wrong with her?

"I'm normally very good at hiding what I'm thinking," she said with a smile. "I guess I haven't been trying to do that with you."

"I'm glad," he told her. "I'm also very good at reading people's body language as well as their faces. Sometimes reading others means the difference between life and death. It's something instilled in me, and it'll never go away. So even if you did try to hide how you were feeling, it might not do you a whole lot of good."

She was about to respond when he closed that gap between them and kissed her again, but this time for longer. Her core heated to a molten level, and her breathing hitched when he pulled away. This man could literally kiss her stupid.

He leaned back, held out his hand, and she automatically accepted it, letting him assist her from the car. He didn't let go of her hand, instead entwining their fingers as they moved inside the hotel and headed straight for the elevator.

Avery was too nervous to talk on the ride up, so she stood next to him with other people chatting away as she watched the floor numbers flash by. A few stops were made before it opened to their floor. She was pleased with the beauty of the place when they left the elevator and moved inside.

They were seated at a window table and Avery smiled as she looked out at the lights of the city and harbor. She loved Frisco, though she knew she wouldn't be there much longer.

She couldn't go far because her relationship with her mother and uncle were too important, but she was on a new career path and that was going to take her somewhere else. She didn't know where and all of it made her a bit sad.

It didn't take long for a waiter to arrive, take their drink order, and hand them menus. She enjoyed a few minutes of silence while she made her selections. She was seriously hungry. The hospital food had been terrible, but she'd been too stressed to eat.

When the waiter came back with their drinks, they placed their orders. Carl laughed as the man walked away. She sipped on her lemon drop and raised her brows. He kept laughing.

"What?" she finally asked.

"You're such a petite thing and you ordered about half the menu. I want to see if you're going to eat all of it."

Some girls might've been offended by his comments, but she just shrugged. "I work out a lot so I can get away with eating more. I love food."

"I do the same," he said. "Though I try to avoid too much restaurant items. I like to know all of the ingredients I'm putting in my body about eighty percent of the time. Then I figure twenty percent I can go crazy."

"Seriously?" she asked, now the one grinning. "That's funny, because my rule is more of a seventy-thirty where I'm super good seventy percent of the time and have crazy Oreo and popcorn nights the other thirty. Plus, I like healthy foods because there's no guilt if I do eat a helping for three."

He sat back, looking completely comfortable. Avery was surprised how relaxed she was. This might actually be the greatest date she'd ever been on.

"Have you lived in Frisco your whole life?" he asked.

"Yes. I went away for college, but my mom and uncle are here so I knew I'd come back."

"Some kids want to leave home and never return," he said.

"I love my mom more than any other person on this planet. My uncle is a close second. There was no doubt I'd live close to them. And I was lucky enough to get work here." She stopped and scowled. "I can't believe I just said that."

"Said what?" he questioned.

"Lucky. I can't stand when people say *lucky*. I wasn't *lucky* to get the job, I *earned* it. I worked my butt off in school and I interned every summer. I graduated at the top of my high school class, my undergraduate school, *and* my law school. I literally had a golden ticket to go anywhere I wanted. It didn't have to do with luck, it had to do with countless hours of studying while others were playing, and a work ethic and drive I'm very proud of."

The waiter seemed to have radar because as soon as her drink was nearly empty he was there to offer another, which she gladly accepted. She wasn't driving so she was free to have as many as she wanted. She never had more than three, but the week had been quite stressful. Her rule could be broken that night.

"You should definitely own what you've done. It's impressive and not a lot of people have your drive." He stopped and reached for her hand across the table. She let him have it. "I'm very glad I've met you." She was locked in his gaze for several moments before he grabbed his glass with his other hand and held it up. "Here's to the start of . . . something."

Her fingers trembled as she lifted her glass. She wasn't able to utter a word as she clicked hers against his, their eyes never parting, their fingers clasping together a bit tighter.

She felt as if she'd just entered a contract, or somehow entered a . . . relationship.

The waiter came with their appetizers, and the spell was broken. Avery let out a relieved breath as she reached for anything on the table to occupy her. She shook her head, trying to clear the cobwebs. She wasn't sure what in the hell was going on. She did know for sure though, that she wasn't in a hurry to make it stop.

Chapter Eleven

It was three in the morning when Chad's phone jolted him from a deep sleep. He'd been a soldier for years. He went from sound asleep to fully alert in one second flat. He looked at the phone number and didn't recognize it, so his urgency slowed as he gazed at the glow from his nightstand.

Now a bit irritated at a possible sales call at approximately 3:00 a.m., he pushed against his covers, his feet tangling, making him nearly tear the bed apart. The phone stopped and in less than a heartbeat it began to ring again, making him growl as he finally managed to untangle himself from the heavy blankets his wife insisted be on the bed.

The things a man did for the woman he loved, he thought, before a smile appeared on his lips. He'd do anything for Brianne. She was his world. His wife, the niece of Joseph Anderson and cousin of his best friend, was stubborn, spoiled, bratty . . . and perfectly amazing. She was truly a gem in a sea of rocks. If she wanted a pile of blankets on their bed, then a pile of blankets was what she'd not only get, but she'd get them with a smile.

It also helped that Chad was a former SEAL and he'd learned to embrace sleeping in all types of austere environments, whether it was on rocks, dirt, water, ice, or scalding hot asphalt. Hell, he'd slept in it all, even in a sandstorm that had nearly suffocated him as he'd been practically buried alive.

It had taken him quite a while to adjust when he'd returned to civilian life and sleeping on a real bed night after night. When he'd married Brianne, he'd felt a bit claustrophobic for a while with her ten thousand pillows and blankets. But his love for her had easily overruled his discomfort — and like he'd always been able to do, he'd adjusted.

Chad grabbed his phone and silenced it as he looked at his wife who could sleep through a damn tornado. She hadn't so much as stirred in all of his struggles. He loved that she was so secure and comfortable with him that nothing interrupted her sleep.

He clicked his phone. "This better be damn good," he grumbled in a fierce whisper.

"Chad." It was just his name, but in that one syllable he was on alert. It was Mark, his best friend of many decades, and the fear and pain in his best friend's voice had every instinct in Chad ready to do battle.

He quickly moved to a room where he could talk freely without waking his wife.

"What's wrong?" Chad asked.

"I'm sorry to wake you," Mark said. "But I need your help."

"Where are you? I'll get there as fast as I can," Chad said. He was already mapping out the inside of his closet, where a hidden false wall contained a safe bigger than an average room. It held tactical equipment to do any job that needed done.

"Let me slow down and explain. Take a seat," Mark demanded. Those words stopped the thundering in Chad's chest. If he had time to sit, the situation wasn't life or death. He could get out of fight mode for at least a few minutes.

"Talk to me," Chad said as he made it to his large living room where a fire was still burning behind a secure screen. He threw a log on, then sat in his favorite chair.

"Someone attacked my mother . . ." Mark began. It took all of Chad's willpower to sit there without interrupting his best friend, but he waited for the entire story, his anger rising as he thought of someone foolish enough to hurt that amazing woman who'd treated him as her own son for many years.

"What's the plan?" Chad asked. He didn't care what it was. He was in. Mark would know that went unsaid.

Mark sighed and Chad let him form his thoughts. He knew what was coming. He also knew Mark needed to state it. "My dad has never asked, never thought of, and never intended to do what he's asking now. None of us have. But *this* is different. This is too close to home. This is a nightmare that won't end until the problem is solved. We need you to make some magic happen. Dad wants a team. He wants a very secret, very intelligent, and very capable team. Whatever contacts you have, whoever you can pull together, whoever is loyal, we want to talk."

Chad smiled. That was something he could do, something he'd been born to do, to lead, to bring together, to do work that protected good from evil. He was the sheepdog willing to take on any wolf trying to harm what he'd sworn to protect.

The world might be fascinated by superhero movies, might fantasize about being Batman, or Superman, or Wonder Woman, but they had no idea of the real heroes in the world. They didn't know they actually were out there keeping them safe, fighting crime, and bringing justice to those who deserved it. And they did it without wearing a cape; they did it without glory.

They did it because they were heroes, and to not do it caused them to wither and die. Almost all of them kept the masses safe in their homes, sleeping soundly at night, knowing only a select few would ever know the heroic story. The world would never thank them, and the real heroes were still willing to do the job.

"We have to get the drugs off the streets, away from the homes of our community, and find out who hurt my mother. We have to do this for more than just my mom. We have to do it for all of the mothers out there. This city won't be run by thugs anymore. This is *our* town, these are *our* communities. It's happened before in our area, and it's getting out of hand. For us to keep sitting idly by makes us just as bad as the men doing it," Mark continued.

Chad realized he hadn't said anything, so Mark was still trying to sell him on it. He nearly laughed. Mark knew him better than that, knew he was in from the moment Mark said he needed help.

"You do know what you're asking for, correct?" Chad asked.

Mark paused for a moment. "Yes, I do. With or without you we won't turn back," Mark answered. Chad smiled. Chad was already making a mental list of who he'd call.

"Consider it done. And Mark?" Chad said.

There was relief and hope in Mark's voice. "Yes?"

"This is the *last* conversation on the phone about this. It's officially beginning."

"Understood," Mark said.

"I'll wake Bree and we'll be on our way. Do you need anything from the house?" Chad inquired.

"Just you guys," Mark said.

"See you soon," Chad said. He hung up and moved to the bedroom where Bree was sitting up in bed. He gazed at her and saw concern in her eyes.

"I came out and saw you by the fire. By the set of your shoulders I knew you needed privacy so I came back here to wait. Are you okay?" she asked.

He moved to her and sat, pulling her into his arms. "I know I tell you often how lucky I am to have you as my wife, but I truly mean it. I love your faith in me, how well you know me, and how much you trust the power of us," he said, grateful to have her in his arms.

"I love you too, Chad. I can't imagine my life without you."

"That goes without saying," Chad said. He then leaned back, hating he had to break this news to his wife. "First and foremost, everyone is alive and well," he started, and her eyes widened with fear, but she didn't interrupt. "Your aunt was injured and your family is gathered at the hospital. She's stable and they don't know more than that for the moment, so let's get dressed and get there."

She jumped from his lap and ran to her closet. He moved to his and they emerged at the same time. She didn't say anything until they were in his truck on their way to the hospital.

When she spoke next he was even more grateful he'd married this woman.

"I don't know what the plan is, and I don't want to know. But thank you, Chad. Thank you for being who you are, thank you for being the kind of man the world can count on," she said. She reached out and caressed his cheek before she sat back, all of her energy taken by simply breathing in and out as they drove what seemed like endless miles to get to their family. They were as much Chad's now as Bree's.

He was mentally scrolling the contact list on his phone, which he pretty much had memorized. Names were popping into the forefront as he crafted a list of men and women he trusted enough to bring in on this mission.

He needed people who'd served, who had top-secret clearance, and who had morals and ethics and cared about their country and their fellow human beings. He wanted experience, and he wanted loyalty.

He'd get it.

He couldn't recruit those who were currently active duty or employed by the government. He couldn't ask any of them, because they'd be required to report it. He had to be smart.

By the time they reached the hospital, he had a list of about a dozen names compiled in his brain. He smiled, happy with the initial crew of men and women he was going to ask. This could grow into something so much more than the Andersons could possibly imagine. Or it could be a one-time job. He wasn't sure in which direction it was headed. From something tragic, something beautiful was emerging.

Chapter Twelve

Avery looked up at the large downtown office building she'd been working at for the past seven years. Mixed emotions flitted through her as she stood outside trying to talk herself into walking inside.

She'd made up her mind, and was more than ready to do this. But she was also finding it a bit harder than she'd thought it would be to execute her decision. She wasn't sure why. It wasn't as if there was anyone inside she'd miss. Sometimes people stayed far longer in jobs they disliked, not wanting to leave their co-workers. That wasn't the case for her.

"Let's do this," she said to herself. She took a fortifying breath and moved forward.

"Great job, Avery," the secretary said as she walked inside. The smile she wore faded as she took in Avery's bruised cheek. Avery ignored the look, getting used to it now. She simply nodded at the woman, her throat too tight to answer.

Then she moved through the offices, ignoring the stunned looks and nodding at those who'd been hard at work for the past few days as she'd stayed home trying to figure out her next move. Only the senior partner was aware she'd been attacked. He'd assumed she'd be back on her feet in a day or two with nothing changing. He was wrong.

She didn't hesitate as she walked into the senior partner's office. He looked up with a grin that faltered for a second, but he recovered quickly, just as she'd known he would. They were attorneys, damn fine ones, and they didn't react. Neither of them said a word about the state of her face. She did attempt to give him the semblance of a smile as she moved to his desk, not bothering to sit.

"There's my all star," he said. "You were supposed to take the week off and celebrate your victory. I should've known better, though. You're a workaholic like me. You might take over my job someday. I wouldn't be surprised at all."

His words sent another mix of emotions through her. On the one hand, it was a dream come true to hear those words. Her dream had always been to be the top dog at an established, well-reputed firm. There weren't many women who claimed that title. She wouldn't allow less than the best for herself, though, and being a woman wasn't a limitation in her eyes. Even thinking that, her dreams had recently changed. She still needed to be the best, but she wanted to do it by helping those who deserved it.

"I need to give this to you," she told him as she handed over a resignation letter. It was short and to the point. She handed him a second letter with the cases in her file. They'd be handed to other competent attorneys in the firm.

He gazed at the letter for several long moments, his smile fading once he realized what it was. When he finally looked up, she saw how the man had become the senior partner of a multimillion dollar firm, how he had so many wins beneath not only his belt, but from those he'd chosen to work at this establishment. It made her respect him that much more.

Three entire minutes passed with neither of them speaking. Though that might not seem long in the scheme of life, it was an eternity in a situation like this. She had to stay strong and couldn't speak before he did. Her letter had said all she'd needed to say. It was up to him what came next.

"Why?" he finally asked. "Were you given a better offer?" The second question was spoken with disbelief. It would be tough for her to get a better offer. She was their all-star junior partner, and her pay and bonuses reflected that.

"Because I can no longer defend the guilty. This position doesn't work for me anymore."

She was shocked when respect entered his eyes as he gazed at her. That hadn't been at all what she'd expected to see.

"You're going to go far in your career," he told her. "It's too bad we're going to find ourselves fighting against you. I'm predicting some disappointing losses on our end."

She could've been thrown into a brick wall and been less stunned. "Thank you, sir, but I'm not sure what my next move is going to be."

"I'll enjoy keeping an eye out to see what happens in your future. Take care of yourself. And, Avery, if you ever need anything, anything at all, please call."

"Thank you again for giving me a chance." He nodded his head. The conversation was over.

She didn't say goodbye. She simply turned around, walked to her office, gathered the minimal personal items she kept there, then exited the building for the final time. It was overwhelmingly bittersweet.

For years, she'd spent more time at this office than at home. She'd lived and breathed being a lawyer. She imagined she'd become a prosecutor somewhere, she just wasn't sure where. She knew she couldn't leave her mother. Her mom was the only person on this planet who loved her. Of course Avery also loved her uncle, but the bond with her mother was the only thing that kept her believing love truly did exist.

Avery was lost after she dropped her items at her apartment. She walked the Frisco streets, unsure of what to do next or where to go. Normally, she'd be studying her next case, planning, looking at her opponents, figuring out her strategy and what she needed to do to win. What did she do now that she had spare time on her hands for the first time in her life? She wouldn't waste much time. She'd at least study law, follow other cases, do things to keep her mind sharp.

But not today.

Today was a day to acknowledge her life was changing. Today was a day to feel a bit of pity for this new path she was on that led to who knew where.

It was only a few hours past dawn, the beauty of the bay lighting up, boats beginning to stir, and people milling about, looking for a place to eat. She moved along the famous Pier 39, people watching, seeing the tourists exclaim over different items they couldn't live without, hearing kids cry over not getting a beloved piece of junk, and seeing young lovers sneaking off to be alone — things she normally didn't pay the least bit of attention to.

When she passed the Wipeout Bar and Grill she saw Carl sitting alone at a table as a waitress dropped off a plate of food. He smiled at the waitress before looking over the balcony, his eyes connecting with Avery's. Her stomach clenched as her reaction to him was instantaneous and intense.

She'd had the best date of her life with Carl. They'd laughed and talked for hours at that rooftop bar. She'd had a little too much to drink, and she'd found herself wishing he'd had a room at that hotel. By the spark in his eyes, the feeling was mutual.

But as he'd said earlier, he wasn't getting a room. At the end of their night, he'd escorted her to the car. With virtually no traffic at that time of night, it hadn't taken them long to get her home.

Much to her disappointment all she'd gotten at her front door was one scorching kiss, then he'd practically pushed her inside before he left. She'd been so disappointed she'd wanted to cry. Then she'd refused to say more than a few words through texts over the past few days. She was finally realizing how stupid she'd been.

But, in her defense, she didn't normally date, and she didn't know the rules. She felt the deep connection between the two of them, but she didn't understand what that meant. And now, here he was. She wasn't sure what to do.

"Join me," he said, barely audible over the noise on the pier. It was a rare sunny day with nearly no wind. It seemed everyone in the city was out to enjoy the warm morning.

Before she could talk herself out of it, she was moving forward, skirting around patrons, and squeezing between tables. She reached him, her heart beating a bit too fast. She could try to convince herself it was from the walk, but she knew it was because of her reaction to *this* man.

Before she was able to sit, she heard a high-pitched female voice squeal. Turning, she saw a bombshell of a woman skirting the same tables she'd just passed. California was known as the land of plastic, and this was its poster child. She was blonde with fake boobs, fake lips, and fake eyelashes. Her skirt was too short, and her tank top showed off her twenty-grand boob job to perfection. And she had eyes for nobody but Carl.

"Well, it's been far too long, sexy," the woman said in a Marylyn Monroe husky voice as she reached for Carl, immediately wrapping her arms around his neck and pressing her plastic body against his. Her leg even rose as she squealed her delight at seeing him. She planted her lips on his for about three seconds, before finally stepping back and giggling. "Mmm, delicious as always."

"How are you, Janine?" he asked, his voice less enthusiastic than hers. But he didn't exactly sound turned off. Avery found herself awkwardly standing there, feeling incredibly foolish. She should've shaken her head at him and moved on. It would've been far less embarrassing than the moment she was now in.

"I'm great now that I see you. I'm meeting my girlfriends, but I have no problem ditching them," she said. Avery had no doubt this woman would drag him from the restaurant right then and straight to her bedroom if he nodded his okay.

"I can't. I have a date," he told her as he looked at Avery. She wanted to correct him, tell him this was far from a date. Of course, according to him, they'd had three dates already, so this might actually be their fourth. She normally wasn't a woman who got confused, but she was finding herself that way right now.

Even in her confusion, there was something Avery really despised in women like this one clinging to him. There was a slightly gleeful part of her that was enjoying that Carl was turning the woman down so he could spend more time with Avery.

The blonde probably hadn't even noticed Avery standing by, but with his words, she turned, her eyes going ice cold now that they weren't on Carl. She slipped her arm around his waist, as if trying to let Avery know he was hers and she wasn't giving up without a fight. She eyed Avery as if she'd judged and found her wanting. It made Avery want to punch her in her veneered mouth.

Avery wasn't going to be the first to speak. She wanted to stand her ground, but she had zero illusions that she and Carl were in a committed relationship — they'd only been on a few so-called dates. He could obviously see other women.

"Don't worry about it," Avery said after a few seconds, glad to be able to put her lawyer face on, so neither party would know how upset she was. "I was simply coming to say hello. I don't have time to stay. I have another . . . person I'm meeting with," she said with a moment of hesitation. Let him wonder about *her* plans.

She turned and walked away, telling herself she didn't care at all that he was a man whore with a cliché woman. Men like him usually had big egos and liked women to fawn over them. She wasn't into those types of games. She'd thought he was different from how much he'd supported her so far — she'd obviously been wrong.

Carl called out, but the blonde stopped him, and Avery was able to make her escape. She fled quickly, hailing a cab, leaving the pier and Carl behind. She wished she could feel a whole lot better about the situation than she did. Unfortunately, all she felt was crappy.

She'd lost her job that day, and even though it had been her choice, it still was frightening since she didn't have a new one lined up, and now she'd lost the guy she'd been pretty dang attracted to. She'd known her time with him wasn't going anywhere so it shouldn't cross her mind again. She feared it would though — she feared she'd be thinking of him for quite some time.

There was only one place she wanted to go when she was feeling this blue. She gave the driver the address then sat back. She wouldn't allow herself pity for long — not long at all. Her new life had begun, and nothing was going to bring her down.

Chapter Thirteen

It had been twenty-four hours since Joseph had been with his wife, and his temper was peaking. He'd been patient, but he needed to hold her, needed to see her face. The hospital was being overly cautious, and he respected that, but enough was enough.

He rose from the chair in the waiting room, his body aching as he walked out to the corridor and moved to the end where a double door was closed. He pushed the button and moved through it, finding himself in a wide hallway with huge windows at the end. He moved toward them, seeing the lights shining down below. The sun had set, and there were a couple of people below, either sneaking in kisses or smokes. He wanted to be outside the hospital walls himself, but he wouldn't leave his wife.

He'd always enjoyed the night when the streets emptied and a person could hear their own thoughts. But right now he couldn't imagine feeling joy. Normally, his favorite time of day was the morning, the breaking dawn of a new day. Anything was possible with a brand new day. Problems from the night before vanished, and the morning light gave a person a new perspective.

He was certain tomorrow's dawn wouldn't be any better than tonight's dusk. That was a humbling and sad thought. For right now he simply felt hopeless. He needed his wife. Yes, that was something most people said, but in his case, it was so much more than words.

Before Katherine, he'd been a lost man. He'd been arrogant and stupid, and had no understanding of love and devotion. Before Katherine, he'd cared only about his next big deal, his next project to conquer. He hadn't wanted to be a family man. He hadn't thought to help the world. He'd been lost without knowing he'd needed to be found.

But from the first moment he'd spotted Katherine he'd known he had to have her. While they might've had bumps in the road, the next time he'd seen her he'd known she'd be his wife and the mother of his children. From that moment on, he'd known his world would never be the same again. To lose her was unacceptable.

Joseph felt someone beside him, but didn't turn. Somehow he knew he didn't want to hear whatever it was they were going to tell him. Though he wasn't normally a man to run from news, or danger, he didn't want this person to speak, didn't want to look at them. He was scared — a completely new emotion for him. He was downright terrified.

"Joseph." Dr. Whitman's voice was quiet, reassuring, and kind — too kind. Joseph knew that tone of voice.

"You promised me," Joseph said, not recognizing his own voice. It was broken, raspy, and didn't have anywhere near the booming quality he was known for.

There was a pause as Dr. Spence Whitman gave Joseph a moment. Joseph appreciated him for that. Normally he was a man to want the bandage ripped off. But the longer he lived in denial, the better off he was — at least for this horrible period in his life.

"I don't like to make promises for this very reason. Before I explain, let me tell you it isn't hopeless, Joseph. I'm going to use some very scary words, and I'm not going to lie to you, but I want you to understand that there *is* hope," Spence said.

Joseph swallowed the lump in his throat. His eyes were burning, and rage was trying to bubble through the absolute grief controlling him. From the second he'd opened his eyes in that chair a few moments ago, he'd known something was terribly wrong. There was a connection between him and his wife that was unexplainable. If she was in trouble, or in pain, he knew. She was the same with him. Their souls truly were connected.

"I can't live without her," Joseph said.

"Why don't we find your family and I can tell all of you what's happening at the same time," Spence said.

Joseph didn't hesitate. "No. I sent them home. I needed some alone time. They fought me, but I won," he said. "I might want to run from this, but I won't. I need to be strong for my wife and for my family. And I need you to tell me. I'll figure out how to tell them."

"Are you sure?"

Joseph wasn't normally questioned. But then again, these weren't normal times. "I'm very sure."

"Katherine's tests have come in. First, I'm going to tell you the positive to this situation. Had she not taken the fall . . ." Spence began, being diplomatic by not saying the word *attack*. Spence stopped and began again. "Had she not been injured, we might not have found this in time to do something."

Those words processed in Joseph's muddled brain. "What might not have been found?" He was beginning to realize there was something more than the injury of the night. His dread deepened.

"Katherine needs a team of oncologists, neurologists, and neurosurgeons. The attack might've initially knocked her out, but the subsequent issues in the chopper caused us to perform scans not typically associated with a concussion," Spence said. He took another pause that infuriated Joseph.

"What are you telling me?" Joseph asked, his voice growing louder as rage began taking over his unending sadness.

Spence sighed. "I've never had such a difficult time giving a diagnosis to a family member." He straightened his shoulders and looked Joseph in the eyes. "Katherine has a mass in her brain. We believe this to be a tumor that signals cancer. We need to do a lot more to have a definitive answer. I do know this won't be an easy journey." He stopped, and Joseph knew that was to allow the words to seep in.

Joseph couldn't breathe.

With those few sentences hammering down on him, he felt his soul trying to escape, trying to fly to his wife, trying to unite with her. Those earlier words of reassurance that everything would be okay had been nothing but a wisp of smoke that was now disappearing into the wind, taking them thousands of miles away.

Joseph had gone through something similar many years ago, and though he'd been in a coma, his family praying over him daily, he hadn't suffered because he'd slept through it. But Katherine had told him how devastated she'd been. He hadn't fully understood until this very moment.

"How bad?" Joseph asked. He didn't want to know, but he couldn't help her if he buried his head in the sand.

"It's bad, Joseph, but it's not hopeless."

Joseph's world fell out beneath him. He had to fight the shaking trying to overtake his body as the doctor's words tried to process in his brain. Cancer? What was happening? How could his world be flipped upside down in a matter of seconds? How would any of them survive?

"Joseph, I've contacted doctors from around the world, the best of the best. You have a unique advantage many families don't, you have the ability to do whatever it takes for your wife. Don't give up. We can beat this. I'm not going to make promises this time, but I'm telling you there's real hope," Spence said as his hand rested on Joseph's shoulder.

Joseph swallowed. He couldn't take even a few minutes to wallow in his grief. He needed a plan of action set in motion, and he needed to move fast. He blinked back the stinging in his eyes, not allowing himself more tears. He could wallow in pity, or he could be a man of action.

"It's sad isn't it, how this world works?" Joseph asked.

"What do you mean?" Spence asked. He was a wise man, and wouldn't assume

Joseph was only speaking of how sad this situation was for him and his family.

"I have all the money in the world. I can hire the best doctors. I can do whatever needs to be done, but at the end of the day it might not be enough. It's sad because there are other people who are in nearly as much pain as I am, and they don't have the resources I have. Maybe that needs to change. Maybe this world needs to find cures, instead of bandaging problems. Maybe I should've cared more about this a lot sooner, then maybe I wouldn't be in this pain now because it wouldn't be a problem. And maybe other people wouldn't have to hear news like this either."

"There are many debates over medicine," Spence said. "Unlimited money goes through it. I think if anyone can solve this issue, it'll be you."

"You might just be right," Joseph said. It was so much easier to focus on a problem and work to fix it than to accept what was happening. "I won't lose her," he added, that famous steel he was known for present in his voice.

"Let me take you to your wife," Spence said.

"Finally," Joseph sighed. He'd been waiting too long.

Suddenly, though, Joseph found he was afraid to see her in a coma, afraid to see her weak and hooked up to machines. But he did *need* to see her. He nodded, no further words left inside of him. He allowed Spence to lead him down corridors to his wife's room.

As he walked, he reminded himself he was the rock of his family. He was the man they leaned upon in tough times. He had to have faith, had to be a rock that wouldn't crack. He couldn't fall, and he couldn't waiver. He was the head of his family. They needed him — Katherine needed him. He couldn't make poor decisions because he was broken. Then he'd fail them all.

He'd follow up on those doctors Spence had contacted. He'd do all in his power to bring them together, to get his wife the best of the best care. He wouldn't lose her, even if he had to make a deal with the devil.

"Here we are," Spence said at a closed door. "Do you want me to go inside with you?"

Joseph shook his head. "Thank you, but I have to do this alone," Joseph told him. Spence nodded, then walked away.

Joseph stood for a moment, forcing himself to breathe in and out, taking in long, deep breaths to calm the beating of his heart. Then he pushed the door open and crossed the threshold. Pale light filtered through the room, and he gave himself a moment to adjust to the dimmer setting. Then he focused on the bed in the center of the room, and his heart felt as if a vice were squeezing it.

He stepped forward, his eyes glued to Katherine's pale face. "Oh, my darling," he whispered, tears overflowing as he moved to her side. His fingers shook as he lifted his hand, placed it on her cheek, and willed her to look at him.

He pushed back strands of her silver hair, taking his time to caress the silky locks as he'd done countless times in their many, many years together.

"Don't leave me, my love," he begged, his legs shaking. He was barely managing to hold himself up in his deep despair. "We've had so many beautiful years together, good and bad, funny and tragic, hard and easy. We have so many more to go. You're my world, my reason for being. It's you and me until we take our last breaths together. Even then, we'll have an eternity in the afterlife. But our kids need us here for now. There's so much more to do on this beautiful planet. Please don't leave me alone. Please don't go into the light just yet. I can't do it without you. I feel as if I can't even breathe right now. Please, Katherine, please my darling, please stay."

Joseph choked on his last words as emotion overtook him. He blindly felt behind him for the chair he'd barely managed to see, then fell into it as he sat at her side, still touching her face and hair, needing to feel her.

He ignored the tube secured in her mouth, and the machines making all sorts of sounds with lights flashing and numbers appearing. None of this seemed real. Part of him was still hoping to wake up from this nightmare he'd found himself in.

But as he gazed at the purple bruise on the side of her precious head, he couldn't deny the events that had taken place. There were four stiches, marring her perfect forehead. The area was beginning to darken, and she'd forever have a scar to remind her that this world could be a dangerous place. She should've never found that out. He should've kept her safe.

"I promise you no stone will be left unturned. I'll get you the best doctors and we'll fight this together. I won't leave your side my love, just as you didn't leave mine when I was fighting to come back to you," he promised.

He hadn't been able to understand how much pain she'd been in when he'd had his heart attack and then been in a coma. He'd apologize to her profusely when she was woke. He'd been unconscious while his family had been tormented. No one should ever feel this kind of pain. It was nearly unbearable.

He couldn't bear to think of what ifs anymore. It was killing him. Instead he focused on that scar, on what had put her in this hospital in the first place. Anger began taking over the pain.

"Those men will pay," he promised. Though even as he said it, he knew the revenge was for him. Katherine would tell him he needed to have forgiveness in his heart. Well, she was wrong this time. Some deserved absolution, but so many more deserved retribution.

"Joseph," Dr. Whitman said from the door. Joseph hadn't even noticed it opening. He looked up.

"She'll wake up, right?" Joseph asked, aware he was practically groveling.

Spence nodded. "Yes. We want to allow her to rest for at least a couple more days. Then the plan is to begin the process of waking her as soon as the initial wounds have healed."

Joseph nodded, then looked back at his wife. She appeared as if she was simply sleeping. If it weren't for the tubes and IVs, and of course the terrible bruise, he could almost pretend they were simply going to sleep together as they'd done every night for close to fifty years.

Joseph didn't hear Spence exit. There was no way he was leaving his wife's side. Exhaustion filled him as he gently cupped his large hand against her delicate cheek. Then he stood, removed his shoes, and rolled his sleeves. He took great care not to bump any wires or tubes on Katherine's bed as he carefully slid in next to her, unable to bear another moment of them not connecting.

He lay on his side, facing her as he reached out an arm and gently cradled her against him. He kissed her cheek before making her a promise. "When we said our vows, I told you we'd spend the rest of our lives together, that I'd love you for eternity, and I'd always put you first. I won't forget those vows. I love you, darling. You're my world yesterday, today, and tomorrow. You stay here with me, and I promise you I won't ever take us for granted again. I'll never assume there will be a tomorrow. I'll live each and every moment with you as if it's our last. I promise to cherish you, protect you, and appreciate you."

He so wanted a response from her, and in his heart he knew he'd gotten one because he felt warmth in his heart. He had no doubt that was Katherine warming him, assuring him she wasn't going anywhere. His eyelids drifted closed as weightlessness washed over him.

He finally fell asleep, his love right beside him.

Chapter Fourteen

Carl watched Avery practically run from the restaurant and he wanted to smack himself. Of course she wouldn't understand the supermodel in front of him was actually dating one of his friends. Yes, she was slutty, and yes, she liked to be the center of attention, and yes, he was *very* aware she inappropriately touched men. It had simply never bothered him before, as he'd never been trying to go after another woman when Janine was around.

"What in the hell was that, Janine?" he asked as he unwound himself from her.

She batted her fake lashes, something he was unimpressed by, as she tried to touch him again. He stepped back so she couldn't. He'd had enough of her games, possibly for a lifetime.

"I don't know what you're talking about," she said.

"Damn, you have the innocent act down to a science. I like that woman you managed to chase away in a matter of seconds. That's beyond uncool," he told her.

She gave him a pouty look, her bottom lip sticking out as she cast her eyes down. He didn't know if it was possible for her to get her feelings hurt. Women like her were a dime a dozen. Women like Avery were a jewel in a crown.

"You're hurting my feelings, Carl. I haven't seen you in a while and I wanted to catch up."

He pulled out his wallet and threw two twenties on the table, his food barely touched and his drink only half finished. But he'd lost his appetite, and he needed to find Avery. He wasn't sure what in the hell was happening between the two of them, but it was something, and he wasn't willing to sacrifice it — especially for *this* woman.

He didn't bother telling Janine anything. He simply turned and walked away. At least she had enough pride to not follow. By the time he made it to the end of the pier he knew Avery was long gone.

Carl knew there was no point in calling; she wouldn't answer. He also knew she wouldn't head home. Where would she go? His best guess was to her mother. He didn't have Bobbi's number. That meant he was going to have to do some pleading and begging to get what he wanted — Avery. He was shocked he was willing to do just that.

He got in a cab and made his way back to the bar where he'd first spoken to both Bobbi and Avery. It was about ten in the morning now, with scattered people milling about the farther he got away from the wharf. It didn't take long to draw close to the bar. The second he passed the alley where Avery had been attacked less than a week before, rage flowed through his veins. That situation could've turned out so much worse had he not heard her cry for help. He was damn grateful he had.

He walked inside, disappointed when he didn't spot Avery or Bobbi. What in the world was he going to do now? He put on his most trusting smile as he approached the bar where a woman about Bobbi's age was working. She looked at him with suspicion, not trusting his smile at all. He was sure she'd seen it many times before from men who wanted something.

"Is Bobbi working today?" he finally asked when the bartender didn't speak. He could normally judge a person's attitude by what they said in their first sentence.

"Nope, today is her day off."

"We're friends. But I've misplaced her number. Can I get it from you?" he asked. He'd been told before that when he put on the charm he had a very trusting face. From this woman's disbelieving look, he was thinking his friends who'd told him that were full of crap.

"You can give me that trust-me smile all you want. I don't give out anyone's number. I think you'd do best to move along," she said as she brought out a rag and began wiping the counter.

"I really need to speak to her. It's important," he pleaded.

She rolled her eyes. "It's *always* important," she mocked. This woman was hardened, and he knew he wasn't going to get her to bend.

"Okay, then let me put it this way," he said as he sat. "I'm not going anywhere until I talk to her. You can give me the number, or you can dial her up, tell her my name, and let me speak to her through your phone. But I *will* be speaking to her in the next thirty minutes."

He made himself comfortable, assuring her he had nowhere else he needed to be. She looked him over, and he was sure she was judging whether she could find someone who could force him out. From the resigned look in her eyes, he determined she didn't know anyone who'd be willing to take him on. He probably wasn't the biggest man she'd ever seen, but there was steel in his eyes that she'd recognize. Hopefully she could tell he wasn't often messed with.

"Fine, but if she refuses to speak to you, I'm calling the cops to get you out," she told him through clenched teeth. Carl didn't push his luck by gloating. He waited as she picked up the phone, turning away from him so he couldn't see the number she was dialing. Just as he thought she would, when Bobbi heard his name she was willing to take the call. The bartender seemed disappointed. She handed it over with reluctance.

"Hi Bobbi, I need to speak with Avery. Today wasn't what she thought it was," he said, hoping the truth was conveyed over the phone. He'd much rather speak in person where he could read body language.

There was silence for a moment before Bobbi spoke, clearly enjoying her power as she played go-between. "Sorry, Sugar, but Avery's emphatically saying she wants nothing to do with you. Yes, she's sitting here now, and no, she's not impressed with your excuse."

Carl let out a sigh, hating that the bartender was listening in on this conversation. He was a private man and didn't like strangers butting into his business.

"Let me explain all of this in person. If you guys don't buy it, I'll be on my way without a hassle," he promised.

She paused so long this time, he began wondering if she'd disconnected the call. He didn't interrupt the silence, just waited.

"Okay, come and explain," Bobbi finally said, then rattled off her address. He heard Avery gasp in outrage in the background before her mother hung up.

He knew to hurry and get there before she decided to disappear. He clicked off the phone and handed it to the bartender, thanking her as he ran from the bar.

He'd win over the girl because there was no other option than to do just that. He wanted her — and he *would* have her. He wished he could explain to himself why he was so obsessed, but he didn't have time to delve into that. Maybe today would end that obsession. Or maybe his obsession would make him unable to resist whatever was going to come next.

Chapter Fifteen
Two Years Ago

Eyes didn't flinch as they were surrounded on all sides. They were SEALs, and they were trained for this. He knew there was only a split second to make a decision. He looked at his teammates and nodded.

"Sleep, pull Morph down the edge of this damn mountain, and cease fire. I'm going to take these guys on a magic carpet ride, and if the fates are with me I'll create a flank," Eyes said. He grinned and gave his brothers a wink.

"Eyes, you realize you're not funny, right? Not in the best of times, but definitely not in the worst." Morph huffed at him, though his own lips twitched, even with the amount of pain he had to be feeling.

"I just have a tough crowd," Eyes replied. He then nodded to Sleep and Morph. Nothing else needed to be said. Sleep would follow his command.

Then he turned, knowing Sleep would follow his orders. He ran directly up the trail, straight at the enemy fire. A lot of men would back down at the danger Eyes was running into. Most people would curl into a fetal position and pray they weren't found. But the best of the best didn't have that option. Eyes might have a hell of a sense of humor, but he'd die for his brothers, and he'd die to keep America safe and free.

As he stealthily moved forward, Eyes focused on the different groups of two-, three-, and four-man teams in varying distances from him. They weren't hiding, thinking they had the upper hand, and there'd be no way any of the American soldiers would run at them. They obviously didn't know SEALs too well.

They were firing steadily, each burst from their rifles causing the internal components of Eyes's night vision goggles to nearly blind him. Unfortunately for the enemy, Eyes had spent thousands of hours of training in situations just like this one. This wasn't even close to his first rodeo where the enemy was doing everything to end him.

Yes, this was bad. But it wasn't the worst he'd seen. He knelt behind a fallen tree and took down two groups of men before they knew they were being fired upon. In order for Eyes to flank the enemy, he had to wipe out the men in front, giving Sleep enough time to bandage Morph and get back into the fight.

A man stepped out and Eyes dropped him with a three-shot sequence. Then it was time to move again. He ran parallel with the fallen tree as he noted four more groups of men, the closest about one hundred yards away.

Luckily for him, they weren't good shots. The fact that some of their men had been taken out was due to luck, not skill. That was a hard pill to swallow for Eyes.

He rounded the top of the large tree and began his way around this group when he heard a sound his brain refused to comprehend. Braking, he turned back to where he'd left his last two team members.

A man was swiftly moving forward, where he'd just sent a grenade at Morph and Sleep. Eyes could hope like hell they'd gotten out of there first, but it had happened too quick. There was little possibility they'd escaped. How in the hell had he missed this man? Shock was quickly replaced with white-hot rage.

Eyes covered the distance between him and the enemy with the speed of a cheetah, and the man had zero chance of escape as Eyes took him out. He didn't pause as he rushed back to where his men had been.

He rushed through the bushes, his nightmare coming to life as he stumbled onto the body that was torn apart. It was Morph, though he was barely recognizable. Eyes checked for life, knowing there wasn't a chance.

Even though their team was the best, they were surrounded on all sides by an enemy firing in every direction. They didn't care if they hit friend or foe. Sadly, they were losing the battle no matter what pep talk he'd been giving himself just a few moments ago.

He pushed down all emotion at another loss and studied the scene, quickly determining by the blast pattern that Sleep must've been sent over the cliff. He was sure Morph had given his life to save Sleep. All of them would do the same.

He looked over the edge, his night vision not able to pierce deep enough to see the bottom, making Eyes aware it was a long drop to the bottom. It was almost surely a death sentence.

Eyes got to work, grabbing Morph's extra ammo, then pulling him into the bushes, hiding him so these monsters couldn't mutilate his body further. These assholes wouldn't use his brother's body for their propaganda to terrorize the world with the horrific things they were willing to do to those who crossed them.

Though he was moving quickly, the time he'd taken had allowed the enemy to merge from the forest and close in on Eyes's location.

He immediately put a new plan into motion, running to the man he'd just eliminated and grabbing his grenades. Pulling the pins, Eyes launched them toward the closest insurgents and ran with all he had in the opposite direction before they hit the ground.

As the two grenades detonated, a barrage of gunfire exploded behind Eyes. He kept moving forward, not even flinching when a few grenades exploded behind and to the side of him. They were throwing all they had at him, missing so far. He wasn't trying to keep quiet any longer, just moving at full speed ahead.

They had no idea where he was, they were just blindly firing in all directions. If he made it out alive it would be a miracle, but he was determined to get back. He needed to let the families of his brothers know they'd died heroes.

As he surged forward he noted the treetops to the right of him were gaining in elevation. He was moving downward. Soon he'd be able to get to the bottom of the cliff, then change direction, and gain more distance from the men trying to take him out.

There was a river down there, and that was his surest escape route. He kept following the path he was on, jumping over fallen logs, rushing through the bushes tugging at his skin and clothes, and keeping his ears out for a possible ambush.

He made it to the bottom of the hill as dawn began to break. Dammit! He'd be a sitting duck in the light. He turned, seeing two insurgents near the waterfall, then heard a noise to his left. He couldn't make out much more than shapes at this point, but guns began firing again in all directions.

Fear wasn't a remote factor. Eyes flashed through all scenarios in a matter of seconds as he ran through a mental checklist of what he needed to do next. He'd either live — or he wouldn't. It was that simple.

He quickly took out the two men near the waterfall, his long shots hitting with deadly accuracy. Then he turned to take out the one closest to him, but before he could fire, a multitude of shots rang from above him. He ducked behind a large tree, then sent a round up the cliff, hearing a scream, knowing he'd connected.

He stepped out, sent a couple of rounds in front of him, then felt his body thrust forward as a round ripped through his shoulder. He hit the ground, but didn't stay there, jumping back to his feet and rushing forward again, pushing the pain aside as he quickly assessed the damage. He'd lost the ability to raise his arm above his shoulder, but other than that, he'd been lucky. It hadn't hit anything vital.

He kept moving, bullets hitting the trees all around him as he returned fire, knowing he was hitting targets when their pained screams echoed through the canyon.

He was getting farther from the enemy when another bullet ripped through his midsection, this hit taking his breath away. He nearly fell, but managed to stay on his feet, managed to keep going forward, although slower. He didn't have to be a physician to know a hit in the torso was critical.

He wasn't sure if it was adrenaline or if the bullet had missed his vital organs, but he barely felt the pain. He wasn't going to stop. If he died, he'd do it on his feet, fighting. More concerning to him than his wounds was his rapidly depleting ammo supply. If he had any chance of escape, he'd need his weapons in full working order.

He concentrated on moving one foot in front of the other, encouraged when the fire behind him grew dimmer. They were following in the wrong direction. A hint of a smile crossed his features as he realized he might just make it out of this.

But that smile was shattered when pain ripped through his body, knocking him off his feet, spinning him in the air. He landed hard on his back, feeling like his leg had been removed. He lay there for several moments, finally able to catch his breath. He didn't want to look down, but had no choice. Relief filled him when he saw his leg hadn't been blown off.

The round that had hit him had been to his right hip. "Dammit!" His thunderous whisper was full of frustration. How in hell was he going to run with his leg out of commission? There wasn't time for him to have a pity party, though. He had to assess the damage.

He ripped off his night vision as the light of dawn hindered its use. A movement to his side drew his attention. This might be the last of the enemy in this area, because the gunfire he heard in large quantities, kept moving farther away.

If it came down to one on one, he knew he'd be the last man breathing.

The movement stopped, and Eyes knew he was at a standstill. He also knew he was losing too much blood to stay conscious for much longer. Rage ripped through him. Was this man going to be such a chicken he'd simply wait it out?

"Show yourself!" Eyes thundered. "Don't hide like the coward you are." He gazed in all directions, his finger on the trigger of his gun, ready for a fight.

Silence greeted his demand.

"Come on!" he cried out again.

Nothing.

He leaned his head back, real pain creeping in. He knew he had to plug his wounds if he had a chance of survival, but if he let his guard down, he'd be shot again. He was in a no win situation.

After several more tense seconds and no more sound, Eyes had no choice other than to tend his wounds. He pulled out his bag of QuikClot and packed his wounds, which quickly stopped the flow of blood in his torso and hip, though he knew the bandaging wouldn't take the place of a well qualified surgeon, which is what he'd need sooner rather than later.

He ripped open an energy bar and practically shoved it down his throat to try to bring some of the energy back that had literally spilled out of him in blood, then using only his left leg, managed to get himself to his feet. He tried to put pressure on his right, but it was useless.

He glanced around at the tree limbs, looking for something to create a brace and make a crutch. He was as quiet as possible, listening for any approaching feet. But he moved as fast as his beaten body allowed, grabbing pieces of wood and making a brace for his leg. He used his paracord to secure it then created a useable crutch. It was as good as it was going to get under the circumstances.

He took his first step; it wasn't graceful, but he was able to move. Pain shot through his entire body each time his right foot connected with the ground, but he pushed it aside. As long as he felt pain, he knew he was alive — that was all that mattered.

He took a few more steps, and his head began spinning. He stopped as he tried to refocus. Then he heard rustling in the bushes, far too close. If the enemy had his gun on him, Eyes was a goner.

He smiled.

He might die, but he'd do it with his head up and a look in his eyes that would haunt his enemy for life.

Lifting his side-arm, taking aim at the bushes where the noise had come from, Eyes hissed out, "Show yourself you mother—"

He was cut off with words that filled his soul with hope.

"Shut up, ya freaking idiot."

That was a voice and a sentence he'd heard many times before. He wasn't sure how it was possible, but unless he was hallucinating all of this, a member of his team was still alive. The intense pain flowing through him told him he must be alive. If this was a hallucination and he was actually dead, there was no way heaven could be this bloody or painful.

Eyes tried to respond to the voice, but his throat closed on him.

"Eyes, do not shoot me!" the voice commanded.

The rustling came closer and Eyes found his voice. "Sleep?"

"The one and only. I'm coming to you," Sleep said, sounding as weak and tired as Eyes felt.

For one of the few times in his life, Eyes found himself speechless. With all that had happened to their team in the past couple of hours, it seemed impossible that he and Sleep were uniting.

Sleep slowly stepped from the bushes, his body as beat to hell as Eyes's. Sleep limped forward, swaying, until they were finally face to face. They gave each other an assessment of the damage to their beaten bodies.

And then they laughed.

That might seem strange under the circumstances, but it was the only way these men knew how to deal with the stress and trauma. The laughter faded as they worked to catch their breaths.

"We've certainly looked better," Sleep said.

"It's a good thing we're so good looking or this might deflect from our overall appearance," Eyes said. Then his face turned serious. "What happened after I left?"

Sleep went right back into soldier mode, giving Eyes a brief rundown from the time the grenade had been thrown until right then. His final words left both of them confused as they stared at one another.

That's when they realized their last gunfight had been with . . . each other.

Eyes didn't even blink as he realized the last three bullets that had ripped through him had most likely come from Sleep's hand. Sleep appeared horrified.

"I could've killed you," Sleep said. There wasn't much that could take down these men, but being the hand that killed one of their brothers would certainly do it.

Eyes gave him the same grin he'd given right before he'd launched himself at the enemy. "Well, I guess it's a good thing you suck at shooting cause I'm still alive . . . for now," he said. Sleep glared at him and Eyes continued. "Just know that you don't get a promotion if you wipe out your commander." He laughed then winced as pain ripped through his torso at the shaking in his stomach.

"I want out of this shitshow," Sleep said. He wasn't finding quite the same humor as Eyes with the knowledge that he could've killed his teammate.

"Well, let's end this homecoming and get moving. We'll lean on each other and move as fast as our broken bodies will allow. I don't want to wait to see if there's a second wave of insurgents or if the first wave smartens up and turns around," Eyes said.

"I think that's the brightest idea you've had yet," Sleep told him. They grabbed onto each other and began steadily moving along the river, staying under cover, but not going deep into the woods again. They knew the water would lead them to civilization.

"You know," Eyes said after a while, "when we make it out of here and are once again on our own soil, I'm never going to let you forget you nearly killed me. You'll owe me for the rest of your life."

"Let's just make it out of here," Sleep said. Then he finally smiled, though it wasn't even close to his brightest one. "I'm sure I'll be picking up your dry cleaning for life."

"Hell with that. I'm going to be living in sweats and T-shirts for a while. There won't be a need to dress up until these wounds heal and we can get our asses back to work."

"Amen to that," Sleep said.

"I think I might have you making liquor runs for me though," Eyes said.

"I don't think I'm going to be running for a while. But as soon as I can, I'll make them for us both," Sleep assured him.

And then they saved their energy as they plugged along, one foot in front of the other. They didn't focus on what was behind them, they didn't focus on the pain. They simply moved forward with a sheer determination to make it home . . .

Chapter Sixteen

Joseph was jolted awake by a loud beeping sound. His eyes popped open, and it took him a few seconds to orient himself as he tried to figure out where he was. Even in his haze, he found himself being careful, grateful when he realized he was in the hospital bed next to his wife.

He'd woken this same way for several days in a row and it still disoriented him. But before he'd fallen asleep the night before, the doctors had assured him they'd wake Katherine soon, very soon. He needed to speak to her, to hear her voice.

A nurse walked into the room and Joseph gazed at her, hoping for good news. "What time is it? Is everything okay?" He eyed the machine she'd just pushed buttons on, making the alarm stop.

"It's ten in the morning," she told him with a gentle smile. "And all is okay. Her IV simply ran out and I replaced it. I apologize, I should've turned off the alarm sooner."

"I'm not getting a whole lot of sleep these days. Any noise will wake me," Joseph told her. He felt guilty every time he fell asleep. What if something happened to his wife and he could've stopped it? He knew that wasn't rational, but he wasn't very sane these days.

"Sleep does much good for the body, so you let me know if there's anything I can do to make it easier for you to get some," the nurse said as she moved over to a flat screen near the head of his wife's bed and began typing. He didn't say anything as she inputted information, not wanting to distract her and maybe cause her to get something wrong. He'd heard horror stories of medicine doses being entered wrong or vitals being incorrect. Those minor mistakes could cost a person's life. He wasn't taking a chance like that.

She finished then gazed at him. "Can I get you anything?"

"No, thank you," he said. He began to carefully pull his arm away from his wife, taking extra precaution not to snag any of her tubes or wires as he extracted his large six-foot-five, two-hundred-ten-pound frame from the small bed. It was a good thing his delicate wife didn't take up much space. Joseph gently pulled himself from the bed, taking caution not to jolt Katherine.

"Has anything changed in the past few hours?" he asked. He had a ping of guilt he hadn't asked that the second he'd woken. He was functioning on very little sleep, though, and that was fogging his brain.

"Nothing has changed as of now. Her vitals have remained stable, and her oxygen levels are good. I'll have the doctor speak directly to you about the plan for today and tomorrow, but I believe we're on track with Dr. Whitman's course of action. The plan is to slowly wake her tomorrow morning."

"Okay, thank you. I'll be here all day. I might need to step out for a few walks and to speak to my family, but as long as I'm not in the way, I'd prefer to spend most of my time in here," Joseph said.

"Of course, Mr. Anderson. I'll have the room cleaned while you're out."

"Thank you. That would be appreciated," Joseph told her.

The nurse gave him a sweet, genuine smile before she turned and left, closing the door behind her. Joseph took a moment to stretch, his entire body aching. He couldn't recall the last time he'd felt so old and almost . . . frail. Neither of those words would be ones anyone would use to describe him.

He was a giant of a man with endless energy. He normally could run circles around men half his age. There was something to be said about how a broken heart could deplete a person. He was beginning to understand how Johnny Cash had withered so completely and quickly after losing the love of his life.

It didn't take long for his eyes to connect to his wife again, lying so still in her bed. Her motionless form left him wanting . . . wanting her to move, to be safe, to be free from that bed. He wanted to see the normal sparkle in her eyes, the sweet curve of her lips that was more often than not in a smile, and the deep flush of her cheeks as warmth filled them. He wanted her healthy, safe, and with him.

Before he could allow his mind to wander too far down that path, he shook away those thoughts. He couldn't get lost in self-pity again. He had too much to do. There were doctors to call, his family to update, and plans to be made.

The only way he'd been able to get any sleep lately was in knowing there were many people working hard as he slept. He was a man who liked to get things done himself. It had been difficult to turn his company over to his eldest son . . . at first. Then he'd seen the child, who'd turned into a fine man, take the reins and run with it, and he'd known he'd done his job as a parent.

His son was more than capable of not only doing the job of CEO of the vast Anderson empire, but of making it better. He knew the team assembling to take care of Katherine would be just as dedicated as he was going to be. It would allow him to rest periodically, making him more capable of being there for his wife as she needed him.

Joseph grabbed his phone off the charger so he could turn it on. He planned to be on it a lot with, texts, emails, video chats, and countless calls. As his device woke, a photo of Katherine filled the screen, her eyes sparkling, her lips open with laughter. He could practically hear that joy coming through his device. He clearly remembered the day the picture had been taken. She'd been laughing to the point of tears as their grandchildren had performed a special play for them titled "*A Thousand Feathered Pigs,*" including homemade outfits, arms and legs going in all different directions, and slapstick humor.

At the end of their performance, the kids had pulled out cans of silly string and covered their grandfather from head to toe in pink, green, purple, and orange strings. Katherine had been snapping pictures, and thankfully, his son had captured the absolute joy on his mother's face.

Their family had many days filled with joy, and this was simply one of those moments, but this picture had been Joseph's favorite from the second his son had sent it. This was his Katherine, this beautiful, joyful, God-fearing woman. She was the heart, soul, and true head of their family. She was the one who made them all want to be better. Life couldn't be imagined without her. He needed to hear her laughter again every single day for the rest of his life.

When his cell woke, it began buzzing, and Joseph sighed as he was pulled from his reverie. When it was done buzzing, he found a lot of texts, emails, and phone messages.

Joseph had spent many, many, *many* years glued to his phone, to his computer, and to his work. Of course, his wife would rein him in, and he was glad she had, because he also hadn't missed out on his children's lives. But to be honest, he'd sat in the bleachers of their games and checked emails, texts, and more, always feeling a need to get just a few more minutes of work done. But a person didn't build an empire by slacking. He'd had a vision, and he'd been incapable of sitting around and hoping it would happen. He'd thrived on building a business that would become more than he'd ever dreamed possible.

But something had changed when he'd retired. It was almost laughable to use those words, because, although he'd stepped down as CEO of the Anderson empire, it had simply freed him to pursue other things in life, such as travelling with Katherine, and even more importantly, helping his friends with their unruly children who refused to give them grandchildren in a timely manner. The latter was the best job in the world.

His Katherine was always saying he was a meddler, but as she found herself surrounded by all of those babies, he knew she wasn't too upset with the results of his planning. She just wasn't too thrilled with the methods he used, well at least in the beginning. Over the years the more grandchildren that were around the less she seemed to complain about whatever methodology he used to get his children, nephews, and close friends' kids married and reproducing.

But something had changed when he'd retired. He'd turned off the technology. He'd no longer been at the beck and call of machines and the blinking notifications so many couldn't ignore. It had been like cutting the strings to a kite, allowing it — and him — to fly free. Now his time, attention, and focus were where he wanted, and more importantly needed, them to be.

The older he grew, the more he realized that time was a valuable resource. He only had so much of it, and he wasn't wasting it on emails and phone consumption. It seemed as if this new generation couldn't make it through a meal without a phone in their hands. That was sad in his honest opinion. The art of a good game, and an even better conversation, had seemed to have gotten lost in all of this technology. Of course, when he did need answers, like he did right now, he was quite grateful a miniature computer fit in his hand.

He opened his family text and typed a quick message to let them know he was awake and ready to get started for the day. *Good Morning. Your mother is stable and her color seems to be a little better today. There's a tiny hint of pink in her cheeks this morning. Please meet me at the hospital in one hour.*

Joseph went to the cabinet and pulled out his overnight bag. His sons hadn't hesitated in giving him whatever he needed to stay with Katherine. He had time for a shower and shave before he jumped into his email. Maybe today he'd hear back from some of the doctors Spence had notified.

Before showering, he sent Lucas a private message. *After the family talks, we'll have the other meeting. Make sure Chad is here again.*

They'd had their initial meeting with Chad, but too many family members had been there, so Chad had assured them he'd begin doing research and they hadn't had time to come together again. Joseph needed that to move forward.

He rushed through his shower and shaved in ten minutes, coming out of the bathroom in Katherine's room, feeling fully alert and ready to take on what needed to be done. Sitting down in the corner of the room, he immediately got to work, feeling invigorated, his mind sharp, and his energy high, grateful to have something to focus on other than feeling helpless.

Joseph had expected a few replies today, but was humbled at what he saw. There were thirty-three responses from sixteen different doctors around the world. There was a group thread where they were consulting with one another, Dr. Whitman taking the lead and replying quickly. It was enough to awe Joseph, and he wasn't easily impressed.

Time was quickly running out before his family arrived. He read each email — twice. He wanted to make sure he didn't miss a single word. Joseph considered himself on the higher end of the intelligence spectrum, but this was an entire new world filled with technical medical terminology, varying philosophies from around the world, and professional recommendations for next steps.

What stood out most to him was that all of these men and women agreed, nearly one hundred percent. Their disagreements were minor. These people were considered the best of the best, highly sought after by every institution worldwide, with degrees from Ivy League schools, training in multiple locations, and innumerable research papers published and validated.

Their research on the brain and how it affected the body was indisputable. And each of these men and women were saying the same thing. They each had a clear plan of action that concluded with what Spence had said. The mass had to be biopsied, but there was little doubt it was cancerous.

From everything Joseph was reading, they'd reached this conclusion based on the size and location of the mass. Though this was terrifying, and some might find it hopeless, Joseph looked at the positive. If he didn't, he feared he wouldn't be able to function.

According to these brilliant minds, with proper treatment and care it was not only feasible, but likely, that the mass could be nearly eradicated, with any remnants inactive and unable to do her more harm or spread to other places.

They had varying ideas on how to remove the tumor and how aggressive to be. There were concerns of complications it could cause. They were still consulting on the best methods. A few were already preparing to travel to see Katherine in person.

The last message was from Dr. Peter Manstein, who worked at Johns Hopkins Hospital in Baltimore. He wasn't able to come for approximately three weeks, which caused Joseph to sigh in frustration. He wanted everyone to drop everything else in their lives for his wife.

Logically, he knew that wasn't possible, but if he thought it would help, he'd hogtie each person to a chair until they had a flawless plan. But from all he was reading, they were telling him this was a marathon, not a sprint. That was something Joseph wasn't used to. His philosophy was that anything worth doing was worth doing immediately.

But Dr. Manstein was the best neurosurgeon in the United States, possibly the world. Of course he was sought after. And if Spence trusted him, he was worth waiting for. Instead of letting his frustration grow at the fact this might take time, he allowed himself to appreciate knowing the best of the best was collaborating on his wife's case.

He created a reply, thanking each of the doctors who'd given their time and expertise, then turned off his phone and sat back, looking at his wife, love radiating from him. The more she felt his love, the more she'd fight.

"Ah, my love, many people are working hard to take care of you. I've promised you the best, and you'll get nothing less. You have nothing to fear because you are loved, cherished, and there's no mountain any of us won't conquer for you. It will be only the blink of an eye in an eternity of time until you're back on your feet, laughing with our grandchildren again."

Joseph felt the stirrings of hope in his gut. He'd once read a study that looked at patients from around the world with similar conditions. The authors of the study were theorizing that recovery rates, with all other factors being equal, were higher for those who had family and/or friends not only visiting them on a constant and consistent basis, but also speaking positively about the patient's outcome. Those who didn't have positivity surrounding them, or didn't have visitors, had a much lower recovery rate — with many of those patients having relapses.

In the end Joseph knew love would carry Katherine over that final threshold back to where she belonged. The medicine would cure her body. Their love for her would cure her soul. She'd wake from this and come out stronger than before. Joseph's job, for now, was to make sure the fear and despair didn't suck him under. His wife needed him to be the man she'd married, not the man she'd first met.

He stood, walked to her bed, and kissed her cheek, telling himself it felt warmer today than when he'd first stepped inside her room days earlier.

"This nightmare will end," he said, squeezing her hand before reluctantly letting go and walking away. His family would be waiting.

There was much to do. The slight smile he wore as he stepped from her room was filled with hope. It was such a needed emotion. It was what would carry them through to the end.

Chapter Seventeen

Carl made it to Bobbi's place in eight minutes. Then he sat in his car and made two phone calls. One just took a minute when he told Jon he was taking the next couple of days off work. The next one took ten minutes. But he kept his eyes on the apartment the entire time so he knew Avery was still inside. And both of these calls had been important.

He felt something for this woman — and he had no doubt she felt something just as strong for him. That meant they needed to find out what that was. The only way to do that was to take her away.

He was shocked to find he was nervous as he walked up the flight of steps to Bobbi's front door. He'd been on missions where bullets were literally flying from all directions, and he hadn't once lost his cool. Now, here he was, hoping and praying he could get a woman to go on an extended date with him, and he felt sweat dripping down the back of his neck.

Damn, the men on his team would be rolling on the ground in laughter if they could see him. He was sure those brothers who were in heaven were doing exactly that.

He knocked on the door, not allowing himself to pause for even a second when he made it to the top of the stairs. It flew open with Bobbi standing there, grinning like the cat that had swallowed the canary.

"I thought you said it would be ten minutes, sugar," she said, leaning against the doorframe, not inviting him inside.

"I had to make a few plans first, but I did make it here in eight minutes," he said, smiling. He *really* liked Bobbi.

"I know. I saw you sitting out there from the living room window. I told Avery I thought you were chickening out. I'm pleased to be wrong. My Avery is one strong woman, and a weak man will never do for her."

He grinned big. "I can assure you I'm anything but weak."

"Well then, I guess I'll let you come inside," she said as she stepped back.

It was a small apartment and his eyes immediately found Avery. She was sitting on the corner of the couch, her face blank, her body stiff. But damn if he wasn't impressed with how she met his eyes. She'd been embarrassed and ticked, but she wasn't going to show that to him. He liked her even more.

He moved with confidence to the couch and sat beside her, leaving only inches of space between them. He immediately felt that pull he'd been feeling from the moment he'd set eyes on her. It was powerful and terrifying, but he was 100 percent in at this point, and it was useless to try to back out.

"That woman is dating a friend of mine. She's a tramp, a horrible human being, and I've never so much as touched her. I have zero desire to do so," he said. He noted the shift in her body, telling him she was listening. "The only woman I have any desire to touch, talk to, and try to impress is you. We had an amazing date the night before last. I'd like to take you out today for an even better one."

There was no point in groveling. He needed to get right to the point and then get her out of the city. He was also very aware of her mother listening. If Bobbi wasn't in the room, he might try to explain to her exactly how he was feeling toward her without any words. His body was rock hard, and his heart hadn't slowed since their kiss two nights before.

Avery was silent for several heartbeats, obviously analyzing his words. He knew the moment she decided to believe him. Her body shifted, the tightness releasing. She gave him a tentative smile.

"I'm sorry," she said. It wasn't what he'd expected, but he'd certainly take it. "I overreacted and should've let you explain. I'm not used to dating anyone more than one time, and my one-time dates have been pretty limited at that. Work has been my life for a very long time."

He felt as if he'd just won a gold medal. Even with her mother in the room, he needed to touch her. He reached over, pulled her into his arms, and hugged her, wanting to do so much more but not willing to disrespect her or her mother by kissing her the way he wanted. Instead, he buried his head in her shoulder, inhaling the sweet scent of her perfume, and thanking the Fates for bringing this woman into his life.

Was it possible to fall for someone so fast? He'd have given an emphatic *no* a month earlier. He didn't believe in love or Cupid. He didn't believe in lasting relationships. His parents had maintained a beautiful marriage, but he'd watched a lot of soldiers go through hell in marriage and relationships. It had cost some of them their lives, because they'd only been half alert on missions, part of their minds still at home. Even knowing all of that, he could feel himself falling for Avery. He just didn't know what that entailed.

"I'm going to take you home where you get fifteen minutes to pack an overnight bag, then we're hitting the road," he said, his voice full of confidence. He was more grateful than ever that he carried a bag in his trunk for emergencies with spare clothes, toiletries, and extra cash. If he needed to leave town fast, he didn't have to go home first.

"You think we go from apologies to spending the night together?" she asked with a raised brow.

He looked over at Bobbi who was in the kitchen not even trying to hide that she was listening. He turned back to Avery. He might as well be honest.

"I'd love for you to stay with me all night, but I don't in any way expect it. I do have two full days of activities planned for us though, and an extra room for you . . . if you decide to use it."

"Where are we going?"

"You'll have to get in the car to find out."

She glared at him, and they remained in a standoff for a solid minute, which was a long time when your heart was pounding and you were waiting to hear a yes or no.

"Fine," she said. "But I don't like surprises." She seemed in a pretty good mood for a woman who didn't like surprises. He decided he'd be the better person and not call her on that. She gave him an evil grin then turned to her mother.

"If you don't get a message from me tonight, assume he's killed me and buried my body then call the police," she said. She snapped a picture of him and texted the image to her mother. "Just a precaution."

He gazed between her mother and her in disbelief, then he cracked up. Damn, he loved these women. They were sassy, smart, and made him smile.

"Good thinking," he told Avery. "And since I'm in the database, if anything should happen the fingerprints will give me away."

"Good. If I die, I want you to have a nice long stay in prison where Mr. T can teach you nightly how it feels to pick on someone smaller than you."

Carl laughed again. "You certainly have an evil side."

"Without a doubt," she assured him.

He stood and held out his hand. She accepted it and stood. Bobbi walked over, hugged them both goodbye, told them to behave, and they walked out the door. The next thirty-six hours were going to either be phenomenal . . . or they'd set him free from his obsession with this woman. He had a feeling it was going to be great, and he'd be obsessed with Avery for a very long time — possibly an eternity.

Chapter Eighteen

Joseph Anderson absolutely loved his family and was grateful for each and every moment he had with them. Normally, he was the first to rush forward to be in the middle of every crazy situation involving family and friends.

Today wasn't that day. Today he was lost. Anyone who'd ever described Joseph knew that emotion was foreign to him. He was a man of action, a man who didn't take no for an answer, a man who went after everything he wanted. Right now, the problem was that he didn't know where to begin, didn't know exactly what it was he wanted.

He left his wife's room and moved slowly through the long hospital corridors until he reached the food court. Activity was buzzing in the large room with multiple stations serving different food and drinks. Conversations took place around him, many medical terms being thrown around along with cries of grief, and muffled shouts of joy.

In a hospital there were so many emotions — grief, joy, relief, and despair. A new baby was born, a beloved child was lost. A family member was cured of cancer, and a grandmother's hand was held as she took her last breath. For every low there was a high, and for every high, there was a low. That was the circle of life that had been happening since the beginning of time. But Joseph never had liked being locked into a box *or* a circle. He wanted to break free. He *would* beat the odds.

He hadn't had an appetite since he'd received the call that his wife had fallen. He knew he should eat something, needing fuel to get through the day, but nothing looked appealing, just as the day before, and the day before that. He wandered for a moment before getting a cup of coffee. While drinking it, he finally settled on an unappealing sandwich. He paid then left the food court, eating and drinking without tasting a thing while he moved through the hospital corridors.

When he turned his final corner, a smile formed as he heard the somewhat hushed voices of his family. The Andersons weren't known for meekness. They spoke with passion and volume. But they could tone it down if need be — but never for too long.

His brother George's voice stood out as Lucas's voice joined in. George was saying something about a boat, and Lucas was bestowing the importance of motor size. To an outsider, it might sound as if they were arguing. But Joseph heard the warmth and love between his brother and his eldest son. They were all more than just family, they were friends, and most certainly kindred spirits. He believed in the power of love, and the power of souls aligning. Family was important to a person's survival.

Joseph was able to stand for a few blinks in time and enjoy the pleasure of gazing at his family. But it didn't last. Once he was spotted, a wave of people moved to him, arms thrown around him, as kisses were laid on his weathered cheeks. He had to fight the emotional bubble that had been enveloping him for days.

"How's Mom?"

"What's the latest information?"

"Is Grandma awake?"

"When can we see her?"

"You're pale. We need to feed you."

"You can't end up in bed next to Mom, Dad. We need you."

Questions and comments were thrown in rapid-fire succession, giving him no time to answer. He simply took it all in for a few moments, grateful to have his family care so much.

He finally took a step back, holding up a hand to silence them. It took a few seconds for the questions and comments to cease before they stood before him, waiting. He took in a deep breath and looked around the lobby.

His eyes zeroed in on an elderly man who met Joseph's gaze. There was so much pain in the man's eyes as he blinked back tears. Time froze for a few heartbeats as Joseph felt the man's grief. Finally, the man nodded, before bending his head and looking down again. Joseph slowly turned back to his family.

"Sometimes life is chaotic and painful, but I'm more grateful now than ever to have each and every one of you here. I'm incredibly grateful to not be alone," he whispered, his voice raw with both pain and joy.

His words seemed to rest heavily on Jasmine's shoulders as her gaze strayed over to the man who'd caught her grandfather's attention. Her eyes filled and spilled over. "Catch me up soon," she said before kissing her grandfather's cheek then walking away to sit next to the man who was alone.

Joseph's heart swelled at the love and compassion in his eldest granddaughter's heart. She'd been raised right. She was the hope of the future. And if there were more out there like her, when it was his time for his eternal rest, he'd be able to go with a grateful heart.

"Sorry for making you wait, but I've been trying to gather my thoughts," he said at last. "Katherine's still in the medically induced coma which they feel is best for her right now."

"Will she be awake tomorrow?" Mark asked.

"If everything stays on track, which they believe it will, they'll bring her out of it tomorrow morning," he confirmed.

"Dr. Whitman gave us a lot of information and I've been in contact with doctors from around the world, and though there's nothing definitive yet, but they all agree with Dr. Whitman that the growth is cancerous. They also believe we can fight it and come out on the other side with her showing no lingering effects. More importantly, I believe this too. I know Katherine isn't ready to leave this family. And we'll be there with her each step of the way," Joseph said, power rising in his voice as he said those words.

His family was still shell-shocked by this news, hoping that the other doctors would've given a different outcome. He knew how they felt. So many emotions flowed through him, trying to overtake him, trying to bring him down. His wife had cancer in her brain. It was unthinkable. It was devastating. But it was fixable, he assured himself.

"When does treatment start?"

"What can we do?"

"Did you check the credentials of these doctors?"

Joseph held his hand up. "Stop." He wasn't allowing the questions to get out of hand again. He had to stay focused. They immediately stopped and waited. It wasn't about power, it was about respect and love. He'd taught his children, as his brothers had taught theirs, to have respect for others, especially their elders. His kids and nieces and nephews had passed that same respect and knowledge down to their children. He prayed it would continue on through the many generations of Anderson offspring.

"We have to be strong for each other, and more importantly, for Katherine. We can't allow our minds to twist this and go to the worst-case scenario. She'll read it in our eyes, and if we appear scared or uncertain, she might not fight like she needs to. We have to trust the doctors and do our own research."

"Do you have the emails from the doctors?" Amy asked.

"Yes, anyone can read them," he answered, handing over his phone.

"I'm going to send them to my email and make copies for the family. That'll help us ask less questions of you."

"That's an excellent idea," Joseph said. "Always thinking of the bigger picture and of everyone else. That's why you're one of my favorite daughters-in-law," he said while giving her an exaggerated wink.

She chuckled before kissing his cheek. "We're *all* your favorite."

"That's very true," he agreed.

"I'll help," Emily, Mark's wife, said.

"That's perfect. The doctors said you can visit Katherine today, but we don't want more than four people in the room at a time, so why don't you all figure that out. Talk to her, and reassure her how much she's loved. Some coma patients have come out of it saying they knew their loved ones were there."

"I'll coordinate that," Jessica, Alex's wife, said.

The group split up, leaving Joseph standing with his sons and his two brothers. "Where's Chad?" he asked. Before anyone could answer, the man of the hour stepped inside the room. Joseph wondered if he'd been waiting.

Chad didn't stop, but moved straight to Joseph and gave him a hug. He was about as large as Joseph, and the hug shared between the two of them would crush most people. It made Joseph smile, a real smile, one he hadn't thought he'd wear again for quite some time.

"Where have you been?" Joseph asked.

"I've been on the phone. Had some business to attend to," Chad said.

"I hope it's good news," Joseph responded.

Chad nodded. "Let's find somewhere private to talk."

Joseph took the lead, taking this group of fine men down the corridor he'd walked earlier, saying nothing as they moved through the halls buzzing with activity. As he moved next to these men he trusted with his life, he felt his attention focus. He was once again filled with rage at his wife being attacked.

A few more turns down the corridor, and Joseph found the room he'd been looking for. They moved inside, and Joseph shut the door. Chad cleared the table in the center of the room and they moved around it, waiting for Joseph to sit. These little signs of respect mattered. It gave consistency in a world that refused to be consistent.

Joseph sat at the head of the table, then everyone joined. For once in his life he wasn't sure how to begin. He lifted a hand, scrubbing his face as he turned thoughts over in his brain. Where to start? Where to start?

"Chad," he finally said, his voice flat as he pushed emotion from it. "I've laid a lot on your shoulders. I'm sorry to do that, but you know there's nothing I won't do for the people I love." He looked the man in the eyes, respect flashing between them. "I need full commitment to this. Once in, everyone at this table is in, which we discussed a few days ago."

Chad didn't even blink as he looked at Joseph. There was determination and fire in Chad's eyes. For a man who'd stood tall in the face of true adversity, having been through the depths of the darkest places on earth, Joseph was almost giving him a gift. Chad needed stimulation, needed to be a savior. It was who he'd been born to be. He was the epitome of the word *hero*.

"Your family is my family, Joseph," Chad said. "Everyone at this table knows I lost mine a long time ago. Mark has been my brother since we were kids, and I look at Katherine as my mother. For most of my life I've been given the gift of acceptance, love, and support from you and everyone in this room. There's no limit to what I'll do for this family."

"You're most certainly family," Joseph said. "Blood isn't the only thing that bonds us. Love is even stronger."

The rest of the group was quiet as Joseph and Chad spoke. "I want everyone here to understand how an operation like this will play out. What we are about to do is technically against the law." He let that sink in.

"But it happens all the time," Lucas said. "I don't think people understand how many private groups protect them in both the United States and around the world."

Chad smiled. "That's very true. But the less the average population knows, the better for most. We want protection, we want security, but the average person doesn't want, or need, to know how that comes."

"I thought ignorance was a bad thing," George said in a mocking tone.

"Nah, ignorance is bliss," Richard replied in kind.

That caused a light chuckle. "Okay, back to this," Chad said, getting all of their attention. "For all of our safety, there will be absolutely zero digital conversations about this group or what we'll be doing. That means no emails, phone calls, or texts discussing this once we get it started. One wrong message of any kind can destroy everything we're going to achieve." Chad looked each person in the eye.

"I understand," Lucas said.

"Seriously," Chad emphasized. "This isn't a game. This is real life. I know I'm the only one here with military experience, but you've all had trials in life. I'm very good at bringing out strength in people. I'm also good at reading who I can trust. I trust *each one* of you. No one outside of this room can know what's happening. It's for our safety and for theirs."

"Including our wives?" Mark asked. He shifted in his chair, uncomfortable at that thought. He'd shared even the worst of his worst with his wife.

"Including our wives," Chad said. "If you can't handle that, then you have to step out of this right now." It wasn't a threat or a warning, it was a choice presented. There were no other options. They had to keep this private.

Not a single person rose. Joseph had known his family would stay. They might not like all of the rules, but they did like the results they hoped to accomplish with this special team.

Half raising his right hand in the air, fingers extended up, Chad kept speaking. "I have five points."

"First," he continued, dropping a finger, "I'm going to create a shell company. Second, we'll need an initial operating budget of ten million dollars." The second finger dropped down, and no one so much as blinked at the staggering sum thrown out.

"The beginning crew will be five, possibly six, members. All are former special forces members who know how to commit, know what to do, and can adapt to any situation." His third finger dropped.

"My initial plan is to drop a member of the team into a business, working undercover. This drug ring that's responsible for harming Katherine is in our town, spreading, and is surprisingly hidden — for now. It's important to get someone in the middle of it. That won't happen overnight. I don't want to be prodded daily for updates. It might take months, maybe even a year. I don't know yet. My team will know more and more as they investigate." His fourth finger dropped.

No one spoke. They waited for that final finger to come down.

"Once we begin, we will not quit until the head of the snake is cut off. I don't quit, not ever. So if anyone has a problem with any of this, we need to pull out now before it begins.

The team I assemble won't quit either. We will go to the end, and we won't accept anything less than absolute victory." His final finger dropped, leaving his hand in a fist, his eyes lit with determination.

Total silence filled the room as they waited to hear what Joseph would say. He felt a measure of joy filter through him. This was the action he'd needed. This was what he had to focus on. This was what he could control, what he could contribute to. This was an enemy he could fight.

"Create the offshore account, and I'll have thirty million deposited immediately," Joseph said. Chad could've asked for a hundred million and Joseph wouldn't have blinked. There was no amount of money that would stand in his way of finding justice for his wife. He also liked knowing there were others who would be helped in their battle against this criminal organization that was taking over their cities, taking over the entire country.

"Dad," Lucas said, interrupting the lock these two men had on the conversation. "I'm in for five," he stated, as if he was talking about five dollars instead of five million.

"Deal me in for five too," Alex shared.

"Five from me as well," Mark mirrored.

"We can't let these kids beat us, can we?" George said as he looked at Richard who nodded his agreement. George turned back.

"I'm in brother. I'll raise to ten," George said with a broad smile.

"Without question — I'll add another ten to the pot," Richard said to the group.

The amount was growing so large there was nothing that couldn't be accomplished. This might go so much further than Joseph had been envisioning when they'd first spoken of it.

"And you know all of us will bring more to the table if it's needed," Lucas said, making everyone nod. Chad seemed to be in a bit of shock. But he recovered quickly.

Joseph would normally argue about others coming into a deal he was making without asking first, but not this time. This time it was for the woman he loved, for the community he'd built. Besides, he also knew any objection he might raise would create a firestorm of protest. They all loved Katherine, maybe not quite as much as him, but that love was fierce nonetheless.

"I believe that is a total of sixty-five million to start. Each of you will have your businesses deposit your share into a hidden line item account Lucas will send. Lucas, you know what to do after that. Once Chad sends over his text confirming the account is active, Lucas will send your guys' thirty-five over and I'll send my thirty," Joseph said as if he was doling out a simple pizza order. Then he paused.

"Wait, that can't do," he said with a scowl, realizing he'd been outdone by his sons and brothers. "I'll do forty mil, so we have an even seventy-five to start."

That produced a chuckle from the group. It was a beautiful sound in this stressful time.

Mark handed a ten-dollar bill to Lucas.

"What was that for?" Joseph asked with a frown.

"I told Mark there was no way you'd let us collectively give more than your donation. He bet me you wouldn't be competitive with this particular task. I won," Lucas said with a shrug.

Joseph glowered at them, then decided not to discuss it further. Instead, he turned his attention back to Chad, indicating for him to continue.

"What are your expected deliverables, sir?" Chad asked.

"That's something I've thought about a lot in the past twenty-four hours," Joseph said. "I don't need to know who's on the team or what they're doing. I don't need to know their whereabouts. I do, however, need updates on progress a minimum of two times a month. That's a hardline for me. You know I trust you, and this has nothing to do with anything other than an absolute need to seeing action taking place. You can pick the time and place we meet as long as it's happening twice a month."

"That's acceptable," Chad said. He looked down for a moment, then looked back up, his eyes looking slightly burdened, but unquestionably serious. "There could be bloodshed, Joseph. At the lower levels of drug rings it's the same every time; there's a lot of violence. People in that sphere shoot first and never think to ask why. This will have a high degree of danger associated with it, and while I pray it doesn't go that route, I'll be honest, it's very likely to turn deadly at some point. That's not something to be taken lightly, and not something I, or anyone I bring in on this, look forward to. Let me tell you, there's no burden heavier than that of taking another's life. The memory of it never leaves you — a constant shadow following you for the rest of time. I'll never, under any circumstance or for any reason, tell any of you if that situation has come to pass." Chad looked over each of the men and let the weight of that information settle on them.

He continued. "The men and women infecting the very fabric of this city won't easily give up. I've seen similar situations in numerous countries. After the bottom rungs are passed, the overt violence starts to fade, and then the financial and political warfare begins. In the end, the culprit is *always* money. Money has a way of distorting reality. Once these power hungry people have it, they don't easily give it up. They'd rather die, though they never think they will. I all but guarantee this: you'll be disgusted and possibly heartbroken when the leaders of this ring are brought to light. It's an almost certainty some of the people in your social circle are involved."

Mark, knowing he was now a part of this by buying into the business, allowed himself to cement his decision to keep this secret from his wife, and asked, "What can we do?"

"For now, nothing. Further down the line, that might change. Ideas are brewing and turning in my mind. I know you all want to help. I know you need to. I'll make sure you can. But for now, please allow me to get this started, to get the team in place."

"In about an hour I'll give each of you a list of codes to use in texts. You'll have to memorize that list before you leave the hospital, then you'll give the list back to me. You won't throw it away, you won't take a photo of it, you'll memorize it verbatim. The first text I send will read, "How is Katherine doing?" Obviously this is never a message I'd text. I'd make the call. That'll let you know the account is set-up and ready to receive transfers. That will also let you know an update is ready to be given."

Joseph leaned back, knowing Mark had done well by suggesting Chad run this team. He trusted Mark's best friend as much as if he were another son. Chad would get results. It was tough for him to not be actively involved, but he understood why he shouldn't be, especially as it was set up. He had his wife to focus on anyway.

He'd been away from her too long already. He pushed back his chair and stood, letting the group know the conversation was finished. They stood with him, all of them united.

Joseph walked around the table and took Chad's hand, shaking it. That was as much binding as they needed to make this a solid contract. "Thank you, Chad. You'll bring my wife's attackers to justice, and the rest of our neighbors can sleep easy."

Chad nodded as their hands remained clasped. "I won't let you down, sir." Joseph saw and appreciated the steel in this man's eyes.

Their project was officially in motion now. Nothing else had to be said. The men turned and walked from the room as silently as they'd entered. They were a sight to behold as they moved through the halls, strong, silent, powerful — united.

Chapter Nineteen

Avery was nervous as Carl's sleek car sped up HWY101 — not because of his driving, but because she knew what would happen that night. She not only knew what was going to happen, but she was ready for it. She was *more* than ready for it, she *needed* it.

She'd gone through a myriad of emotions over the past week, and though this was moving at the speed of light, she suddenly didn't care. She wanted the comfort of being in a man's arms — especially *this* man's arms. She had no doubt he'd take away her worries and flush them down the toilet. She had a feeling he was incredibly skilled at pleasing a woman, unlike her last lover who'd been okay but not mind-blowing like in her romance novels.

When Carl pulled off the road beneath a sign that announced a private winery spa resort, her core clenched. She'd heard of this place, and it had rave reviews for privacy, spas, activities, and food. It didn't get better.

His powerful car wound down the road and pulled up to the main lodge. "Do you want to wait or come with me while we check in?" he asked.

Though there was nothing wrong with her spending the night with a man, she found herself shifting in her seat. She shouldn't care what the reception desk attendants thought of her, but suddenly she felt as if she were wearing a scarlet letter on her chest.

"I'll wait," she said with a smile, hoping her nerves weren't showing.

He nodded then walked inside. He was back within minutes, holding an envelope.

"We're all set," he told her, jumping back in the car. But before he started it, he reached for her, pulled her to him, and gave her the best kiss of her life. By the time he let go, she was shaking in her seat. He looked a bit unsteady himself, which made her feel better.

They drove through the spa grounds, then took a road to the right, leading them down a narrow road. After several minutes, he pulled up to a huge cabin. When he stopped the car, she could hear water flowing nearby. The air smelled sweet and mellow, and she was in love with the place even without stepping inside.

He climbed from the car, immediately walking to her side and opening the door. "After you," he said, holding out his hand. She loved that he did that. It made her feel feminine and respected.

A wide wrap-around deck circled the huge place. If the outside was this good, the actual cabin had to be phenomenal. He opened the door and waited for her.

It was perfect. She smiled from ear to ear as she walked through the cabin that had two bedrooms, as he'd told her, with a large spa bathroom in the main one that was every girl's dream come to life. It also had a nice kitchen, a living room with a fireplace, a game area with a pool table, and best of all, a huge back deck. She stepped out the patio doors. She could live on the deck with its large hot tub, lounge chairs, and stairs leading into the vineyard the spa was famous for.

"How did you find this?" she asked, completely entranced.

"I asked my buddy for the best resort around. He grew up in this area. I'd like to take all the credit, but Jon picked the spot," he admitted.

"You have smart friends," she assured him, laughing. He'd dropped their bags off, but she wasn't going to look to see if they were in the same room or not. She knew she was staying with him, but she wasn't sure she wanted to know if *he* knew that. She wasn't sure if she wanted him to be a respectful gentleman or a commanding alpha and kiss her until she was senseless. She'd find out by the end of the night.

"Are you ready for the adventure to begin?" he asked as he stepped up behind her. He was so close she could feel heat radiating off his body. She didn't answer right away, and he slipped his arms around her, his fingers clasping together on her stomach. She relaxed, her body resting against his. Heaven — pure heaven.

Avery closed her eyes and simply enjoyed the feeling of being in a great place with an incredible man holding her. That was something she hadn't thought she'd wanted, but now that it was happening, she realized she'd been missing out.

"What are the plans?" she asked. He squeezed her a bit tighter as he leaned down and kissed her neck. Shivers ran through her as pleasure filled her body.

"You'll have to come with me to find out," he said, his voice a rough purr that rumbled through her.

"I'd be happy to stay right here the entire time," she said. "I can't imagine how any of this can get better."

"I figured you'd be a much harder woman to please," he said with a chuckle.

"Some might say I'm high maintenance, but I disagree. It's the simple pleasures in life I love most, like sitting by a fire and watching a sunset, or dangling my feet over the end of a dock with a fishing pole. I love tranquility because most of the time my life is chaos."

He was still behind her. "You fish?"

She sighed. "Not really. My mother made me when I was a kid. She wanted me to study and be the best, but she also insisted that I had to have a kid day once a week. So on Sundays we'd walk to the water with a second hand fishing pole. I'd dig up worms, and we'd have a picnic. It was pure bliss. When school was beyond stressful in college, I'd take that same pole down to the water, dangle my feet over the dock, and cast it for hours. I'd feel guilty about wasting time, but then, once in a while, I'd get a big trout on, and all of my worries faded. I haven't fished in years. Maybe that's why my stress grows higher each week."

"We'll have to change that," he told her.

"Maybe we will."

"As much as I want to do nothing more than sit here and hold you, if I don't get you out of here now, we're going to miss our appointment . . . and end up seeing nothing more of this place than the bedroom." Heat warmed her insides as she squeezed her thighs at his words. Sadly, he let her go and stepped back.

She turned and saw the passion in his eyes, making her feel better that he might be suffering as much as she was. She'd always read that anticipation made sex better. Maybe those people who said it knew what they were talking about, because she'd never been this turned on, not even while watching that famous scene in Top Gun — and she'd definitely been turned on during *that* hot kiss.

Once they left the cabin, their day was filled with activity. It began at the spa, where she received an incredibly healing ninety-minute massage with Carl only ten feet away. There was something very sexy about knowing he was naked on the table next to her, only a thin sheet hiding his beautiful body. She was also very aware she was nude as well. She had to push those thoughts from her mind before she embarrassed herself in front of the masseuse currently kneading her back.

He next took her on a hot air balloon ride. It had been both terrifying and awe-inspiring, flying high over the beautiful vineyard, feeling weightless as their guide explained the history of Napa Valley. And best of all, Carl held her the entire time, her back pressed against his chest, his hands caressing her stomach, brushing the undersides of her breasts, and making her so hot, she felt as if she'd explode without her clothes ever coming off.

They'd barely touched the ground when a golf cart picked them up and took them to a private room where they enjoyed a wonderful best wine tasting. She'd never been a big fan of wine, but now she might invest in a vineyard.

Was the wine that good, or was she simply that happy?

She'd felt joy each time she'd won a case, each time she'd advanced in her career. But this was different. This was an unexplainable joy swirling through her from the inside out, making her smile, relax, and burn at the same time.

The sun was setting when they stepped out of the dark wine tasting room, and Carl took her hand again as he led her to the veranda of the main building where gas fireplaces were scattered between tables, giving off an ambience that whispered romance.

They sat at a corner table where he pressed in close, his hand resting on her thigh as the waiter took their drink order. She was so wired she couldn't make small talk as she gazed blankly at her menu.

"You decide," she finally said. The words weren't computing. *Never* in her life had she been this distracted, *never* before had she been unable to read. What in the world was this man doing to her? She liked it, but she was sure she shouldn't. Her brain felt as if alarms were ringing and she was about to have a permanent meltdown, all files erased.

"Hmm, a challenge. I think I can do it," Carl said as he glanced again at the menu. The waiter came back and Carl tasted the wine, approved, and waited for it to be poured. She grabbed her glass and took a large swallow while Carl gave their food order. She wasn't sure what he'd picked.

As soon as the waiter departed, she was saved from having to speak when a group of colorfully dressed men and women stepped onto the stage at the front of the patio. Music began and she was mesmerized as they began to dance. The stunning lifts, twirls, and tricks were good enough for the stages of New York.

"I've always wanted to be able to dance," Avery admitted. This wasn't even something she'd told her mother.

"It's never too late to learn. I have a few moves I'll be more than happy to teach you," he said, his fingers trailing higher up her thigh with each pass of his hand.

This place embodied seduction. The wine, the music, the lighting, the entire atmosphere was an aphrodisiac. She was his, and he had to know it by now.

"No, it's a silly dream. It's foolish to put so much time into something that won't help you in life. It would be fun, but work is more important than fun. Work gives a person security and purpose. Dancing is . . . well, it's *just* dancing," she finished, not knowing what else to say.

"I disagree. No one on their deathbed praises how much they worked. What people speak about is their love of family, the fun adventures they took in life, and those moments that took their breath away. The people who were workaholics always have regrets."

"Those who don't work at all must have regrets too, because they can't afford to take adventures. It's crucial to work so you can live, so you can have a roof over your head in a safe neighborhood with food on the table," she argued.

He laughed. "There *is* balance in life, Avery. Trust me, I've been a workaholic most of my life. But in my line of work, I learned early on that I also had to let off steam. We all do that in different ways. Some look for thrills, and some seek peace. And healthy people have a little of both."

"There might be some truth in that, but it's hard for me to let go."

Appetizers were set before them, and she absently reached for one. She slipped it in her mouth and flavors exploded on her tongue. Her full attention was drawn to the plate.

"This is amazing," she said. "What is it?"

He took a piece and chewed, sighing in delight. "It's shrimp ceviche, a favorite of mine, and this is probably the best I've had." Maybe his hormones were on the same path as hers and everything tasted better, looked better, smelled better, and felt better.

"I agree," she told him. "I've never had it before, but now it's going to be a favorite." She took another piece.

"We'll work on balancing your life," Carl said, bringing her back to their conversation. She chewed thoughtfully before speaking again.

"How do you know we'll be around each other long enough for you to help with anything?" She hated the vulnerability in her tone. She respected strength and pounced on weakness. But with this man, it seemed she was in an upside down world.

Carl took a moment to answer. But when he did, his words made her heart thunder.

"When I moved to Francisco, I wasn't planning to start a relationship. I love my freedom, love going anywhere at anytime," he began. His pause lasted a while, but she sensed he had more to say. "Meeting you definitely wasn't in the plans, but I'm glad plans have a way of kicking your feet out from beneath you, because there's no place I'd rather be than right here, right now, with you."

"I've felt the exact same way my entire life. Relationships are messy. I've done a bit of dating, but even that was too much work. I prefer to focus on my career. But I'm at a crossroads right now, sort of floating into the sky like we did earlier in the hot air balloon. And I'm finding that I *really* like being with you. I don't know what that means." Maybe she shouldn't drink wine. It was making her too honest. That could be a dangerous thing, being an attorney. Honesty was subjective in her line of work.

"Since this has been a surprise for both of us and we don't know what will happen, I think the best thing we can do is not question it. Let's just see where it goes. Let's enjoy each other, stop fighting the feelings, and live for the moment. We might find it's something we like more than total organization," he suggested.

Carl fell quiet as the music stopped and the dancers bowed and left the stage. She watched them walk away as she processed his words, then turned her focus to the closest fire pit, watching as the flames danced on top of the rocks, colors shifting and crawling over one another.

Could she live in the moment?

Could she allow herself to be that free?

She'd been doing it all day, and she felt pretty good about it.

"It scares me," she admitted.

"What scares you?" he asked. His fingers crawled even higher on this pass on her thigh, his pinkie finger whispering across her lower belly. Goosebumps sprung over her arms as she squeezed her thighs shut to ease the pulsing. If she didn't get relief soon, she might embarrass both of them with cries of ecstasy as she came from nothing more than his words, his breath against her neck, and his fingers gliding across her clothed body.

"I like you. It scares me how much I like you," she said, her voice husky, her words barely above a whisper.

Before he could answer, the waiter brought their salads. She'd lost her appetite, which was something new, but she picked up her fork to have something to do with her fingers. Otherwise, she was afraid she was going to pull him against her.

"I like you too," he said before leaning down and brushing his lips at that sweet spot where her neck met her shoulder.

Her nipples were hard, her core wet, and her body on fire. She kept placing things on her fork and bringing it to her mouth, but she wasn't tasting the food, wasn't hearing the quiet music playing over the speakers, and wasn't seeing anything around her. All of her senses were tuned to the man beside her — and she wanted dinner over.

The next hour was both pleasure and pain as plates were taken away and new dishes placed before them. Neither of them ate much, even though the food had to be phenomenal if their first dish was anything to judge by.

Finally, finally, *finally*, Carl stood and held out his hand. There was zero hesitation on her part as she took it. Neither of them said a word as they walked the peaceful, romantically lit trail back to their cabin.

She was shaking as they made their way along the path. She wanted to stop, wanted him to kiss her, wanted so much more than that, but she knew they were both on the edge of a cliff, and the second she was in his arms, they wouldn't stop. If he kissed her right then, they'd be naked on the trail where anyone could walk by.

The second they were inside the cabin, Carl pounced. The door was barely shut when he pushed her up against it, his body pressing into hers, letting her know immediately that he was as turned on as she was — and from the feel of him against her, she'd be very happy with what she saw when his pants came off.

His head descended, and his lips consumed her. She clung to him, her tongue battling his as their hands slid all over each other.

"Hot, I'm so hot," she cried when he released her mouth, his lips trailing over her jaw, then moving down and licking and sucking on her neck. Her legs were close to giving out.

"I'm so turned on I'm not sure I can control myself. You might not believe this, but I've never lost control like I'm about to now," he growled, stepping back from her. She chilled instantly, and took a wobbly step in his direction.

His eyes were on fire, his fingers clenched. The sight of him nearly losing control was the best damn aphrodisiac she'd ever known. It made her feel wanton and beautiful — and more importantly, desired.

"Give me a second," he begged, taking another step back. Those words made her feel something she hadn't felt before — powerful. This man, this giant hero of a man, was losing control . . . all . . . because . . . of . . . her. Something came out of her she didn't know she possessed.

She licked her lips, his gaze zeroing in on the action. She took another step forward, and he took another back. She reached for the hem of her shirt and began tugging it up. His eyes moved to the bare skin showing on her belly. She pulled it over her head and tossed it.

His eyes dilated.

She grew bolder.

She reached for the button on her pants and slowly undid it.

He groaned.

The zipper went down and his breathing hitched. She pulled her pants down, then kicked them off, standing there in her lacy red bra and matching panties. Never had she done something so bold with a man. Never had she felt confident enough to put herself out there where she could be rejected.

He was shaking as she stood before him.

"I'll apologize now," he growled.

And then he was no longer moving away. He took three large strides and she was lifted in the air as he pulled her close. She wrapped her legs around him as his mouth slammed against hers in a punishing kiss.

Her fingers tangled in his hair and she held on tight while his hands squeezed her bare butt. They groaned together as their tongues lashed at each other, both of them losing control.

She hadn't felt them move, but suddenly he was pushing her back, her eyes flying open as she flew through the air before landing on the soft, comfortable bed. She wasn't alone for long. He dove on the bed with her and his mouth took hers again as his fingers traced down her body, squeezing one breast, rubbing his thumb across her throbbing nipple, before moving along too soon to trail across her stomach.

He didn't stop.

His fingers kept going, easily slipping beneath the elastic of her panties and sliding over her slick heat. Her back arched from the bed as she opened her thighs and threw her head back, letting out a cry of pleasure.

He took the opportunity to trail his lips down her neck while his hands trailed to her back and undid her bra, pulling it off and tossing it. His lips replaced the lace as he sucked and licked her swollen nipples until she screamed. She'd never screamed before, but she couldn't help it with this man — she couldn't control her reaction, and what he was doing to her.

He moved down her stomach, then ripped her panties away, and without pausing, spread her thighs and buried his head where she wanted it most. The first swipe of his tongue had her screaming again. If she hadn't been so utterly turned on, she might've been embarrassed at the nearly immediate orgasm that ripped through her after a few swipes of his incredibly talented tongue.

She shook as wave after wave of pleasure washed through her — but he didn't stop. She tried to pull away, the pleasure so intense it was painful. But he gripped her hips tighter, his fingers squeezing her butt as his masterful tongue continued to swipe and twirl, and his lips sucked and caressed. Then, she cried out again as a second orgasm began just as the first ended. He plunged a finger inside as he sucked hard on her core, and she let go, her body shaking, colors flashing before her eyes, and a moan echoing off the bedroom walls.

He slowed his tongue as he pumped his finger in and out of her while she squeezed him, the orgasm taking all of her energy, making her feel as if she were floating on clouds.

When the last of her shaking stopped, she opened her eyes, the movement difficult. She'd never been so exhausted in her life. But as soon as she saw Carl standing next to the bed, hovering over her, his clothes gone, a sheen of sweat covering his beautiful chest and his eyes completely wild, she felt her body stir again. She wasn't sure how that was possible.

Her eyes trailed his thick chest, his incredible abs, and then lower to his rock-hard, well-endowed arousal. Her legs twitched with delight. Holy moly, she wanted him buried deep, *deep* inside of her.

She lifted her arms, needing his weight against her, needing more from him, needing it all. He didn't hesitate as he reached over to the nightstand and grabbed a condom, slipping it on before climbing on the bed, his body hovering over hers.

"You're incredible," he said, his voice a low growl. "I'm barely holding it together. I'm so scared of hurting you." He leaned down and kissed her, shocking her when his kiss was soft, his tongue brushing over her bottom lip. She lifted her hands to his bulging arms, feeling the tremor in his muscles. He was tense, telling her he was losing control, but he wasn't. He was gentle and taking care of her.

"I want you — I want it hard, I want it all," she told him.

At her words, his eyes flared, and she'd swear under oath she saw flames dance in their deep blue depths. His gentleness came to an end as he pushed her thighs open, slipping between them.

His mouth crashed into hers as he pressed forward in one smooth motion. She screamed against his mouth as her legs wrapped around his hips, allowing him to sink fully inside. Then he stopped, his breathing heavy against her mouth as tremors shook his large frame.

She shifted as she adjusted to his thickness. She was full without a single millimeter of space left. And she was wet and hot. He didn't move until she did, allowing her to adjust to him. Her fingernails dug into his back as she shifted her hips, letting him know she wanted more — letting him know she was ready.

Then he kissed her again as his fingers dug into her butt and he began thrusting. He moved steadily in and out, in and out, in and out, and then built up speed and depth, faster and faster, his strokes alternating between deep and shallow. And just like that, she was yanked over that cliff again. It wasn't a build up, it wasn't a *little* pleasure. It was a freaking storm that blew right through her, her core exploding, her body set on fire as she was ripped apart from head to toe.

Her neck flipped back, her scream so guttural if anyone was walking by, they'd think a murder was taking place. She clenched around him so tightly he couldn't move as she shook and flexed, her orgasm growing stronger instead of diminishing.

He let out his own cry as he pumped, barely able to move within her as her walls clasped him tight. But with another thrust, his yell chorused with hers as she felt him pulse over and over within her.

The flashes of lights she'd seen earlier were nothing compared to the lightshow flashing behind her lids in those glorious moments of pleasure. They stretched on and on as she clung to him, her arms and legs vices around his body.

It took minutes for the intensity to allow her to let go. With the final shudders of her body, she went lax, her arms falling, her legs going limp. Her head was still spinning as her lips turned up, her smile bright. And then she shocked herself when a laugh burst from deep down in her diaphragm.

Carl slowly slid off her, making her moan as he pulled from her. She instantly felt empty, but she'd been filled with so much pleasure she couldn't stop the giggling. He pulled her against him and scowled.

"Should I be offended?" he asked, his voice raspy, raw, and absolutely beautiful.

"Oh no, no, no," she said between giggles. "I didn't know something like that could happen. I didn't understand why sex was so coveted. I knew release was good, but I didn't know a release could be *that*," she said, her breathing shallow, her body on fire.

"Yeah, I didn't know either," he said, sounding confused.

She wasn't going to push that one. She wanted to believe it had been just as spectacular for him as it had for her. She knew it had been great, but she suspected it was great for him every time. But she'd rather think it was a connection shared between them and no one else. That made all of her pleasure buttons fire on red.

He pulled her closer to his side, her head resting on his chest. She wanted to talk more about what had just happened, but she felt as if she'd run a marathon and couldn't keep her eyes open.

She was still smiling when she fell asleep, secure in his arms, his hands tracing her slick skin. She didn't want to ever move from this bed. She didn't want to leave this man's side. He'd literally sexed her into submission — and the scariest part of all was that she didn't care.

Chapter Twenty
Two Years ago

Eyes flashed the pretty blonde reporter his most brilliant smile and gave her a wink that turned her cheeks a sexy shade of pink. She licked her red lips before glancing down at the notebook on her lap and shifting in her seat.

"I saw her first," Sleep said in a loud whisper.

"Yeah, but I'm cuter than you," Eyes replied with a laugh. He looked at the reporter who might be trying to stay professional — but was failing at all the attention she was getting. "Who's cuter?" Eyes demanded.

She opened and closed her mouth, and there was no doubt in Eyes's mind that this woman had never had an interview quite like this. He was surprised since she covered foreign military bases. The men knew how to be serious, but they also knew they needed to laugh in the downtime or they'd never make it through the days of hell like they'd experienced in their last battle.

"Let's just stick with the interview," Courtney Tucker, their very sexy reporter, said.

"Sorry, can't do it until you answer," Eyes said, crossing his arms across his massive chest.

Courtney let out an exaggerated breath as if she were dealing with overgrown children instead of the heroes she'd thought she'd be interviewing. That was her fault for making assumptions.

"I'd say you're equally average," she said, giving them both a look that could've wilted lesser men. She was attempting to put them in their place. It was quite amusing and very impressive in Eyes's opinion. He was going to have this woman.

Sleep laughed before slapping Eyes on the back. "I'd say she was talking about you there. I know I'm far from average."

"I think she's challenging me to prove her wrong," Eyes said, his predator instincts on high.

Courtney rolled her eyes, looked at her notes, and tried again. Both men decided to humor her when she asked her next question.

"It took you three days, and an incredible twenty-two miles, before you were found one mile from Operating Base Blessing, the small base made up almost exclusively of the US Army 173rd Airborne Brigade, correct? How did you do it?" That was directed at Sleep, who leaned back, his mouth closed.

Some of the humor fell from Eyes's gaze, but he was the one to answer. "We put one foot in front of the other."

"There are those saying that history lessons will be written about you, that healthy men with unlimited rations of water and food would've made it no more than thirty-seven miles in that terrain. They are saying the world will call you heroes and learn from your techniques. They're talking about having you guest speak at colleges and boot camps, other countries wanting to know what it takes to do what you did. How does all of this attention and fame make you feel?"

"We wanted to survive. There wasn't another choice. It's not about glory, it's not about ability. It's sheer determination to honor our fallen men," Eyes said. Sleep was remaining oddly quiet.

Courtney looked back and forth between them, shock and awe in her expression before looking back at her notebook. They could see the interview wasn't going the way she'd wanted it to go.

"I know you guys wear your emotions close to the sleeve, but seriously, it has to make you feel something knowing that parents will talk to their children about determination and always giving it their best. Coaches will give speeches on teamwork and getting through the toughest of times. And then they'll say your names. You have to feel something about that," she pushed.

Finally, Sleep responded. "The military trained us, and the SEALs made us brothers. That's what gave us the knowledge to survive. That same will is in everyone, some need more training than others, but we *all* have it. Also, if we'd disappeared, our fallen brothers wouldn't have been found, and they needed to come home and be honored."

"Will you participate in the parades being given for your fallen comrades?" she asked.

It wasn't often that Sleep got choked up, actually it *never* happened. But at her words, he found himself having to clear his throat. He hadn't allowed himself to think about the men who'd been lost, because he'd had to focus on recovery. He decided to be honest.

"I don't know if I'll be able to," he admitted.

"Me neither," Eyes said.

Compassion flashed in the reporter's eyes before she looked back at her notes. She cleared her throat and dug through her notebook and pulled out some pictures, handing them over. Both Sleep and Eyes smiled as they looked down.

"They've tied yellow ribbons on the light poles, on car antennas, and around the rails of porches in the small towns your brothers are from. They're being honored, and it's all because you made it back home and told their story," she said.

They looked through the pictures showing the caskets being offloaded, the American flag draped proudly, members of the military and White House saluting. Other pictures showed citizens draping ribbons proudly, some saluting, some crying, and some smiling as they told stories to one another. They say a picture is worth a thousand words. They were absolutely correct.

"Thank you for these," Eyes said.

"Of course," Courtney replied. She did something she never normally did and reached out, squeezing Eyes's hand. He gave her a look of appreciation, and something flashed between the two of them. He wasn't sure what in the hell it was. Obviously, she didn't understand it either, because both of them looked away at the same time.

"Once you were found, you were immediately flown to Landstuhl Regional Medical Center just south of the Ramstein Air Base in Germany. Do you remember the flight?" she asked, getting back to her questions.

"We both faded in and out the entire time we were walking through the mountains and while we were being flown to the center," Eyes said.

"We were later told we'd both lost nearly half our blood, just under three liters. Basically we were walking zombies. They quickly administered blood and medicine in flight, not having much hope we'd make it to the hospital," Sleep said as if he was talking about nothing more meaningful than the weather.

"But they didn't understand our will to survive. Maybe it was good they hadn't yet questioned us about our fallen brothers, or we might've felt our mission had been completed, and we would've headed into that pretty light that had been calling to us for days. But a soldier doesn't quit in the middle of a battle, and ours wasn't finished," Eyes added.

"Yeah, we spent days in and out of operating rooms. I had an infection in my lungs, and they were worried I'd need a transplant. But I'm a god, and with a bit of food, a lot of blood, and some sweet, sweet nurses, my body responded the way it was supposed to. The docs repaired my shattered ribs, replacing two of them. I think they said eighteen fragmented pieces were taken out. I talked them into keeping a piece," he pointed out as he pulled the chain holding his tags, away from his neck, a piece of bone proudly displayed there. Courtney shuddered at the sight before turning to Eyes, possibly hoping his story wasn't so gruesome.

"Don't forget all of the wounds across the rest of your body that had to be cleaned, stitched, and stapled shut," Eyes said. "You have some new scars to brag about."

"I don't mind scars, they're a reminder I survived, and proof of what I can endure next time," Sleep said with a shrug.

"How bad were your injuries?" Courtney asked Eyes, her expression softening. Yep, something definitely going on between the two of them.

He gave her his trademark grin as he leaned back. Looking at either man right then, a person wouldn't have a clue what hell they'd been put through.

"I was so much worse off than this wuss," Eyes said. Sleep rolled his eyes. "I got hit in the shoulder, but that wasn't bad. I have the same maze of stiches all over my body. But what really got me was the hip shot," he said with a look at Sleep. Yep, he'd never live that one down.

"You walked in here, so it didn't disable you," Courtney said as she looked at his hips, waking up a certain part of his body. She seemed to realize what she was doing and jerked her eyes back to his face, her cheeks flushing again. He winked.

"There's a pea-sized piece of the bullet still in there, but it's not a concern. My mobility is fine, but they say there's been tremendous muscle damage. I can walk and jog, but my gait is off. I can't put as much pressure on it. But I think I can work through it in time." The determination shining in his expression was undeniable.

"What will you both do now that you've been medically discharged?" Courtney asked. Both of their smiles fell.

"We've done the required physical therapy, and we've done our homework. Once a SEAL, always a SEAL. We might've been forced out for now, but we'll figure it out," Sleep said. The hardest thing for a SEAL to do was walk away from the fight. But they'd both been given no choice after the beating they'd endured.

Sleep knew that Eyes's hip was constantly hurting him, but he tried to hide the pain. He might flick him a lot of crap about shooting him, but he didn't want his brother to actually feel bad about it. If they made it a joke, then it wasn't traumatic. That's what SEALs needed to do in order to survive the hell they endured on a regular basis.

"You're about to leave for America for the first time in over six months. Are you excited?" Courtney asked.

Their grins returned. Sleep answered. "Hell yes we are. I'm sick and tired of people asking how I'm doing and wanting to poke and prod at me. We go from the medical center to the base and back again. That's been our life for months." He went quiet and Eyes knew what he was thinking even as Courtney voiced it again.

"What will you do when you're home?"

Eyes answered this time. "You'll have to follow up to find out." The look he gave her could've melted her clothes right off, but he left it with that.

After speaking, the two men stood. The interview was over. Courtney didn't try to stop them. It wouldn't have done her any good.

"I thought for sure you'd ask for her number," Sleep said when they turned a corner.

"How do you know I don't already have it?" Eyes replied.

"Did you snag her phone? I must've missed it," Sleep said, his brows furrowing as he thought back over the interview.

"I have ways of getting information," Eyes assured him.

"I guess you *are* a bit of a man whore," Sleep acknowledged.

Then Eyes grinned before asking his next question. "Hey! Did you hear?"

Sleep rolled his eyes, knowing what was coming. He tried to scoot forward before Eyes could continue. He made it a dozen yards when Eyes yelled across the room.

"Hey, Sleep!" The people milling about the room stopped and turned to look between them. Sleep kept on moving. "Sleep!" he called even louder.

He turned back around and had to laugh at the stupid grin on his brother's face.

"What is it?" Sleep asked.

"I was just thinking about that time you shot me, what was it? Oh, yeah, three times," Eyes said as he rubbed his hip and winced, though the laughter in his eyes couldn't be covered.

Sleep refused to respond to his friend. He just stood there waiting for Eyes to finish his little show.

"Come on, Sleep, I know you haven't forgotten, even if you've been hit in the head one too many times. But just in case" — he raised a hand — "you shot me here, and here, and here." He pointed at his shoulder, his back, and his hip. "I want to thank you for all the attention I've gotten from the nurses because of your shooting skills. There have been some hot ones. I especially loved the sponge baths."

The men in the room began laughing, used to this comedy routine. Though, they never knew exactly what would come out of Eyes's mouth from one moment to the next, they did know it would entertain.

"How about you get the yoga guru you've used for years to come give me some extra special therapy. I hear she's a brunette.

I've always had a thing for long, dark hair," Eyes continued.

Sleep gave him a taunting grin right back. "I've been given specific instructions by my guru that I'd have to shoot someone a minimum of seven times before I was allowed to give out her name."

The other personnel in the room didn't even try to hide the fact they were watching the two of them. Several chuckles surrounded them in the large hall.

"Ha! With the way you shoot, I could've been hit another twenty times and still be in the same shape I'm in now," Eyes said.

Sleep rolled his eyes and Eyes winked. Sleep held up his hand with a special finger sticking up. Then they both joined in the laughter of the room. They loved the men and women on this base, but they were more than ready to go home.

What came next, neither of them quite knew. But it was sure to be an adventure.

Chapter Twenty-One

Those who said the Anderson family didn't do things big had never actually met the Andersons. They were known for being a billionaire family that owned a lot of businesses, provided hundreds of thousands of jobs, and were generous philanthropists.

But what was known most about them was that they truly loved each other. There wasn't in-house fighting, there weren't battles over money. They didn't cheat, they didn't lie, and they didn't betray one another or anyone else.

And when the Anderson family needed to be united, there was no question that's exactly what they'd do.

It was the morning Katherine was coming back to them. The doctor's were bringing her out of her coma, and though the family knew they couldn't all be in her room, they needed to be at the hospital, close by and together.

So together they came. They arrived at Mercy Medical in droves. Wave after wave of men, women, and children came through the double doors where they were escorted to a huge conference room. The one they'd used on the first night wasn't big enough for this gathering. This time they needed a stadium.

They came in pairs, in fours, and in sixes. Sons and daughters, cousins, nieces, nephews, and grandchildren. They continued pouring in, the parking lot full, the hospital staff in awe at the sheer quantity streaming inside. And when they thought it was over, more showed up.

They brought hope and love, along with balloons and flowers and handmade cards. Their written messages were of love and healing. The smallest of the grandchildren had balloons tied to their wrists, the bright colors and messages making those they passed smile even through their pain. This family was beautiful, and they were enough to lift all the spirits of those inside the walls of a place no one wanted to come to.

By the time Joseph and Dr. Whitman arrived in the conference room, it was a sight to behold. Dr. Whitman stood in the doorway, his mouth open, his eyes wide. He'd seen the Anderson family many times at several events, but never in such a small space. At the Anderson mansion it wasn't quite so overwhelming.

Joseph rushed forward, a smile on his lips. He loved his family — couldn't imagine losing a single member in it. He'd been blessed beyond measure that, so far in life, he hadn't had to suffer the loss of any of them before their time. Yes, there had been loss, and yes they'd grieved, but so far they'd been blessed beyond what anyone could hope.

"Good morning, my lovely family," Joseph said, his voice booming through the room.

The kids squealed as several rushed forward, hugging his legs. He patted each one on the head as a chorus of greetings flew his way.

"Katherine is doing beautifully. Her color is perfect, her stats are better than we could've hoped for, and we're all set to wake her in exactly one hour. It'll take a while before she can have visitors, and she might be confused for a bit, so we need to have patience, but this means she gets to come home soon, and when she does, she'll be expecting a lot of visitors," he said, tears in his eyes, a wobbly smile on his lips.

He looked at the kids who jumped up and down in excitement to spend time with their grandpa and grandma, or their aunt and uncle.

"Now, let's all quiet down and listen to the good doctor who's been more than wonderful with my sweet Katherine," Joseph commanded. The room instantly quieted.

Dr. Whitman nodded as he stepped forward and began speaking. "Good morning. This is quite the crowd," he began. A chuckle filled the room before they quieted back down. "To add to what Joseph was saying, Katherine will be quite groggy and maybe a bit forgetful. Don't take it personally, and don't call it out. Give her time. This has been traumatic for her. We'll play it hour by hour on how she's doing, and if and when she can have visitors. We all know we can't keep Joseph out of there, so the rest of you will just have to be patient."

There were a few disappointed murmurs, and Dr. Whitman smiled as he held up a hand.

"Now, now, I get enough of that from Joseph," he said, his eyes sparkling. "I honestly don't see many issues. Her stats are great, and she's ready to come back to the real world. Besides," he said with a wink at the group who knew Joseph so well, "I need to get this man out of the hospital so my staff won't be terrified and quit on me, and so I can have my own coffee. Every time someone brings me a cup, it's gone before I can reach for it. Joseph has built in radar for when a hot cup is delivered."

Chuckles accompanied his words as knowing nods were seen throughout the room. They all did know Joseph well, and that sounded exactly like him.

"I'm afraid to ask, but are there any questions?" Joseph asked when it was clear Dr. Whitman was finished speaking.

Most of the family shook their heads. There were a lot of questions, but they knew Joseph had been bogged down with enough already.

Wyatt stepped forward and tugged on Joseph's leg. "Grandpa?" he questioned.

Joseph knelt. "What is it, Wyatt?"

The room was quiet as one of the younger of their family members looked up at Joseph with wide eyes. Technically Wyatt was his great nephew, but all of the kids called Joseph Grandpa, and he loved it. There was no difference in his mind how his family members were related. They were just flat out his family, and he was grateful for every one of them and every minute they had together.

"Can you give this to Grandma? I miss her kisses and cookies. I want her to feel better. Make sure she knows I gave it to her. I wrote on the teddy bear myself. And she really needs this."

Joseph's smile overtook his cheeks as Wyatt handed him a balloon, a teddy bear with *Wyatt loves you* written on it, and a can of silly string.

"Is that so she can shoot Grandpa?" he asked as he hugged his grandson.

"Yep," Wyatt said with a mischievous smile.

After Wyatt was done, a bunch of the kids moved forward, making a pile at Joseph's feet of goodies and balloons that floated to the ceiling. Soon, it was covered in all of the colors of the rainbow, and the floor was filled with love and wishes from these beautiful kids. And there were so many cans of silly string they'd be able to decorate the entire hospital. He was thinking that wasn't such a bad idea.

Joseph had to choke back tears as he looked out at these kids looking back at him with such love and hope that he couldn't help but feel the same.

"Look up," he said with a smile. They leaned their heads back and gasped. Even a few of the adults followed suit. "A rainbow is a promise from God, and it's a message of hope. And you have made a rainbow right here in this room. We'll take these balloons to Grandma's room so your rainbow is the first thing she sees, and it'll bring her good luck," he finished, his words choked, his voice horse from holding back tears.

When he got back to his feet, which definitely took longer than normal these days, he looked up and found Jasmine close by. But instead of the sweet smile she normally wore, there was a glint in her eyes he didn't quite understand. He raised a brow and waited.

She slowly pulled up her hand, and in her palm was a can of silly string. He nearly lost those tears he'd been holding back. He had to look away and cough a couple of times, loving that his family wouldn't call him on it. Then he looked back at all of them and the first laugh he'd had in a week escaped his throat.

"You've made me feel better. I love you crazy people. And let me warn you that if there are any attacks of silly string, retribution will be swift and hard," he said as he looked from one child to another, his eyes finishing with Jasmine, who looked back with utter innocence — the little faker.

The kids giggled. They knew there wasn't a mean bone in their grandpa. They had no fear, and he had no doubt he'd soon be covered in string from head to toe. And as long as his Katherine was there to watch and it brought her pleasure, he'd gladly wear a hundred cans of the sticky goo.

"Joseph, let me send a cart in to collect all of these goodies," Dr. Whitman said, then shook his head. "Make that two carts." He turned and called out to a nurse what he needed.

"I love you all and we'll keep you updated," Joseph said as he and Dr. Whitman left the room, both of their arms loaded down with gifts.

"Nurse Thomas, can you take the lead, collecting all of these items and decorating Katherine's room, including the balloons so she has a rainbow on the ceiling and can wake up to something beautiful?" Dr. Whitman asked.

"It will be my pleasure," Nurse Thomas said as she followed the carts into the overwhelmingly crowded room. Joseph and Spence laughed when they heard her gasp.

"She wasn't expecting that many items, was she?" Joseph asked.

"No, and you noticed I didn't tell her, didn't you?" Spence replied. They both chuckled. "I'll buy the staff a five-star dinner when you depart. They've earned it."

"That's for sure, my friend, that's for sure," Joseph said.

They reached Katherine's door and Joseph's heart fluttered. Today was the day. He'd finally get to hear his sweet Katherine's voice. There was no better gift anyone could give him.

"Okay, Joseph, I'm going to talk to the team and make sure all the i's are dotted and t's are crossed. We'll walk you through the process again before we do what's needed," Dr. Whitman told him.

Joseph pushed away his nervousness. It would be fine. With Katherine back, everything would be more than okay. There was no way there'd be complications. He wouldn't allow it. The nurses passed by and emptied their arms of the goodies just in time.

Before Doctor Spence Whitman could leave, Joseph grabbed his arm, stopping him. It wasn't often Joseph had a hard time speaking, but this was one of those moments. He cleared his throat then spoke from the heart.

"I want to thank you for staying when I know you were supposed to go back to Montana. I truly appreciate that you saw Katherine's case all the way through to the end. There's no possible way for me to ever repay you, but I mean it when I say, if there's ever anything I can do, don't hesitate to ask."

Spence smiled as he patted Joseph's shoulder. "You're family, Joseph. You've done more for me and my family than can ever be repaid. This was only a small thank you from me. It's been my pleasure to be here. And we aren't quite finished, so let's cross that line together," Spence said, his own voice a bit choked.

Both men turned away, clearing their throats. Then Spence went to consult with his staff, and Joseph went to his wife's bedside.

"We're going to be just fine, my love. I promise you we have many more years to live together, many more memories to make. When it's our time to go, we're going to do it together, and then we'll watch over our family from heaven. But it's not time yet, so you just cooperate with the good staff here who've been taking such great care of you. I'll get to hear your voice soon, and then before we know it, we're both going to be rocking in our favorite chairs with our grandchildren crawling all over us."

He leaned down and kissed her on the cheek, loving the warmth of her skin. She was healing. She was truly healing — and he was a thankful man.

He reached out and held her hand, his fingers trembling. Then he moved his other one to her cheek and cupped it, his thumb gently tracing her chin. He closed his eyes and bowed his head.

"Please, please let her come back. I know she's special, and I know she'll one day sing with the angels, but I need her right now, and her family needs her. So please give her back to me. Please," he prayed as a lone tear slipped from his closed eyes and landed on their joined fingers.

A nurse walked in and quietly pulled a chair up behind Joseph, then took his arm to help him sit. He wasn't willing to let go of Katherine. He was scared even though he refused to acknowledge it.

He was left alone again, and time stopped having meaning as he whispered words of encouragement to this woman he loved so much.

"It's time, Joseph." The words were uttered quietly, and Joseph looked up to find Dr. Whitman, and a team with him, moving toward the bed. "Are you ready to talk to your wife?"

"More than you know," Joseph said.

"Okay then. We have Deek Hurns, who's our respiratory therapist, and Ms. Rills and Ms. Bradford who have been Katherine's nurses most of this past week. We all love your wife and can assure you she's in good hands."

Joseph listened to them explain the process one more time, but he didn't really hear the words. He was too busy looking down at his wife, silently begging her to stay with him. He leaned down and kissed her one more time. "I'll talk to you in just a few minutes my love."

"Okay, Mr. Anderson, can you step back so we can wake up your wife?" Nurse Bradford asked. He squeezed Katherine's hand one more time, kissed her knuckles, and then reluctantly let go.

Spence moved over to him and placed a hand on his shoulder. Joseph stared at his wife as the very competent team worked their magic. "It's going to be okay, Joseph. Take some breaths in and out," Spence calmly said.

Joseph let out a rush of air he hadn't realized he'd been holding. His head was a little light and Spence led him to a chair and had him sit. He still didn't take his eyes off of his wife.

The next couple of minutes were a blur. Medicine was administered, her breathing tube removed, and orders and numbers were conveyed to the team surrounding her bed. Something was said about breathing, and he stared in horror at her chest. It wasn't moving. His body began shaking.

"It's okay, Joseph. This is normal," Spence said.

And then, just when Joseph began to feel pain in his heart, just when he thought he might be having a heart attack, the most miraculous thing happened — an audible breath filled the room — and Katherine's chest moved.

The nurses and therapist were talking to her, holding her hand and saying words that Joseph couldn't compute. He was shaking all over. For just a moment there, he'd thought she was gone. He knew beyond a shadow of a doubt that he could never go through that again.

"Go to her side now, Joseph," Spence said as he stood and helped Joseph to his feet. His knees were shaky, and it took a second to take a step. He hadn't realized how tense he'd been.

"Open your eyes, my love, please let me see your beautiful eyes," Joseph begged.

And then . . . and then . . . she did.

Her lids fluttered up, then down, then up, then down, and finally up. She blinked several times, and the nurse moved to dim the lights. Katherine's body shifted as she gazed around the room, trying to focus on something.

Joseph was filled with shock, confusion, love, joy, sorrow, but most of all raw happiness. He tried to speak, but his throat was tight. He cleared it and tried again, but still, no words came out.

"Katherine, it's Spence Whitman. You're okay, Katherine. You're in the hospital, and you're okay," he said gently. "We just woke you up with a bit of medicine. Your throat is going to be tender because we had a tube in there to help you breathe, but I'm looking at your charts right now, and your vitals are great. Joseph's right here with you, but he's a little emotional. He's missed talking to you. Can you nod at me and let me know you hear me?" he asked. His voice was calm and gentle, and not only was it most likely soothing to Katherine, but it had the added affect of calming Joseph as well.

Joseph gazed into Katherine's face as she nodded at Spence. Then she looked from the doctor to Joseph, and his heart exploded with joy when her lips wobbled up the slightest bit and her eyes filled with tears.

"I'm here, my love, I'm right here," Joseph said, not even trying to stop his tears this time. His Katherine was awake, and she knew who he was. This was the greatest day of his life. He'd never take advantage of one more day he had to spend with this woman who was the center of his universe.

She opened her mouth to speak, but only a croak came out. That little sound still filled his heart with joy.

"The whole family is here, all of them, my love. You have a rainbow of balloons the kids brought you and all sorts of presents throughout your room," he said. "Look up, it's a rainbow. It's a promise of healing, of restoration, of a new beginning."

She looked to the ceiling and smiled, her eyes lighting up the tiniest bit. He was going to buy each of those kids a pony for giving his wife this peaceful moment.

A nurse quietly handed him a tissue, and he swiped at his face. Katherine's smile grew bigger as she wiggled her fingers while trying to move her arm. Joseph knew what she wanted.

He lifted her hand and placed it on his wet cheek. "I'm sorry, my love. I've been so scared. I need you so much. I need to tell you that I love you every single day. I need to hear you tell me you love me every day. And I don't care about any of the other words spoken, just as long as I hear your sweet, beautiful, patient, kind voice," he said. More tears fell from both of their eyes.

She opened her mouth again to speak, but no words came out, and Joseph briefly glanced at the nurse. "Why can't she speak?"

"Give it a few minutes, Mr. Anderson. She's still waking, and just needs a bit of patience," the nurse replied.

Katherine smiled as her eyes cleared a little more. The confusion was waning. "He's not known for patience," she whispered, her voice ragged, but the most beautiful sound he'd ever heard.

"Oh my love," he said, "you know me better than anyone else on this planet." He leaned down, gently placing his forehead against hers, inhaling her sweet scent, and even more importantly, feeling her hot breath against his lips. He pulled back just a tad, then gently brushed his lips against hers.

"It's been too long since my lips touched yours," he said.

She smiled. The staff was still there, monitoring her progress, checking her vitals, and making sure everything was going smoothly. Joseph didn't mind one bit.

"What happened?" Katherine asked.

Dr. Whitman was the one to answer. "What's the last thing you remember?" he asked.

She frowned as she tried pulling the memory out. "In the car. Going to the vet's center," she said. Her throat was hurting, so she was using fewer words. The nurse placed a straw in her mouth for her to sip water.

"Anything else, Katherine?" Dr. Whitman gently pushed.

"No, nothing," she replied.

Katherine shifted on the bed, trying to make herself more comfortable, and the nurse jumped into action, coming over and fixing her pillow, then bringing the bed up to more of a sitting position.

"I'm sore," she said as she shifted, trying to find comfort. "Thank you for helping. Sorry I'm so weak."

"You're a lot stronger than you realize, Mrs. Anderson. You're a true fighter," the nurse replied before stepping back.

"Yes you are, my love. You're so strong," Joseph said. His chair was moved closer, and he sat, his head at the same level as his wife's. There was nothing that would make him let go of her.

"Tell me what happened," she demanded, a bit of her normal strength coming into her voice. Joseph heard angel's sing at her words. He was getting his wife back.

"Darling, you got to the center, and a couple of men attacked you," Joseph said, anger flashing through him at having to utter those words. "You were in and out of consciousness and brought to this hospital. They've had you in a coma to help you heal. It's been a week since I've heard your voice." He choked on his last words as more emotion filled him.

She looked confused. "What?"

He repeated his explanation, willing to do it a hundred times if necessary. He wasn't going to tell her about the tumor. There was no way. He'd do that later. But she shocked him when she gazed at him with love and remorse.

"You found out about the tumor, didn't you?" she asked, gently squeezing his fingers.

"You . . . you knew?" he gasped, not knowing how to feel about her words. He was in shock. There was nothing they didn't share with one another.

More tears fell down her cheeks. "I'm sorry, my love. I've struggled for months with how to tell you. I went to the doctor three months ago because I didn't feel like myself. I was tired, forgetting things, and frankly a bit scared. He did a scan and found it."

Joseph was too stunned to say a word.

"I'm sorry you found out when I couldn't be there to hold you. I was trying to protect you. I was wrong to do that. If it were in reverse I'd be furious with you," she said before a sob escaped and her frail body shook.

Dr. Whitman took the staff and left the room, giving them privacy as they shared this moment. They'd be close by.

"Darling, I'm not mad at you. I could never be mad at you. I just have to prove to you that you can always trust me, that you can always come to me. I understand why you didn't. You know how much I love you, and you know how scared I am. But, my love, if I've learned anything this past week, it's that there's no end to what I'll do to keep you with me. We'll fight this together, and we'll win. You've always been by my side when I've needed you. Now, it's my turn to be by yours. And I will. I won't leave you for a second. You truly are my world, and we'll get through this together," he said. He then leaned down and kissed her. This time she kissed him back, their lips whispering together, their love strong, their devotion unbreakable.

The staff came in and checked on them over the next couple of hours, and Katherine grew stronger by the minute. Spence agreed to let her go home in two days if she remained stable.

A few of the family members came by, but it was too much, too soon, so once they were all assured she'd be home soon, they reluctantly went home. Joseph stayed at her side, not willing to ever leave her again.

She grew stronger each hour that passed. Soon, Joseph would take her home where he'd have a full staff to ensure she didn't so much as sneeze without a lab analyzing the germs.

This was just another bump in the road of their beautiful life together. They'd get through it just as they'd gotten through every single other trying event. He wasn't at all worried. Or he wasn't allowing himself to acknowledge that he was worried.

When it was time to take her home, he held her the entire car ride. He carried her into the house and straight to their bedroom suite then out onto the balcony and sat down, keeping her secure in his lap.

Lucas quietly placed a blanket around them, then gave them some much needed privacy. Katherine had enjoyed all of the love from her family, but now it was time for them to be alone.

He held her as she fell asleep in his arms. Her nursing staff was there to monitor her, and their family filled the rooms of the giant mansion, but none of that mattered right then. All that mattered was his wife was in his arms.

Joseph looked up to the sky and said one more prayer.

"Don't take her from me. Please, I beg of you. Please. I don't ask for much. I work hard for everything I want and need. But I'm pleading on my hands and knees that you let her stay with me," he whispered.

Just then three shooting stars passed through the clear night sky, side by side. And Joseph smiled. If that wasn't an answer to his prayer, he wasn't sure what would be.

Chapter Twenty-Two

Carl Schwartz sat on his back deck, overlooking the bay as the sun set in the sky after an absolutely beautiful day. Coals were heating in his grill, and his bottle of Hop Valley's *Citrus Mistress* was ice cold; perfect flavor and temp, easily going down the gullet.

Life didn't get much better than it was right then. He kicked back in his chair, his mouth watering at the thought of a good meal. He'd been thinking a lot about life in the past couple of weeks.

He took another sip of his beer before he sighed. He was thinking so much about himself, his life, and his past because, well, because of a . . . woman. Never before had he gotten hung up on a woman. As a matter of fact, he'd been disgusted with his friends when it had happened to them. He'd called them weak or whipped.

If only they could see him now.

Shaking his head, he sipped his beer again. Instead of focusing on the colorful sunset while thinking of his favorite baseball team, he thought about his life. Carl was a fairly simple man — for the most part. If a battle wasn't going on, he seemed like any ordinary man living in a chaotic world.

He didn't spend money on frivolous things. He wouldn't exactly call himself a penny pincher, it was more that he was a practical man without a lot of wants or needs. When he needed something, he bought it — when he didn't, he passed it by. He figured the world would be in a much better place if all people followed this philosophy.

What in the hell was the matter with people who felt a need to buy two thousand dollar shoes? What happened if they stepped in a crack on the first trip out of the house and destroyed them?

On the other hand, a gun was a practical buy. That made sense to him as it did to most of the men he called friends. It was something he could hunt with, providing food for himself and others. It offered home protection, and it had the added bonus of entertainment when he went target shooting. He didn't mind spending hundreds, or even thousands, of dollars on a gun and ammo.

He bought the necessities of life: food, clothes, toiletries, furniture, weapons. They didn't need to be fancy, unless of course, it was to splurge on a nice, thick, juicy T-Bone. Some might think Carl was one step away from poor by the way he chose to live. His truck was ten years old, his home a thousand square feet, though it did have a nice large deck in the back with a spectacular view of the bay. He did splurge when it was necessary, and a peaceful place to sit and relax was certainly necessary.

His briquettes ready, he got up and uncovered the steak that had been marinating for the last two hours and took it out to his Webber grill — which, in his opinion, cooked better than those overpriced feed store thousand dollar brandname grills. He set the steak on the hot bars while continuing his musings.

From the way he lived, he could understand why people wouldn't know he had more money in his bank accounts than he'd ever be able to spend. Not only was he wise in his spending, but he'd found he was a pretty smart investor.

He'd been raised right by working class parents who'd always provided for their children without spoiling them. They'd had food on the table for every meal and practical clothes for them to wear. They hadn't been name brand, and that's definitely where Carl had learned his lifestyle.

When he'd been forced out of the military due to his multitude of injuries, his financial security had given him time and options to figure out what his next step was going to be. He'd been far too young to retire, and though he didn't mind a game of golf or taking a day to go fishing, it wasn't something he wanted to do on a daily basis.

He needed action and adventure.

He needed stimulation.

When Jon, aka Eyes, had called him approximately six months after they'd left Germany, it hadn't taken long for new life to spark inside him. He'd been lost after coming home. Jon had told him he had a possible job for him that couldn't be discussed unless he accepted — just what Carl had been waiting for.

Carl had been back in Philly since his release, where his family had raised him. If he wanted to take the job Jon was offering, he'd have to move to San Francisco, a place he'd never been particularly fond of.

While the pull to be back home had been strong, being there hadn't been what he'd expected. He'd lost his sister to a drug overdose as he'd been recovering from his injuries in Germany. That had nearly done him in where the insurgents hadn't been able to.

His parents had been taken from him a few years earlier in a car accident caused by a drunk driver, which was what had led to his sister's drug addiction. She'd felt abandoned, not only by them, but by him since he was gone far more than he was around. He had a lot of regrets that he hadn't been there for her and hadn't been able to take more time with his dad after he'd retired.

Carl had missed out on a lot of family life while serving his country. But he had no regrets about serving. Without men and women willing to serve, people like his parents and sister wouldn't have the freedom to live their lives the way they wanted. His dad always reminded him of that when Carl lamented about missing out on a holiday or a big family occasion. Hard work and service — be it to God, or mankind, had been instilled in him early in his childhood.

It hadn't taken him long to accept Jon's job offer. Philly would always be home, but maybe if he wasn't there daily, it wouldn't be a reminder of everything he'd lost. Maybe if he was away, he'd be able to remember all of the good things he'd grown up with instead of the tragic ending.

Carl had easily packed his meager possessions into the back of his long bed Ford F150 with room to spare beneath the canopy and began his cross country trek to the West Coast. When he'd gotten there, Jon had told him the story of how his new company had begun.

Carl was ripped from his thoughts as a timer went off. Why was he lamenting the past? It had to be those two days with Avery, four days earlier, and it had been better than anything he'd ever had before. It was making him think about his entire life.

How was it that one woman, one small, competitive spitfire of a woman changed his entire belief system in such a short time? He thought about how his dad had proposed to his mom after five days. His father had told him that when you knew, you just knew. Their love had been strong for thirty years before their life had been taken too soon. He had no doubt they'd have made it to a seventy-five-year anniversary if they'd been able to live out their lives.

But Carl wasn't in love.

No.

There was no way he was in love after . . . how long had it been? Two weeks? Three weeks? He didn't know. The man who could tell time by looking at the sun wasn't quite sure how long he'd been seeing this woman. What was she doing to him?

His timer went off again and he jumped to his feet, shaking his head. He'd lost his appetite which was ridiculous.

He took his steak off the grill and carried it inside where he covered it to let it rest, allowing the juices to slowly release. People who cut into their steak right away disgusted him. Why buy a perfect cut only to destroy it in the cooking process? There was nothing worse than dry meat. He'd had enough of that in his MREs, which he'd been grateful to have while on mission.

Restlessness filled Carl as he paced his deck, wanting to go to Avery. He was trying to figure out his feelings for her, and instead he found himself aching, needing to hold her, needing to talk to her, needing to figure out why he was feeling how he was feeling.

Forgetting about his steak sitting on the counter, Carl walked inside his house, then moved to his garage. He went to his garage door and flipped on the light.

His tools, golf clubs, and hunting gear sat neatly on a shelf in the back corner. But a person wouldn't even notice that stuff as their eyes would be fastened to the black Audi R8 Spyder that was a pleasure to open up on the road. With all of the custom upgrades, the final price had been two hundred thirty-five thousand dollars. His first thought as he'd presented the cashier's check for the fine automobile had been that it had cost three times more than his father's one and only home purchase.

Surprisingly, Carl had never had regrets about buying it. He loved his car, but he still kept his sturdy truck. One of Carl's stress relievers was finding back roads to test the power of his fine machine.

Looking at the car, Carl knew what he needed right then was a fast drive. He had to get this fog out of his head. He had to figure out why his life seemed to be spinning. Was it time to leave his job? Was it time to move on? Did he want to leave San Francisco? Did he want to leave Avery? What was happening to him?

Forgetting all about his perfectly grilled steak, he decided he needed speed more. He jogged inside the house, grabbed his wallet and keys, then slipped into the buttery leather seat of his car before revving his engine.

For just a moment he turned the car in the direction of Avery's place. On their way back from Napa Valley, she'd insisted on having the top down and she'd laughed with joy as she'd held her hands in the air, her cheeks pink, her eyes lit, her smile heart-stopping.

What wasn't to love about her? There was a connection between the two of them he couldn't deny — didn't want to deny. But she was helping her mother at the bar that night, so he didn't want to distract her. Her uncle wasn't doing well, and that was cutting into their time together. He felt selfish for missing her, for wanting to take all of her time.

Instead of heading to Avery, he found his way to HWY101. At night, there wasn't as much traffic, and he luxuriated in the cool wind blowing over him while the heater kept his body warm. The farther he got from the city, the freer he felt.

No stress.

No flashbacks.

Nothing but wind and a smile on his face. Damn, he needed to do this more often.

He was about a hundred miles from Frisco when a notification lit up on his console, *new text from Eyes.*

It was still hard for Carl to use Jon's name. In the military, at war, or preparing for missions, they always used call signs. Hell, some men never knew the real names of members in the military.

Carl hit the button to read now and a voice message came over his speaker: *Stop everything you're doing, make sure you're sitting down, and take a call coming in to you in less than five minutes.*

"Alrighty then," Carl said out loud before replying with a simple, *OK*.

The music began again where it had been paused for the message, and Carl hit his blinker as he slowed enough to whip into a driveway off the road. He moved down it, noting the overgrown foliage. It was abandoned.

Perfect.

An old barn was about half a mile down the rock driveway, and he moved up next to it, parking. In exactly five minutes his phone rang with an unknown number. He clicked the send button.

"This is Carl Schwartz," he said in a clipped voice.

There was a short pause. "Carl, thanks for taking my call. My name is Chad Redington;

I have a matter to discuss with you that requires discretion."

"I'm alone, you can talk," Carl told him, immediately respecting the man's tone of voice. He'd bet every last dollar he had, which was a lot, the man was military or former military.

"Eyes notified you I'd be calling, so you know he gave me your information," Chad began. The fact Chad was using Jon's name as Eyes confirmed this man was military. "I'm looking for five or six former operators to do undercover work. Eyes and you were recommended by Secretary of Defense Whitaker who sent the information through Commander Glass."

Carl was officially impressed this man had access to the Secretary of Defense. He certainly wasn't a nobody. This was growing more interesting by the second. He didn't say anything, waiting for Chad to continue.

"I know Mike well," Carl said, speaking of Commander Glass. He'd been his and Jon's lead on three different missions. He was smart, focused, and as loyal as it got. There were fewer Carl trusted more than Mike Glass.

"You've done some work to reach me," Carl said. "You certainly have piqued my interest. What can I help you with?"

"I spoke with Eyes last night. He had to clear some things before he could confirm or deny. He just confirmed five minutes ago. He also said he cleared your path if you choose to come. I'm sure you understand I can't tell you what this is about unless you accept, but I can tell you I've reviewed your files and believe this will appeal to you. The money will be more than equal to what you're making now." He paused, and before Carl could say something, he continued, a smile sounding in his voice. "The action will be more of what your previous profession provided."

With the sort of connections this man had, Carl wasn't surprised he had access to Carl's and Jon's records. He just wondered how deep that access went. He also knew it was pointless to ask. This was a need-to-know basis.

"Tell me what you can," Carl said.

"I can say I have an issue that needs people I can count on to get to people who are impossible to find. All of this will remain off the books, zero records kept, and the team will remain in the shadows. We don't have a timeline yet, but it won't be in SF. You'll have to move. And I can't tell you for how long. All expenses will be paid for the move and compensated beyond that. All living expenses are also provided. The perks of this job are unlimited. If you accept I'll tell you the location."

"How long do I have to decide?" Carl asked, knowing the answer.

"Six hours," Chad said.

Carl laughed. "That was longer than I thought, I was expecting you to say five minutes ago." He paused for only a moment. Eyes was in, and he was intrigued. It meant a new location, but he was learning that just meant a new adventure. "I'm in," he added after only a few heartbeats.

Chad seemed to let out a relieved breath, but Carl might just be imagining that. "I'm glad to hear it, Carl." He paused for a moment, perhaps to write something down.

"Okay, this is as much as I'll say on the phone. We're going to be breaking apart a major operation. I'll need you to report to the private hanger at SFO Monday morning at 0600. You and Eyes will arrive in Seattle at 0800. Further instruction will be provided later.

"Okay," Carl said. "And Chad," he added before the man could hang up, "call me Sleep."

"Thanks, Sleep. Last thing before we hang up. Everything you need, and more, is already provided, so you can pack your old life up. We'll have to secure your phone and computer if you have one. Those personal items will always be left at your civilian location. When you're on campus, you'll only use what we provide. We are fully underground."

Chad didn't give Carl a chance to reply, he simply hung up. That was nothing unusual when speaking to men in power. Carl sat for a few minutes, thinking of how much his life was going to change again. Excitement was brewing in him. He hadn't realized he'd been needing a change. He should've known with how restless he'd been.

As much as he'd spoken to Avery about work not being life, it wasn't necessarily true. If you weren't satisfied in the thing you did for a third of your day, then the rest of your time diminished.

He revved his engine back to life, made a three-point turn, then headed back toward home. He had a little bit of time to think about what was going to come next and what needed to be done before he left San Francisco for an unknown amount of time.

He'd thought of Avery the second he'd hung up the phone. He hadn't allowed his relationship with her to factor into this decision. What did that mean? The closer he drew to the city, the more anxiety he felt.

Had he just made a mistake?

Could he actually leave this woman behind?

Would she be willing to move without him telling her what he was doing and why he was abruptly moving? It was too soon to ask her to do that, wasn't it?

He didn't have a single answer to any of those questions.

He turned his car when he got into the city — not in the direction of home, but straight to the bar. There was no way he'd sleep that night unless they talked. His entire future might hang on the conversation they were about to have.

Chapter Twenty-Three

Chad Redington hung up his phone, his final person confirmed. He'd been on calls, emails, texts, and in meetings for the past week straight. He'd gone through several devices, each destroyed after being used. He'd only slept three hours in the last forty-eight.

Chad absolutely loved his wife, would die for her in a second, would go to the ends of the world for her, and there was nothing on the planet that could make him give her up. Even feeling that way, it had been a long time since he'd felt this type of stirring in his blood, this much adrenaline running through him.

This new mission — this life — this operation was what he'd been meant to do. He loved working in the shadows, he *needed* to lead men through the depths of hell and back through the tunnel of life onto solid ground again.

It was indescribable to be given the gift of an unlimited budget and a team of soldiers he knew were not just able, but also willing to give their all — *needing* to give their all just as he needed to.

This team would accomplish goals, find truths, and help those who were forgotten. There were so many, himself included, who lived in a bubble and didn't see the tragedies that happened on US soil. He'd seen them everywhere he looked when he'd first come home. But over the years, he'd stopped looking.

Now he was back.

He was who and what he was supposed to be.

And he was lucky.

He had a wife who supported him, trusted him, and held him as she told him she believed in him. Some women might realize their husbands weren't telling them everything, and snap to judgment — but not Bree, not his wife. She knew anything he was doing was for love of family, love of God, or love of country.

This operation was about to begin.

It had taken a week to put together once the money was in and the contacts had been vetted. He'd secured five individuals to start his team. He was damn impressed.

The dossiers from their respective military records had been awe-inspiring. Chad had seen a lot of good and bad in the world. He'd seen things that would make people stay awake at night, checking and double-checking their locks on every window and door. He'd seen things that would make grown men cry and children never believe in magic again.

Tragically that had only been in foreign lands. But lately it was creeping through America's back door. It had to be stopped. And he had just the team to begin deconstructing the chaos evil was slipping through the shadows.

Chad rose from his chair, gazing around the empty room that was the center of his operations. It was completely secure, virtually impossible to locate without knowledge, and becoming his second home.

He leaned down, hit print on his computer, then walked over to the large machine as it began spitting out paper, full color pictures in the top corner of each set:

Name: Jon Eisenhart
Call Sign: *Eyes* — He sees all, even at the back of his head.
Branch: Former Navy SEAL
Age: 36

Physical Description: 5'11" Dark Brown Eyes. Olive Skin. Right Handed. Bullet wound scars on right shoulder, two in torso, left hip. Distance runner, sleek, muscled, and unstoppable. Master of multiple weapons including guns, bows, knives, and spheres. Multiple blackbelt Jiu Jitsu. Two tattoos: left calf a snake, right forearm a map with his own special places designated.

Background: Was lead operator during Operation Mountain Anvil, survived bullet wound injuries, walked five days before finding help. Medical discharge from Navy. Wildly decorated; including multiple purple hearts and a Navy Cross. Seen most live fire action of all on team.

Attributes: Natural leader, even of leaders, always makes the right decision no matter the situation. Sees many moves at once. IQ: 149

Family: Two parent household, two younger siblings attending college, one at Princeton, one at UCLA. Dad professor of economics at Stanford University, Mom runs non-profit organization for women seeking business loans. Parents don't support military career. No other close family.

Name: Carl Schwartz
Call Sign: *Sleep* — due to knocking guys out with one hit
Branch: Former Navy SEAL
Age: 34

Physical Description: 6 foot, brown eyes. Pale skin. Right handed. Prototype: shredded body, works out seven days a week, maintains balance with speed and strength, and yoga learned in Nepal. Scars from severe fall during Operation

Mountain Anvil; long scar at bottom of rib cage where two ribs were removed, multiple puncture wound scars on back. No tattoos. Black belt Jiu Jitsu. Heavy weight boxing champ for military.

Background: Passed every test ever put in front of him on first try. Has a story for every situation, seems to know a person in every city, and will fight any man at any time.

Attributes: Quick-witted, confident, and can turn from carefree to stone-cold, steely-eyed, focused, and lethal in less than a heartbeat. IQ: 133.

Family: From Philadelphia, Pa. Dad was blue-collar construction worker, taught love of God, country, and work. Iron hand. Mom was a homemaker, humorous, loyal, and loving. Grew up in a very tight-knit family. Both parents passed away — drunk driver. One sister, died of drug overdose year and a half ago.

Name: Tyrell Rice
Call Sign: *Smoke* — gets in and out of all places without a trace.
Branch: Former Army Delta Force
Age: 38

Physical Description: 6'4" Dark Eyes. Light brown skin. Right Handed. Built like a brick and as fast as a cheetah. Four scars on abdomen where he was stabbed by a kid trying to get into a gang, killing Tyrell was the initiation target. San Francisco 49ers helmet tattoo on right bicep. Master of Krav Maga. Record holder for dead lift in the military. There isn't a gym with enough equipment to give him a good workout.

Background: Spent most of time in covert operations in toughest parts of the world. Played football for Virginia Tech, NFL for two years, broke left wrist and it never healed correctly. Went into the military. Served ten years. Got out to make more money in the contractor world.

Attributes: Always has a smile on his face. It's up to the person he's smiling at to know whether it's friendly or deadly. Not afraid to speak his mind. People are naturally drawn to him, his whit, his humor, his appeal. Large as he is, moves as smooth as a ballerina, and as quiet as a church mouse. IQ 139

Family: Only child to a single mother in SE DC. Mom worked three jobs from the time he was born to ensure he went to a great school. Uncle took on father figure role, but died during Tyrell's rookie season. He made enough money in NFL and military to give his mom a much-

needed retirement. She fought him on that. He has mad respect for women, and will take a man down who tries to abuse or demean one.
There'd be no help for one who came near his mother.

Name: Steve Bregon
Call Sign: *Brackish* — due to swimming naked and drunk in Lake Maracaibo, Venezuela, costing him two weeks jail time, which he says was worth it.
Branch: Former Army Intelligence Support Activity
Age: 39

Physical Description: 6'1" Hazel Eyes. Permanently tanned. Left-handed. Baby-face — often gets carded. Shoulders as wide as a truck and hands stronger than a bear trap. Long, thin scar full length of right forearm from barbed wire accident as teen. No tattoos. Minimal trained fighting, plenty of bar fights, men are easier to throw than cows.

Background: Muscular body is from time spent wrestling cattle and building fences for miles on end as a youth. Math genius has two speeds — 50,000 mph or 0, with no in between. Got out when his parents' health started failing. Highly sought after for tech skills.

Attributes: There isn't an electronic system he can't hack, break, solve, or build. Worked on nearly all of the electronic communication devices the military has made over the last twenty years. Speaks English, Spanish, Portuguese, and French. IQ 158

Family: His dad is retired Navy who married a Puerto Rican woman. He grew up in the middle of nowhere Texas with four sisters and five brothers.

Name: Hendrick Meeks
Call Sign: *Green* — due to being youngest at every stage of his career.
Age: 32
Branch: Former US Navy SEAL — Sniper

Physical Description: 6'2" Blue Eyes, brown hair, light tan skin. Right handed. Spry, wiry, muscled, and lean. Hair just long enough to comb and always stay in place. No known scars, no tattoos. Can shoot any weapon, has hunted since he could walk. Prefers long guns. Only hand-to-hand knowledge via military training.

Background: Was able to join Navy at age seventeen, got through SEALS as youngest ever. Youngest confirmed sniper kill in combat, youngest to hold command leadership position, and youngest to receive Medal of Honor. Nothing and no one could slow his trajectory. He never sought it, it just happened — like everything: easily.

Attributes: Quiet, reserved, and always watching. Sizes up everyone in a room in less time than it takes to walk across it. Got out of the military to start his own company, took it public, and made over $100 million after only two years. Recently started another company. There are murmurs of him getting into politics, but he denounces it every time asked. Can find a way to get just about anyone to do what he asks them to do. When he does speak everyone listens. IQ: 144.

Family: Parents divorced when Hendrick was 3. Dad was an absent drunk, but non-violent, mom checked out emotionally as she was disappointed with her life. One sister and one brother who still live in same town. They have zero ambition. Grew up in Oxbow, Oregon. Town so small there's no school.

Chad sat back and smiled as he looked at the sheets. This was just the beginning — a solid team with unyielding men. It would grow. But this was a damn fine start.

As with all of their operational papers, these sheets would be destroyed. There wouldn't be a trail left for anyone to find. Well, he was sure Steve could pull any of it out of thin blue air — but *that* was why he was part of their team.

He'd contacted seven others, but they'd chosen not to join. It had worked out in the end just as it was meant to. The combined skillsets of these men made them an unstoppable force, their combined knowledge and skills an asset to any organization. Individually they were great, together they were unbeatable.

Jon and Carl were flying in together from SF, landing in Seattle at a private airport at 0800. Waiting for them was an unmarked vehicle, keys inside. It wouldn't take them long to find them. He smiled. It wasn't a test; he knew these men well enough to know they'd laugh when they figured out he'd hidden the keys.

A message would come to them when they landed, letting them know where the command center was located. Joseph had given them a building that wasn't in a traceable name. When on the mission, they'd stay there. When away from the mission, they had private quarters. No visitors were allowed at the command center; no one outside of their group was to know the location.

Tyrell Rice was coming from Washington DC. Steve Bregon was flying in from San Antonio. They were both arriving at the private hangar at 1000 and 1015 hours. They were aware they were meeting and taking the vehicle left for them. Same format on how to get to their location.

The last team member, Hendrick Meeks, had been spring bear hunting in Northeastern Oregon. Hendrick had received his call just as he'd been driving over the top of the mountain. In another minute, he'd have been out of cell phone service. Chad was glad he'd call when he had, because that minute would've cost him the slot, and this team was better for having him on it.

Hendrick had been hesitant to join the team. He'd already conquered the world, so it was tough to entice him. Money hadn't been a factor. He had more than enough, and it simply accumulated more interest than he needed to spend. He might be rich and he might be a genius, but he was a simple man in a complicated world. The deciding factor for Hendrick had been the probability of becoming a hero. He'd conquered a lot in his life, but saving those who were forgotten was something he hadn't realized he needed to do until this offer came to him.

He'd agreed to arrive at the intersection of I-90 and I-495, just outside of Bellevue, at 1200 hours. His truck would be taken to his new residence in the Seattle area, and he'd switch to a company vehicle to come to the base.

Not one of the teammates had argued about the way they were arriving, not one had asked questions. Each and every crewmember knew how an operation like this one worked, and they were 100 percent in.

Chad took the papers to his incinerator and tossed them in. His team would be there soon. It was about to begin.

Chapter Twenty-Four

Avery was dead on her feet. She'd been helping her mother for three days, working twelve-hour shifts, getting her ass slapped, having indecent proposals thrown at her and sloppy drunks puking at her feet. Never in her life had she been more grateful that her mother had pushed her to do well in school.

She couldn't imagine doing a job like this for the rest of her life. It was more than enough motivation for her to get back to practicing law and quickly figuring out what she was going to do next. The one great thing about this experience was she appreciated her mother a heck of a lot more now.

There was a break in demands coming at her as her mother moved back behind the bar. Avery grabbed her, pulling her in for a sweaty, heartfelt hug. She didn't want to let go — not ever.

When she finally pulled back, her mom was grinning. "What was that for?" Bobbi asked. "Not that I'm complaining."

"I just love you more than you can possibly understand. I don't think I tell you enough how much I appreciate you and how much you sacrificed so I could live my dreams.

I promise you, I'm going to make up for that. You're not going to be doing this kind of work much longer," Avery said, feeling tears sting her eyes.

"Idle hands are the devil's play tools. I don't mind a hard day's work. It means I'm capable of doing it and blessed to have all I need," Bobbi said.

"Mom, you've put in more than enough hard work. Maybe it's time for you to go back to school. Isn't there something you want to do other than this?" Avery asked.

Her mother looked stunned at her words. They stood there for a moment, and when someone called out to them, her mother gave the man a stern look and told him to wait a damn minute.

That made Avery smile. She'd wanted to say that for three days straight. The man surprisingly listened. Her mother did have that look in her eyes that told everyone not to mess with her. He was wise to obey.

"I've never thought about that. No one has asked me before," Bobbi finally said. She moved over to the counter and told the man to place his order fast. He was subdued as he ordered a couple of beers. She poured them then turned back to Avery.

"What is it?" Avery asked.

"I always thought it would be fun to work in an office where kids come in, like a receptionist at a dentist office, or even better at a school. Kids are so pure, and it would be amazing to start and end my workday with children instead of drunk adults," her mother said.

"Then you're going to do just that, Mom. We're going online and looking at exactly what you need to do to work in a school," Avery insisted.

"I can't do that. I'm too old, and school costs too much money," Bobbi said as she waived her hand in the air.

"I have so much money, it's not even funny," Avery said as she stomped her foot. "I'm not taking no for an answer. You gave me everything I needed in order to have a beautiful life. If you don't accept my gift, I'm going to be on you twenty-four/seven, not giving you a second of peace. I'll move back in with you, play loud music with a group of people and party all night . . . and leave dishes all over the house. I'll hate it, but I'll do it, because I know you'll hate it more." Avery crossed her arms and glared at her mother, daring her to argue.

Bobbi laughed before hugging Avery again. "You are *definitely* my daughter. I'll compromise by agreeing to look into it," she finally said.

Avery wanted to argue further. But she decided the door was open, and that was a good start. She'd get her mother into school, and she had a feeling she was going to watch a butterfly emerge from the cocoon she'd been in for Avery's entire life. It would be beautiful to witness.

Before she could say anything else, the air shifted. Avery didn't have to look up to know Carl had stepped inside the bar. Her stomach clenched, and she automatically squeezed her thighs together as heat stirred. Just knowing he was nearby awoke her body in a big way.

She looked up as he moved to the side of the bar, not bothering with sitting down. He came behind the bar, pulled her into his arms, and kissed her — kissed her like he meant it. When he let her go, she was a bit wobbly on her feet. She ignored the catcalls coming their way.

"Well, that was a hell of a greeting," Bobbi said with a laugh. "How do I find some of that?"

Carl laughed as he let go of Avery, then pulled Bobbi to him with a warm hug. Avery's heart enlarged, if that was possible, seeing him being so good to her mother. She looked at the two of them, then felt sick to her stomach as a realization hit her in the face like a car slamming into a brick wall at ninety miles per hour.

She loved this man.

It was impossible, yet it was true. She wasn't sure if it was real, but she knew she loved him. She'd missed him like crazy ever since they'd parted, and he was always on her mind. She even dreamed about him. In an incredibly short amount of time she'd fallen for him, and fallen hard. She didn't know what in the hell she was going to do about it.

He let go of her mother and moved back to her. "May I steal her away for a few minutes?" he asked.

"Shelly just walked in the door. Take Avery home. She's been here since nine this morning," Bobbi said.

"You've been here since eleven. I'm not leaving closing to you," Avery said, hands on her hips.

"You're fired . . . for tonight," Bobbi told her daughter. "Now get out of here."

And just like that, Avery was being pushed from behind the bar, Carl's hand on her back, not giving her a chance to argue further. Before she could blink, they were outside and he was moving across the street where his truck was parked. He took her to the passenger side, opened the door, and lifted her inside.

She was so stunned she didn't try to fight him. By the time she snapped out of it, he was in the driver's seat, and the truck was pulling out onto the street.

"Did you just kidnap me?" she asked, feeling oddly pleased about it. She should be furious.

"Yes, I did," he said, looking her way for a second as he gave her a tight smile.

Now that they were out of the dim lights of the bar, she could see something was wrong. He was wearing a smile, but it was off. It didn't reach his eyes.

"What's wrong?" she asked. She suddenly realized she didn't want to know. She had a bad feeling she wasn't going to like it at all.

"Let's get you home first and then we'll talk. You're still the most beautiful woman I've ever laid eyes on, but the fumes coming off of you at the moment could stop a truck driver," he said with a chuckle. There was a bit of mirth in the laugh, but he was holding back. She was horrified at smelling bad. She lifted her shirt up and took a whiff, then gagged.

"Ugh, I smell like a mixture of beer, grease, puke, and smoke. I'm one sexy mama right now," she said while rolling down her window. The cold air was much preferred to her own odor. Thankfully, her place wasn't far.

Carl parked and she was still unbuckling when he came to her door and opened it, helping her down, and holding her hand all the way to the door. She was grateful her neighbor wasn't out on the landing, to not only smell her, but to see her bringing a man to her apartment. She was a grown woman, but still . . .

"Grab a drink from the fridge. I'll be back in fifteen." She walked away, then turned. "Make that thirty. It's gonna take a while to get this smell out of my hair."

She disappeared into the bathroom, her stomach tied in knots. Something was wrong, something was *very* wrong. She wanted to hide out in the bathroom, but she'd never been one to run away from problems. It was much better to confront them, get them over with, and move on with her life.

It was odd though, she thought as hot water washed over her, because a couple of weeks ago she'd wanted nothing to do with this man. Now that she had a feeling it was going to end, her heart was breaking.

It took three washings to get her hair smelling normal and two body scrubs to feel clean, but she finally stepped from the shower just as it was turning cold. She dried off, spritzed her body, then brushed her teeth and hair. It had been thirty minutes. She couldn't put off going to the living room any longer.

She came out wearing her favorite flannel pajamas, not trying to seduce Carl. As much as she wanted the relief of some incredible sex, she wasn't going to be pathetic. If this was their last time together she was determined to hold her head high and not let him see how much she was hurting.

Carl was sitting on the couch, an empty beer bottle on the kitchen counter and another almost empty one in his hand. Yep, it was bad. He was using liquid courage.

"Please just tell me. It's obviously something big, and I'd rather receive it straight forward without any pretty little words," she said after grabbing a bottle of wine and a glass. After their trip, she was officially hooked on wine.

She set the bottle on the coffee table, wanting it close to her, then opened it and poured herself a very generous glass before she sat back on the opposite side of the couch, her legs curled beneath her. She held the glass like a shield as she guzzled several big gulps. She was proud of herself for looking him in the eyes.

"I got a new job," he said. She could tell by his expression the job wasn't in SF.

"When do you start?" she asked, taking another long swig of wine.

"I leave Monday morning at 0600 hours. I won't be back to SF for a long time. I'm not sure how long."

Avery felt as if her insides were being ripped apart and there was a physical pain in her chest like she'd been stabbed. She'd never fallen in love before, hadn't realized how much joy, or how much pain, it could bring. Knowing this now might actually make her a better attorney.

She could empathize more easily now that she was going through it.

"I appreciate you telling me and not just disappearing," she said before finishing off her glass of wine. She leaned forward, refilled it to the top of the glass, and sat back again.

"Avery, there's something between us. I know we haven't had a lot of time, but there's something real here. I don't want to let it go," he said. He finished his beer, then stood, moved to the fridge, and grabbed another before coming back to the couch. This time he sat next to her. But her back was to the arm of the couch and her feet were up, creating a shield between them. She was barely keeping it together.

"Yeah, I can't explain it, but there's definitely something here. But life happens, Carl. It's not your fault, it's not mine. We're adults and we have to go where we need to go," she said. Her eyes filled with tears and she madly blinked them back. She was able to, but barely. If she kept talking, she had a feeling the tide would overflow. Once it began, she feared she wouldn't be able to stop.

"When I'm settled, come to me," he said, his eyes lighting as if he hadn't even considered that option before this moment. She opened her mouth to speak, but he held up his hand to stop her. Her throat was so tight with emotion she was grateful to not have to answer right away.

"I'm serious. There's something great between us. Let's not give it up. I'll be settled in a couple of weeks, a month at most. You're starting a new career. Do it in a new place. Sometimes that's the best thing you can do," he added, excitement filling his voice.

She realized he wasn't telling her where he was going. She decided not to ask. She didn't want to know because she knew she'd be tempted to do just as he'd asked. But either way her heart would break. She had to choose between him and her mother. And the bottom line was that her mother had been there her entire life while Carl had been in it only a short time. She couldn't leave her mom — it wasn't an option.

They were silent as he read her body language, read the refusal in her eyes. She knew the moment he was aware she wouldn't go. His shoulders slumped. He finished his beer in a few pulls, set it down, then leaned back against the couch. She drained her glass, the buzz giving her just enough relief to do what she truly wanted to do.

She set down her glass, unwound her legs, then straddled his lap. Their eyes locked, hers filled with sorrow, his with regret and surprise.

"Love me for tonight," she said. She leaned down and kissed him, a whispering of lips that was gentle and filled with pain and love. She was telling him without words what he meant to her. It only took a couple of seconds for his arms to wrap around her, his fingers climbing into her hair as he held her close. They kissed for long, agonizing, beautiful minutes before she leaned back again.

"I want you to make love to me like it's our last time, and then I want to wake up and find you gone. I can't have you here in the morning. I can't take it," she begged.

"Avery, I can't do that," he said.

"Please, I need this. If you have any feelings at all for me, then you'll do this," she said, those damn tears finally filling and spilling over, dripping down her cheeks and over her chin, landing on his shirt.

He reached up, gently wiping them away before cupping her cheek. He didn't say a word, but he nodded. He stood, cradling her in his arms, then moved down the hallway, easily finding her small room.

He moved inside and gently set her on the bed, gazing at her as if he was trying to keep a snapshot in his mind. She did the same with him. She wondered if it was better to know it was your last night with the man you loved, or worse. She was getting a goodbye, but the pain was excruciating.

She sat and watched as he stripped away his clothes, revealing his beautiful body to her in agonizing slowness.

"Oh, you are a masterpiece," she said with a sigh.

He smiled at her, but again, there was no true joy in the expression. "You, my darling, are the masterpiece," he corrected after all of his clothes were off. He pulled her back to her feet and into his arms. He gave her another long, slow, aching kiss before reaching for the buttons on her pajama top. He undid them one by one, the back of his fingers grazing her skin, heating her, waking her up.

He parted the shirt, then pushed it from her shoulders before tracing his hand down her chest, his fingers grazing her nipples, circling back, pinching them, then holding the weight of her breasts in his hands.

"Absolutely breathtaking," he sighed, before bending and taking a hard nipple in his mouth, sucking and licking it until she was putty in his hands.

Then he pushed down her pants, and she kicked them away, sighing with pleasure as he pulled her back to him, nothing between their hot skin now. He kissed her again, this time more urgently. She reached up, holding on tight as her tongue danced with his.

When he pulled back, they were both panting, their eyes dilated, their bodies ready for each other. She looked away, feeling shy as she spoke her next words.

"I'm . . . um . . . I have an IUD if you don't want to . . . um . . . use a condom," she finally stuttered, horrified at how she was speaking. Her entire life depended on the way she communicated.

"I very, very, *very* much don't want to use a condom," he said, pulling her to him again and kissing her harder. She squirmed against him as her sadness dissipated and lust took over. She pushed against his straining erection.

He moved, and the two of them fell onto the bed, their mouths crashing together as their hands caressed each other. She couldn't get enough of him. He ripped his mouth from hers and began moving over her jaw. His tongue swept down to her neck, and he started going lower.

"No!" she said, pulling his face back to hers. "I need you inside me now." She had to have this connection, she had to have it immediately. She didn't want foreplay.

He reclaimed her mouth as he positioned himself between her thighs. And then his kiss slowed as he pushed inside of her, one beautiful inch at a time. She felt tears build again as he moved in and out of her slowly, pulling back all the way, before sinking back deep. He did it over and over again while his lips caressed hers.

The buildup was slow, strong, and mesmerizing. She opened her eyes, and found him looking at her as his mouth whispered over hers. He kept it gentle, moving a little faster, their breaths mingling, their hearts racing as they pressed against each other.

He pushed in and out, and then she fell . . . and fell . . . and fell.

The orgasm rocketed through her at the same time as his. She felt his heat and the strong pumping of his release as her walls clenched around him, their gazes never breaking. He was still moving within her as the floodgate opened, and tears streamed from her eyes.

He bent down and kissed her again as the last of their pleasure floated away. He turned them, still buried within her, but taking his weight away. And then he just held her as she cried out all of her sorrow while lying in his arms.

Eventually she fell asleep, their bodies still entwined, her heart broken.

When she woke up at dawn, he was gone. There was a rose and a note.

I'm not giving up. This is too great to let you go.

That was all. No signature. No other words. She pushed down the hope those two sentences brought her. It was over. She had to accept that.

It was over.

She'd repeat it again and again until she believed it.

She cried herself to sleep once more . . .

Chapter Twenty-Five

Chad walked into the room, looking like a man in charge. He'd done this before, and he had no doubt that first impressions mattered. These men were the best of the best, and if he wanted their respect and loyalty, he needed to earn it.

"Men," Chad said, nodding to each person as he looked them in their eyes one at a time. Each one nodded back at him. So far so good.

"Thank you for being here. I'm Chad Redington. Finally, we're face to face. I'll assume each of you have read your respective packets."

He paused for a moment as the men nodded. "Good. As you can see, we're going to get our hands dirty. Seattle could've kept sinking into a black hole with drugs, murder, and kidnapping, but the criminals screwed up. They messed with the wrong family. And that's what brings us here."

He didn't bring up Joseph's name. It wouldn't take long for them to figure that out, but he liked to see how good these men were. He had no doubt they'd be testing him too. He'd be disappointed if they didn't.

These men were disciplined. They waited as they leaned back in their five-hundred-dollar office chairs. None of them, Chad included, had ever had such a luxurious base of operation. Things were starting off on a very solid note.

Chad continued. "The operation, in terms of technicality, is no different than what each of you have been involved in at some point during the last ten to twenty years. But this goes deeper. As stated previously, this is completely off the books. We don't report to government or military leaders. This is privately funded, and our only oversight is from ourselves and our consciences. That frees us to do what needs to be done to get this scum off the streets."

At those words, the men sat up a bit straighter. He again looked them each in the eye, and they smiled, nodding back at him. None of them liked the proverbial handcuffs that had been tied around them their entire careers.

Chad smiled back before blanking his expression. "Each of you knows how serious this is, especially since we have to weave through those first doors. We're going to slip inside some, kick some down, and do what we all do best in order to crawl our way up to the top of the organization. I don't want you to mistake our hands being untied to being stupid. We all have family, we all have people who count on us. Let's make sure we finish our mission, or possibly multiple missions, and then retire the right way, where we get old and gray, fat, and get to sit on porches with our grandkids."

"I'm not getting old," Eyes said, his smile cocky. Hmm, the first to speak up, Chad thought. He'd been wise in choosing him for a leadership role.

"Alright, before you jokers start in on the fish stories and measuring, let's get the official crap out of the way. Then we get to have some fun." He was between fifteen and twenty years older than these men, but being with them was taking him back to the good old days. They might not think they'd get old, but age was just a number. He could still swing his wife around the dance floor . . . *and* the bedroom.

"Memorize those packets, because they *will* be destroyed. We get rid of all paper trails as soon as possible. That's where Brackish comes in. He'll keep track, and he'll get the correct info into the hands needed when the time is right."

Chad moved on. "Your *official* jobs are as listed in those packets," Chad pointed out, holding up his fingers and wiggling them. "We have an official office for a fictional shell company where your false jobs will be filed. That's how you get your paychecks. We have to keep the government happy, so they know you're still working and paying them your hard-earned money." That elicited a bunch of groans. Chad had yet to meet anyone who liked taxes. Military men hated them more than most. They were fighting for people's freedom while the government continued to hold its hand out for more and more for its pet projects a lot of citizens didn't want to participate in but had zero choice in the matter.

"Something's wrong, Chad," Sleep interjected while papers lay scattered before him.

"What is it?" Chad asked.

"Well, it's kind of embarrassing," Sleep began. He kept his face pointed at the papers as if he was looking for something. "I see my beneficiary, and see my bank accounts, and then this crap over on this line, but I peeked over at Eyes's paperwork, and it's clear I'm not the beneficiary on it. There's a mistake because this sorry loser has no other friends. I figure since Eyes is such a pain in the ass, these other men you've pulled into this have to be just as burly, having no friends, either." He dramatically swept a palm face up, showcasing each man at the table.

Chad waited, knowing there was more — and he wasn't wrong.

"I haven't saved a dime in all my years working, since the government takes half and the rest goes to hookers and whiskey. I want to make sure my retirement plan is in place before we head on out into the big bad world." A huge grin overtook his features as he attempted to innocently bat his eyes — he wasn't pulling it off.

"Shit, Sleep, everyone here knows I'll live at least forty years longer than you," Eyes replied with a grin, then slapped his friend hard enough on the back to send most people sprawling. Sleep didn't move an inch, and didn't flinch, though the sting was felt all around the table.

"I'll get on that right away, Sleep. HR will be notified, and the paperwork changed," Chad told him. He was grateful he'd gotten the two friends involved in the project. They'd make a great icebreaker for the rest of the team. Men who liked each other were stronger and smarter.

"Don't worry, Sleep, I'll make sure that work is done just right," Brackish said with a wink that had a chuckle exploding from the whole table.

"Never mind. I take it all back," Sleep quickly said, holding up his hands in surrender. They'd each read one another's profiles, and all of them knew Brackish could erase them in a matter of seconds if he chose to. Sleep's quick retreat caused another round of laughter.

"Alright, alright, let's get this show on the road," Chad said. He wanted the men to bond, so he wasn't going to reel them in too much on this first meeting. But they did have a lot to get through. They were still relaxed, a lot more relaxed than when he'd first entered, but they were also paying attention. Good.

"As you can see, this conference room will be our main operating center. The sixteen monitors on the wall at the end of the table will be our eyes when we're not in the field. The glass board on the wall behind Eyes and Sleep connects to the computer system. It will show us anything Brackish wants to feed to it from the servers, or to be honest, from anywhere he damn well feels like pulling something." Steve smiled, and the other men gave him a thumbs up.

"The white board behind me is for quick updates and brainstorming sessions. Above my head is a screen that comes down if we use the projector. Smoke, Brackish, and Green, behind you is the cork board to hold photos, newspaper info, and other vital information."

"I thought we burned everything," Green said with his cocky little grin. Oh, he was going to be a lot of fun to mess with. Chad was sure he was used to it, but this was a whole new world, and he was the little boy on the block. He might be lean, but Chad was aware of the power of this kid. He'd read up on what he'd done.

"Green, you're playing with the big boys now," Chad said. "Pay attention."

"I can answer this one," Brackish said, interrupting.

"Be my guest," Chad told him, stepping back as Brackish stood. He looked around the room and grinned.

"We all had to use our thumb to get into this facility from a secret pad that the average person wouldn't notice. Of course, that made me immediately look around as I've created many of those devices. If you look into the corners of the room, and in a few nooks and crannies, you'll see little boxes. Those are explosives. It's virtually impossible to get into this center, but if the impossible happens, and it's breached, and a code isn't entered within sixty seconds, this place will be no more. There won't be time for the intruders to gather anything and make it back out before the building and all that's inside it goes up in flames."

"What if someone managed to capture one of the team and come in with them?" Smoke asked as he laughed. He didn't think that was possible, but it was a good question.

"Did you notice the hallway was an exact ten-foot box?" Brackish asked.

Tyrell, aka, Smoke, shook his head, obviously annoyed with himself for not being more alert. He'd known he was on friendly ground, so he hadn't been watching as much as he should've been.

"That was a body scanner. Let me suggest you don't get captured, because if someone pushes their way in with you, nobody is coming back out, therefore, to answer your question, whatever is on that bulletin board will be burned . . . in one way or another, just don't get burned with it," Brackish finished.

The men's smiles never faltered. They were far too confident to believe they'd ever be captured. And if that *were* to happen it would end in death. Sure, they might die, but not before they caused a hell of a lot of pain to the other side.

"I was wondering how long it was going to take you to say something," Chad said, not showing Brackish how impressed he was.

"I figured out this place in less than a minute," Brackish bragged.

"Brainiac," Green muttered, but the grin he wore showed no ill will.

"This is the beginning, men," Chad said, taking back control. "Anything you want, or need, is at your fingertips. Let's make sure we don't take advantage of that. I know if you suddenly want twenty AKs, and ten thousand rounds of ammo, you're probably planning a boys' weekend, which is fun, but not on our benefactor's dime. Now, saying that, if you're busting your asses and getting things done, this benefactor will reward you in more ways than you can imagine, so you just might receive an order for something like that out of the blue."

Green's eyes glazed a bit at the thought of that much ammo and unlimited shooting time. Chad chuckled. He had a feeling he was really going to love this mission.

"Hey, Eyes, ask for that one-armed, one-legged hooker you got all hot and bothered for when we were in Djibouti," Sleep said.

The table busted up.

"Nothing wrong with a one-armed, one-legged hooker," Green said as he stood and thrust his hips back and forth with one hand behind his head. "There's just more room for the thrust."

Smoke chucked a paper wad dead center on Green's nose. "Nobody wants to see your hips moving, little boy. Leave the thrusting to the men with the right equipment who *know* how to use it."

"Oh, I know how to use it," Green assured the group. "And I have plenty of satisfied customers."

"Aren't the fairy tales supposed to start later?" Eyes asked through his laughter. "Cause that's about the biggest fish story I've *ever* heard."

Chad kept on going as if nothing had been said. "There's a gym here and a weight room." He stopped and looked at Smoke. "I think we stacked it high enough to even satisfy you," he added with a wink. Smoke grinned, looking as if he wanted to jump up right then and there and test Chad's theory. Chad knew for a fact he'd stacked those plates high enough. Smoke was a beast, and if he didn't burn energy someone in the world was going to pay for it.

"We also have a gourmet kitchen that I have a feeling will never get used," Chad said.

"Really?" Green asked, perking up. "Will it be stocked?"

Chad hadn't been expecting to get surprised, but he was. "I have some basics in there, but make a list and I'll have whatever you want brought in."

"Do you cook?" Sleep asked, suddenly very interested. Chad hid a smile. These men were confirmed bachelors, though that might be changing in Sleep's case if Chad's sources were correct — and they were *always* correct. But the other men were definitely bachelors, and a home-cooked meal was the epitome of happiness to them. Otherwise they lived on takeout or poorly cooked selections they tended to throw away before giving up and ordering pizza.

"Hell yeah, I cook," Green said. "My father was a loser, my mom worthless. I had siblings, so I learned to cook really well."

Chad wasn't surprised it was Green who was the first to open up with some honesty, even if he was doing it in a cocky way. These men had to be willing to die for each other, and that required trust and walls coming down. It wasn't an easy thing to do.

"Sweet," Eyes said. "I don't mind some good food, not one little bit, especially if there's a gym to burn it all off."

"I'll make a list," Green said, grabbing a piece of paper.

"You're writing it down. Why not use the iPad?" Brackish asked as if paper and pen was a foreign thing to him. It might just be.

"I like making lists. I get sick of electronics," Green said.

Brackish flew back in his seat as if he'd been shot. "Be still my heart, take the words back," he said in a dramatic voice.

The team once again laughed.

"We also have a shooting range, though it's not going to be nearly good enough for you, Green, so that's something I'm working on," Chad continued. This team was bonding much sooner than he'd expected. Maybe they had been waiting for this type of mission. Maybe they'd found themselves.

Green was busy making his list, so he didn't look up to notice the respect showing in his team members' eyes. He was a skilled marksman, his longest kill at just over twenty-five hundred yards. It was an impossible shot — unless you were Green.

"There are intercoms throughout the building, and nobody but Brackish could possibly break into them from the outside. Your rooms are on the top floor, and you all have more than enough space. It won't be anything like the bases we've all slept on, in, and around. There are times we'll be here a lot, but times we'll barely pass through. When we're here, I want it comfortable."

Chad looked over at Eyes who was sizing up the entire team, analyzing them and the space. He'd have them all figured out within a week, knowing their strengths and weaknesses. He'd be the leader, hands down, and he'd have the team's respect.

"Does anyone have any questions or comments?" Chad asked. Eyes immediately stood. Even Green stopped writing and paid attention. Good. Very good.

"We've been here a couple of hours already, and from what I see, we all have unique skills. You've assembled a fine team. We've read your reports, but what I'd like to hear more about is your strategy," Eyes said.

"We'll get to that," Chad said. "Very soon. For now, the mission is for you to get to know each other, to be comfortable with your teammates and this facility. You can come in and out this week, but make sure nothing inside these walls leaves unless it's for mission purposes. Make sure you don't use call signs when not on a mission. You will be living two lives from this point forward. You'll have two identities, two different job titles, and two different residences. I know each of you can handle that. If you couldn't you wouldn't have been invited in. This week, the mission is to bond. Now, let's get out of the conference room and look at the facility."

Chad stood, and the rest of the team came to attention. He looked at them and smiled. "Have at it. This is your place now. Nothing is off limits."

With that, the men exited the room. Chad had no doubt that within an hour, two at most, these men would know routes to escape the building, know every nook and cranny to check for security, and be prepared for outright war if it came knocking. There was a fight headed their way, and they'd be more than ready for it.

Each room was stocked with all types of clothes they'd need from luxury suits, to jeans and polos, to sweats and tanks. They had all of the essentials and several luxury items. But Chad could tell this team couldn't care less about any of that. What they cared about was doing the best damn job they were capable of — and that was pretty much everything. They had secure phones, secure computers, and unbreakable software — well, unless it was Brackish breaking in.

Chad ended their first day together by leaving another packet with a bit more information then headed out. It had been a very long week — a very long week indeed. He wanted nothing more than to sit on his back deck with his wife cradled in his arms and a cold beer beside him.

He'd have more action than he could stand soon enough. He was taking the quiet moments when he could to appreciate the life he was so blessed to have with a woman he'd do anything for. He got into his car and hit the gas. It was time to head home.

Chapter Twenty-Six

Avery was shell-shocked as she stood in the hospital room with her mother. There were no words to express how she was feeling. This had been the worst possible week of her life, and it kept falling further and further into an abyss she was sure she'd never be able to climb out of.

"Oh, Sweetie, it will be okay," her mother said as she pulled her in tight and hugged her. They sobbed out their pain together.

The doctors and nurses had departed fifteen minutes earlier, apologizing for their loss and offering to make calls or send them anything they needed. They hadn't been able to say a word.

Avery let go of Bobbi and turned, facing the bed where her uncle lay so very still. They'd removed the tube they'd used to try to resuscitate him. None of their efforts had worked. He was gone. She couldn't believe it. This man, this larger-than-life man who'd been her hero, had been stolen from her.

She walked over to the bed and sat on the edge, lifting her hand and trailing it down his cheek. He still felt warm. He was a bit bruised, but he looked as if he was simply taking a nap. She so desperately wanted him to open his eyes, look at her, and tell her this had been nothing more than a nightmare.

But he didn't do that. She moved her hand to his chest, pressing her palm against it, praying the doctors were wrong, praying for a miracle, praying she'd feel the steady thump of his heart signaling that he was still alive, that he'd live another thirty years so he could make her laugh and hold her when she cried.

But his chest didn't move. His heart didn't beat, and oxygen didn't fill his lungs. She leaned down, pressing her forehead to his as her tears dripped down on him. She shook as her sobs broke free.

"He's no longer in pain, sweetie. We're in pain because we didn't want to set him free, but we can't be selfish. We couldn't expect him to keep hanging on just for us. He was hurting every single day, but he stayed for us. You did the right thing by telling him we were okay, that we loved him. You might be his niece, but I assure you, in his heart you *were* his daughter. Love him like a father, and be glad for him that he's no longer hurting, that he's up in heaven playing his guitar with the greats."

Her mother stopped as her own sobs ripped from her. She kept one hand on Avery's shoulder and the other on her brother's chest, her fingers twining with Avery's. They stayed that way for a very long time as they cried out their grief and said their final goodbyes.

When they could manage it, when they finally accepted that it was just his shell lying on that bed, that it was no longer their beloved family member, they got up together and walked from the hospital room, arm in arm. They didn't say a word as they exited, both of them needing to inhale fresh air. They'd been in the hospital for the past twenty-four hours, and it had become a prison.

Once they stepped outside, Bobbi reached into her purse and pulled out a pack of cigarettes. Avery was shocked when she lit up. Bobbi sent a grimace her way.

"I know, I know. I don't smoke all of the time, but I'm going to give myself a break right now," Bobbi said with a frown.

Avery's shoulders sagged. She wasn't going to lecture her mother, not after what the two of them had just gone through. But she had to say something. "I can't lose you too, Mom. That's all I'm going to say."

Bobbi took a few more drags, then looked at Avery and let out a sigh as she moved over to a receptacle and stubbed out the cigarette. Then she pulled the pack from her purse and tossed the package away.

Avery rushed to her mother and gave her a hug. "Thank you, Mama, thank you for loving me enough to stay healthy. I couldn't handle losing you. I'd break into a million pieces and never be the same again."

She wholeheartedly meant her words.

"I know, baby girl, I know," Bobbi said.

They began walking away from the hospital, not caring about their destination. They didn't want to be in a cab, and they didn't want to be indoors, so they needed to walk.

"I don't know what to do next," Bobbi said after they moved along in silence for a solid twenty minutes.

"We're moving away from this city," Avery said.

Her mother stopped and looked at her. "What do you mean we're moving? This is our home."

"We have nothing left here, Mom. And I don't want to be in that bar without him. I don't want to be in this city anymore. There's so much pain. We need a fresh start."

"Is this about Carl? Why don't you just call him?" her mother asked. It was good for both of them to talk about anything other than her uncle, to focus on anything other than death.

"That's over, and this decision has nothing to do with Carl. He's in my past now," Avery assured her mom.

"Baby, it's only been a week, and he's tried to call you so many times already we've both lost count," Bobbi pointed out.

"I won't do long distance, and besides, I don't even know where he is. For all I know he's back in the military and already halfway around the world," Avery said.

"I don't think so. He wouldn't be calling you if that were the case."

"Well, it doesn't matter anyway. It was beautiful, and amazing, and it made me realize love isn't a myth. But it *won't* work. So I'm moving on with my life. I won't try to erase him, I'll just try to appreciate what we had, and possibly in the future try to find something that resembles it," Avery said.

"Honey, a love like that is once in a lifetime," her mother said. "Trust me, I know."

The utter sadness in her mom's voice broke Avery's heart. She wrapped her mom's arm in hers and they continued to walk.

"Yesterday I got a job offer to be a prosecutor in Seattle. It pays far less than I was making here, but considering I have zero prosecutor experience, I figure I can't be that choosy. And I like Seattle. I love all of the islands, and I love that it's still out west without being in California. Please, Mom, please let's go. I won't go without you, and I want a do-over," Avery pled.

Her mother looked at her, obviously wavering as she considered her choices. Avery decided to push a little more.

"Uncle Tom left you everything, his bar, which you know Emilio is begging to buy, and his life insurance policy, which is more than enough for all four years of school for you if you want a degree. It's more than enough to make you comfortable for a long time. And that's without me helping, which I'm more than happy to do. Let's move to the outskirts of Seattle. We won't stay in the city this time. Let's find a nice small town and live a good life."

Bobbi smiled at her, and Avery felt some of her pain lift. It would be a very long time before she was whole again, but a new start in a new place would take her quite a way down the road to recovery.

"You know what, you're absolutely right. Let's do this. There's nothing holding us here. Neither of us owns a place, and the bar can be sold fast. We *can* leave. I don't know why I was so set against it," Bobbi finished.

"Because we're both stubborn as hell," Avery said with a tearful smile.

"That we are. Maybe I can even get you to call that man of yours and see if you two can work out a compromise," Bobbi said as they continued walking, enjoying the fresh air. Now that their time in SF was limited, they wanted to soak it up and say goodbye to it all.

It took them a couple of hours to make it home. Avery stayed with her mother that night. They had a lot of planning ahead of them, but for now they needed to grieve. Tomorrow was a new day. Within a month, they'd have a whole new reality.

Maybe, just maybe, Avery could forget about Carl. She wasn't sure that was possible as she dreamt of him every single night, but for the sake of her broken heart, she hoped she could.

She closed her eyes and woke up with tears streaming down her cheeks. This time her dreams were filled with her uncle holding her as he'd done when she was a child, telling her to follow her heart, telling her he was fine, and he needed to know she was as well.

His final words had been to not allow love to escape like he had . . .

Chapter Twenty-Seven

The sun was just rising in the sky as Chad turned onto the unmarked driveway out in the middle of nowhere. He began the long drive to the bunker as his clock clicked over to 0600. It had been a week since he'd left his men to bond, to find their footing, and to ensure they wanted to be there. It had been tough to not check on them, super hard to not call, and almost impossible not to sign in to the videos and see what was happening.

But he'd managed it.

When he made a sharp turn on the road, he was met with the sight of all five of his men jogging just ahead of him. They were in formation, looking like a team that had been together for years instead of days.

He slowed and watched. They knew someone was there, but they also knew it was him, not a stranger. He wondered if they'd spotted him from the road. They had to have. He was either losing his spotting ability that he'd missed them at the turnoff — or his team was just that stealthy.

Green was in the back of the line. He pulled out, sprinted to the front, fell back into formation, and set a new pace for the other members. After about sixty seconds, Brackish, who was in the rear, pulled out, and sprinted to the front, slipping into the lead position, and setting another new pace.

Smoke was next in line. Exactly sixty seconds later, he stepped out, and Chad realized why his call sign was smoke. He had to have left skid marks in the gravel, his feet moved so quickly. He was in front of the line in about one-point-two seconds. Chad was driving twenty-four miles an hour and Smoke would've run circles around him at that speed. He set the new pace, a bit faster than the old one. They were probably praying for the next runner to move forward — if Eyes could even pass them.

Smoke's chart had said he was fast, but holy hell, that was roadrunner fast. Unless you were witnessing speed like that, you had no clue what fast truly meant.

Eyes pulled out next, and, in seconds, it was clear the injury that had sent him packing from the military was still a bit of a problem — not enough to prevent him from doing this job well, but enough that a man like him would be furious at even the slightest limitation. Chad was told that Eyes didn't complain — not ever, but Chad had no doubt Eyes was feeling pain as he sped to the front of the running line, took his place, then slowed the group down.

Chad knew all about the damage too many soldiers suffered, especially now that the veterans facility was up and running. The bone and muscle damage Eyes had suffered after being shot wasn't able to fully heal, and certainly not enough to give him the same level of fitness he'd had before the event. Chad was amazed the man was still jogging. But then again, men like Eyes pushed past the pain. He wouldn't stop unless his leg literally fell out from beneath him — which *was* a possibility.

Chad passed the group, who all lifted their arms, but continued running. He watched in his rearview mirror as Sleep took his turn from last to first. The light was still bad, but Chad caught a glint in his mirror. He squinted as he tried to figure out what was happening.

And then Chad laughed aloud as he heard Sleep yelling. He was wearing a smile as he passed each team member, giving them a hard slap on the ass as if he was a football coach.

"Good game!"
"Nice step!"
"Try again!"
"Seahawks suck, Cowboys rule!"

Each slap was accompanied by a little hop and skip from Sleep as if he was just as surprised by the slap as his team members were. But Chad had a feeling this wasn't the first round of mischief from Sleep as he heard groans and curses echo through the night air from the four men he was slapping.

Chad was still chuckling as he turned another corner and lost sight of the men. Their voices faded as he picked up speed. He wouldn't mind parking and joining in on their morning run, even though he'd already run ten miles that morning. He refused to get soft, especially working with men like this.

He pulled up to their building and Chad gathered his securely locked briefcase, then went through the security measures to enter, and after several minutes, stepped through and made his way to the conference room.

The motion activated lights turned on and he set his briefcase down. He looked around the room, noting that this was most likely the last time this place would be so sterile . . . and empty — or at least the last time until *this* mission was complete.

Soon the monitors would be on, the white boards filled with information, and the men walking in and out. They'd add more people to their team, more analysts, more data driven people, and hopefully, more undercover operatives. He wanted this to grow. He wanted this mission completed, and then he wanted to keep going. He envisioned an America that was peaceful, a place where the good guys always won.

He, in no way, wanted to take away free choice or people's rights. He just wanted the scum of the earth to evaporate. Word quickly got around in the criminal world, and if his team did their job right, he had no doubt he'd chase these people back into the holes they'd crawled from.

He was restless in the building all alone. He'd done it for a week straight before his team had arrived, but now it felt different. He moved to the kitchen and fired up the Keurig, filling a cup to the brim and taking a long swallow of the hot, black liquid. Then he moved back to the conference room.

Between 0623 and 0626, the team entered the room, each freshly showered and holding donuts and coffee. He'd missed the donuts. Sleep was the last one in, and he carried a large box, setting it on the table. It was loaded with sugary deliciousness. Chad didn't hesitate to reach in and pull out a maple bar.

He appreciated a team that knew how to be on time. He appreciated it more when they were early, even if it was only by minutes.

"Good morning," Chad said as they circled the table, each taking the exact same seat they'd held the first day they'd met. "How has your week gone?"

Eyes was the first to speak. "We've gotten a lot accomplished. We've been scouting the territory and like what we're seeing. It would be very difficult for someone to spot this place except from the sky, but we ran the mountain two days ago and were higher than the building; it's been cleverly disguised so unless a pilot knew what he was looking for, he wouldn't even glance at this space."

Chad smiled. They were correct. Even where they parked was hidden from the sky. This operation was all about being stealthy. If they couldn't manage to hide themselves, how were they expected to infiltrate anything?

"How was your week, boss?" Smoke asked, leaning back in his chair as he devoured what appeared to be his third donut in the past few minutes. The man was fit as hell, so Chad didn't think a hundred donuts stood a chance in his system. They'd burn up going down his massive throat.

"It's been good, but call me Chad," he said. He couldn't stand the term *boss*. It was ridiculous. The men nodded. Respect was ingrained in each of them. That was a very good thing.

Chad hit a button, and at each seat a piece of the table opened, computers popping up.

"Now, *that's* bad ass," Green said as he gazed at the computer, then bent and glanced underneath the table as he looked for levers. They were built in. He wouldn't find them.

"Ah, it's old technology," Brackish said with a wave of his hand. "Seen it, done it."

Chad was sure there was nothing much that could impress Brackish when it came to electronics, but he decided it would be his mission to find a way to shock the man, even if it took years.

"Let's get started. Fire up the computers. When they wake, open your respective files. Your individual missions are loaded."

Chad consumed his coffee while the computers woke. They might seem slow, but they were moving at the speed of light, they were just scanning every conceivable hack attempt before they unlocked.

Chad was excited, *very* excited. This was the first official day of operations. They were going to find the person responsible for his second mom getting attacked. All who were involved would definitely pay — and it wouldn't be gentle. Taking down the entire empire was sweet, sweet icing on top.

Chad finished his coffee, disappointed the delicious brew was gone so soon. He might have time for a refill. Before he could get up, Smoke spoke up again.

"With the way you drink coffee, I'm thinking your call sign is Chug." He leaned back with a wide smile.

"Chhuugggg," Sleep said, drawing out the word and slapping his fist on the table.

"I like it," Green said.

"Chug, Chug, Chug. Chug," Brackish chanted like they were at a freaking frat party.

These men really were overgrown teens. Of course, Chad's team had been the exact same way when he'd been on an elite SEAL team.

There wasn't a chance of escaping a call sign once a team gave it to you, so Chad went with it, shrugging as he rolled his eyes. He couldn't stop his grin though. He loved enthusiasm. He continued speaking as if the last minute hadn't just happened.

"I don't like wasting time on useless tasks," he told the team. "So we won't be sitting around talking about the things we'd like to do, nor will we be gathering copious amounts of information and sifting through files for hours. This team has been built for action, for speed, and to bring people to the light to answer for the destruction of their fellow brothers and sisters in a community that deserves to be protected."

"Hell yeah, I've never been a bookworm," Sleep said. Chad didn't correct him, but he knew Sleep had a high IQ. The entire team had IQ's that were border line genius, they just acted like mouth breathing knuckle draggers most of the time because it was an easy ploy to throw people off of what was under the surface.

Chad continued. "This mission truly hits home for me for a number of reasons. I'll share need-to-know info at a later time, but just know that I'm with you one-hundred percent from beginning to end. I'll either be here, be in contact with you, or be within range every single day."

"No days off, Chug?" Green asked.

"No," Chad replied. "We don't have days off, we don't have vacations, we don't take breaks. However, saying that, you're undercover, which means your life is one big day off." These men were like most soldiers. Bullets could be flying and they'd be cracking jokes as if they were at the beach, sipping on margaritas. Their hardest day felt like a day off.

"Brackish," Chad said as he looked at their tech guy. "Your mission today is to go through each piece of technology in this space. I want you to start in the server room, and then go through everything that has a blinking light. Here's a list of equipment," he said, handing it over.

"Do you think there's a breach?" Brackish asked, excitement lighting his eyes. He was hoping for a problem because he had no doubt he'd not only be able to fix it, but go after anyone who came even close.

"No, I don't think you'll find a thing, but this will be a routine task. As good as you are, there are others just as hungry out there. Maybe they're good too, and they just haven't been found," Chad told him.

Brackish scoffed. "Not a chance," he said, his lips turned up in a cocky smile, not even remotely worried. "But I'm on it anyway,

Chug. By the way, here's my list," he added, handing over a two page list of groceries, and a list of some needed electronic components.

Chad looked at the list and laughed, at first softly then full-bellied. The rest of the team looked quizzically at him as they waited to find out what was happening. Brackish didn't lose the cocky grin.

"I should've known you already had your assignment," Chad said when his laughter stopped. Brackish pulled out an identical copy of Chad's list . . . from his top-secret server.

"You have a new assignment," Chad said. "Secure my computer so even *you* can't get into it."

Brackish's eyes widened and he rubbed his hands together. "Now, *that's* an assignment," he said, utter delight flashing in his eyes.

"I'm glad to bring you joy," Chad said with a roll of his eyes. It was going to be difficult to stimulate this team member. He was going to have to put some real effort into it.

"Now that we worked through that," Chad said before focusing on Eyes, then Sleep, then Smoke. "You three will make your way through the areas where we know drug use is the highest. I want you to go from South Park to Rainer Beach to Othello, Beacon Hill, and then Yesler. You'll have no problem finding people to talk to if you blend in. This is an info-gathering mission — not a takedown. I want names. I want ringleaders. I want information. And I *want* something to sink my teeth into."

"I like my mission," Smoke said. "Do I get to smoke a doobie?"

Eyes and Sleep chuckled. Chad rolled his eyes knowing that he used the word *doobie* as a nod to the slang for the older generation, which Chad was put into.

"Why don't you keep yourselves safe, and if you do buy drugs, store them for analysis. Also, if you get caught purchasing drugs, you're a citizen. We'll get you out, but your names are your names, and it'll go into the system until we can clean it out," he added.

"Yeah, that'll take me two point three seconds," Brackish said. "Police computers are the biggest joke known to man."

"Nice," Sleep said, fist bumping Brackish. "Guess I can break any laws I want since it will all just disappear anyway."

Chad tried to keep his smile away as he sent a firm stare at Sleep. "We won't be clearing any records of stupidity, *only* if you're caught while on assignment."

"Ah, you're no fun. I guess that hooker and cocaine night is off limits," Sleep said with a sigh.

It only happened for a moment, but Chad saw the look of pain flash through Sleep's eyes. He covered it quickly with another joke that made their team laugh. Chad wondered how long it was going to take before Sleep went after the girl he'd left behind. He had a feeling it wasn't going to be long at all. They might just have their first team wedding. He wondered if Avery would be able to handle the men. Though she wouldn't know what they really were, she'd definitely know them.

These guys wouldn't just work together, they'd become best friends, leaning on each other for everything, standing in at weddings, becoming godparents, and standing by each others sides at funerals. They'd be closer than blood. They'd be brothers.

Chad had a feeling Avery was just the girl for Carl, aka, Sleep. He had a feeling she wasn't only strong enough, but loving enough to handle the isolation a career like this could bring to a spouse.

Chad looked next at Smoke. "You'll also have some time in Holly Park. We'll disguise you with some facial alterations and fake tats of IGC and BNC, and I'm not kidding here. If it gets sketchy you get the hell out. We'll put on another disguise at a different time and try again later. Don't be a hero. I know that's impossible for you to comprehend, but we need you alive and working, not a hero and dead."

Smoke and Chad stared each other down for several moments, until finally Smoke nodded. That was good enough for Chad. If they didn't take each other at their word, then they weren't a team.

"Green," Chad said, bringing his youngest member to attention. "I've set you up to immediately start working at Fork Creek Shipping. This company is on Harbor Island. They touch nearly every container that comes into Seattle. This is a key position."

Chad pulled out a thick packet of papers and tossed it to Green. "Here's a breakdown of the company, your position, your business history, and the players we've flagged. Some are lower rung, and some are at the top. We have zero doubt that a majority of the drug transportation is coming in through the port. What we need you there for is the how, what, where, when, and who."

"On it, Chug," Green said. Chad couldn't tell if the man was happy or not about his assignment. It might take him a bit of time to read Green. He gladly accepted the challenge.

"In the locker to the left are two duffels, Green. Grab those."

Green set the heavy bags on the table.

"Have at them," Chad said.

Green opened the bags, then whistled. The smell of money washed through the room. The men barely blinked at the staggering amount of cash sitting in front of them. Impressive, Chad thought.

"This is your petty cash," Chad stated. "Use it for whatever is needed on a day to day basis. There's one and a half mil in unmarked bills. There's no accounting, no receipts, and no tracking of any kind on this money. Use as needed for any part of your mission."

Still, the men barely blinked. It was as if there was nothing more than a box of ones sitting in front of them. Chad was used to a world filled with money, but there had been a time when he hadn't known where his next meal was coming from. He wondered how he would've reacted seeing over a million dollars in cash sitting in front of him when money had been scarce. He realized he'd most likely have had the same reaction as this group of men.

"Okay then, we're coming to a close. The most important aspects of the beginning of this mission is to gather and validate information. We don't track our activities, but we do track the criminals. If drugs are purchased or sold, note the date, the time, the place, the price, and of course, the person. You'll be given fake names, so dig deeper. Find the real names, and find out who they interact with and where they go. And we'll test all drugs, so records are important. We can trace them through formulas."

"Easy to do, Chug. I'll have multiple secure, and most certainly unbreakable, sites by lunch," Brackish said. Chad had a feeling

Brackish was only half in the meeting. He figured the other half of his brain was already building those accounts, so as soon as the meeting adjourned, all he'd have to do was type some numbers into his computer.

"Hey, Chug, quick question," Sleep said.

Chad sighed, barely stopping himself from rolling his eyes. He knew something was coming. "Yes?" he said. But when he looked at Sleep again, he realized the man wasn't joking — possibly for the first time since he'd met him. "What is it?" he asked, his tone changing.

"I know we all agreed to be here for the same reasons. We want to work for the people of this beautiful area. We need to get a job done, and we need to save this country. Like each man sitting at this table, I'll complete my mission. I'll go to the end whether that's with a satisfying conclusion or with a bullet to my head . . . But the question I have . . ." He paused as he hung his head. He seemed to be in deep thought. Chad's eyes narrowed. It was too much. He'd been right in the beginning. This man just couldn't remain serious for too long. He didn't try to stop what was coming though.

Sleep looked up. "Do you think you can find that hooker from Djibouti that Eyes wanted to marry? His life has never been the same since."

"Mother Fu—" Eyes's response was cut off by an elbow to the ribs by Sleep, taking his breath away. "Really?" Eyes said, his glare lethal. "Twice! That's twice in a row, Sleep. Payback will hurt and you won't know when it's coming. I can promise you *that*."

The entire table burst into laughter, including Chad. If you couldn't beat them, then you had to join them. Smoke spit something green out. What in the hell was in that cup he was drinking from? Chad might not want to know. The ugly goo on the table made the team laugh that much harder as Brackish quickly scooted backward before he was covered in slime.

After a few seconds, Eyes shrugged, and joined in the laughter. He loved Sleep even if he wanted to gut punch him on occasion. He'd rather have a friend who was a pain in the ass than one he didn't trust or one he grew bored with.

None of these team members had a problem with their funny bone. That would make their darkest days find some light. It was essential in their line of work.

As he sat with these men who were forming a strong bond, he couldn't help but look back at his own youth. He'd made some close friends that, to this day, he'd die for. Mark Anderson was his best example of a lasting bond. They were brothers even if not by blood.

Who the hell cared about blood? Who the hell cared about color? Who the hell cared about anything other than love and loyalty? He glanced around the table as the team flicked each other crap, and was proud of what was happening. The men had been put through hell on earth with their teams. They'd taken bullets for others — and they'd do it again without hesitation. None of them cared about color, race, or religion. They were brothers. That was it. It was just that simple. They all bled red, and they'd all give their blood to save another.

The group settled down and Eyes looked at Chad. "We're gonna need different rigs. The black SUVs will blow our cover quicker than a Vegas hooker on a Friday night."

"Easy. Tell me what you want and they'll be here by the end of the day."

"I'll need, at most, a few hours with them," Brackish said. "They'll be equipped with hidden GPS, video, audio, and a few extra bells and whistles you can try to find." He was easier to please than Chad had realized — just give him new toys and he was smiling.

"You geek," Sleep said, but the words were spoken as he fist bumped Brackish.

"Bad ass, man," Smoke added, giving his own bump. Then he turned to the team. "Make sure it's tall. I'd rather ride around in a minivan, than try to fold myself like a pretzel into a flipping compact."

"Why don't you take charge of picking the cars?" Eyes said to Smoke.

"Make sure they're a bit beat up," Sleep said. "Anything yuppie will get us robbed, and anything nice will get us carjacked, blow our covers, or both."

"They can be old, but the engines need to be top of the line. The last thing we need is a breakdown in the middle of a bad situation. Protect the radiator with bulletproofing," Eyes added.

A few more comments were made, and then they were done. Chad stood up, and his team rose with him.

Respect.

He absolutely loved the respect.

"Meeting adjourned. Time to get started," Chad announced. "I'll check in daily, but unless something significant happens, we'll all come together in another week."

He walked from the room, pleased when he heard the men talking and planning, excitement clear in their tones. He knew things were going to go extremely well. He slipped into his private office and made a few calls, arranging for the items the men needed.

When he was done he slipped out the door, very aware the men would know of his movements. His job for the day was done — at least with the men. His job for the project wouldn't be finished until the drug ring was shut down.

It was only just beginning, but it was taking off with a great big bang.

Chapter Twenty-Eight

It had taken exactly thirty days for Avery and her mother to pack up their lives, get into a moving van, and hit the I-5 freeway that would lead them straight to Seattle. In that long month, a single day hadn't passed that Carl hadn't tried calling her. She'd nearly caved several times and picked up the phone.

But for the sake of her mental health, and her broken heart, she hadn't been able to answer. The job offer she'd received had held strong even when she told them it would be at least a month before she could start.

It was a small firm on an island outside of Seattle called Gig Harbor. She was excited. She absolutely loved that she wasn't going to have to deal with traffic, that she could walk outside in the middle of the night if she wanted, and that she could even get a dog. Oh, the novelty of having a pet for the first time in her life.

Once the idea of a pet came to mind, she hadn't been able to push it away. She'd been to the shelter three times in a month, sweet little brown eyes gazing at her from kennels, begging her to take them home. She hadn't allowed herself to take one. She couldn't stand it when people made rash decisions, got an animal, then decided a month or two later it was simply too much work and the pet that had bonded with them was now a nuisance.

She looked over at the seat next to her and smiled. Her mother was gazing out the window as they crossed the border into Oregon. Her sweet new baby, Cynder, sitting on her mother's lap. Yep, her last visit to the shelter, just two days earlier had been her breaking point.

There was a litter of eight-week-old French bulldogs curled up together in the kennel. A sweet, pure black little girl had looked up when she'd stopped in front of the cage. The pup slowly walked over, her head down, her eyes looking up. She'd come to the door, and Avery had knelt down and placed her hand there. The tiny thing had given a little whimper and licked her hand.

The other puppies had all been claimed, so there was no way Avery could leave her in there feeling abandoned. She'd picked her up, and Cynder had licked her chin then cuddled into her chest and fell asleep. It had been all over after that. She'd walked to the office, filled out the paperwork, and spent the entire afternoon at the shelter playing with, and holding, Cynder. She wasn't leaving until she was approved so she could take her baby home.

She hadn't wanted to take a chance of losing her.

They hadn't been apart for a single minute since then. Yep, she was that annoying pet owner she'd once rolled her eyes at, letting her dog sleep in her bed. She curled up right behind her neck, and Avery would swear her puppy purred.

She'd called her mother from the shelter, and her mom had met her there. They'd left, heading straight to Pet Smart, and Avery had practically bought out the store. Cynder had a pink bed, a purple bed, and a princess shaped domed bed. She'd have multiple rooms in her home, so she needed comfortable places for Cynder to sleep when Avery was working or doing things around the house.

She'd also bought doggie stairs, so Cynder could climb up into Avery's bed, then wiped out a shelf of doggie toys and chewies. She'd researched the best food and picked up a few bags, just in case they didn't have what she needed in Seattle and she'd have to order more online. She didn't want to take a chance of running out. She'd even gotten her sweet little food dishes that had princess crowns printed on them.

Her favorite purchase had been the pretty pink harness with a matching leash. She planned to walk Cynder morning, noon, and night. She was hoping the smaller firm she was going to work for was pet friendly, because she planned on sneaking Cynder inside. She couldn't imagine leaving her pup home all day. She'd go crazy missing her. Her mom could watch her, but Cynder was Avery's dog, not her mother's, though her mom was growing pretty attached to her granddog.

"She's fine, just like the thousand other times you've looked over here," Bobbi said with a smile.

"I miss her," Avery said, reaching over and scratching Cynder right behind the ears. Cynder's eyes half lifted as she stretched her tiny legs out and yawned before curling right back up in her little bed that was sitting on Bobbi's lap.

"You're going to make a dang fine mama one day," Bobbi said. "You've already fallen head over heels in love with this baby. Imagine how you'll feel about your own child."

Avery shook her head. "I don't think I'll be a mom. I love working too much. Kids take a lot of time," Avery said.

"Many people feel that way, but something happens to us women when our bellies start growing. Those maternal instincts kick in, and it's all over after that," Bobbi assured her.

"We'll see," Avery said

They continued chatting their entire drive up the corridor, stopping several times to grab a snack and walk Cynder. The closer they got to their new home, the more alive Avery began to feel.

She was constantly sad, missing Carl so much it hurt, but she hoped that would eventually fade. He'd called her three times the day before, and on the last call her finger had hovered over the green button on her phone. The need to hear his voice had been overwhelming.

As much as she wanted to let this man go, if she was still thinking of him in another thirty days, *and* he was still calling her, maybe it was more than she was trying to tell herself it was. Maybe it truly was love. If it had simply been lust, or was nothing more than a fling, wouldn't she be over the man by now? Logically, that made sense.

It was just past six in the evening when Avery made her final turn onto the island of Gig Harbor. She'd looked at images online, but they didn't do it justice. She was in awe as she moved down the street. Her mother apparently was as well.

"Wow, Avery, I think I'm going to love it here," Bobbi said.

Cynder woke up and put her paws on the door as she looked out the window. Bobbi kept a hand on her harness as she rolled down the window and let the puppy sniff the sweet sea air.

"Yeah, this is pretty amazing," Avery agreed. Concentrating, she followed her MapQuest directions to her rental home. She was looking forward to purchasing her first house, but she'd never do that online. She'd decided to rent until she figured out where she wanted to reside permanently. Surprisingly, housing prices on the island were a bit less than in the Bay area. She wasn't complaining about that — not one little bit. She had a massive amount of money saved, but she was afraid to spend too much of it. She never wanted to end up broke and homeless. She'd never forget her early years and how hard her mother had had to work to keep a roof over their heads.

She'd bought some nice shoes and several ridiculously priced bags, but a house was a whole different matter. That was hundreds of thousands of dollars versus thousands.

It didn't take them long to find the rental. It was a perfect little three-bedroom house right on the edge of the water, with a fenced yard and a great back porch. Best of all, it was in a quaint neighborhood.

She pulled into the driveway and shut off the engine off. She reached for Cynder, who immediately nuzzled her neck and licked her chin, making her giggle.

"You're such a sweet little girl," she praised. Then she looked her puppy in the eyes. "We're home."

The rest of the night was hard work as they unloaded the moving van. They didn't have a ton of things, as neither of them had too many collectables, and the place Avery had rented in SF had been furnished already. The place her mother had rented there had been filled with a lot of throw-away furniture.

Avery had found the rental in Gig Harbor the first week she'd decided to move there, then had ordered furniture to be delivered. Luckily, it was a key code entry, so she'd had it all set up, making life much easier for her mother and herself. But they still wanted all of the boxes in the house so she could take the van back the next day.

Her car hadn't been anything to write home about, so she'd sold it and figured she'd get a new one her first week in Seattle. She'd chosen to live on Gig Harbor because it's where the law office was, and it would be an easy walk to work. Her place was only a mile from her work. She'd even bought a doggy stroller with a rain hood so weather wouldn't be a problem. Her new life was about to begin.

By the time they got to bed that night, Avery was exhausted. However she was still lying there, unable to sleep. She'd had a hard time sleeping most nights because she thought of Carl from the time she climbed into bed until she finally conked out, and then the man had the gall to invade her dreams. She always woke up thinking of him too.

But it had been a long day, and eventually she was out.

The next morning went smoothly. She made it to the law office that only had two other attorneys: the owner of the firm, and a man who was about to retire, who showed her the ropes.

Just like that, she was sitting there by herself as she studied some cases. Her first week would be learning the firm, learning about the area, and getting her feet dipped into the water. It was so odd to go from a bustling firm to this tiny private practice. But since they were letting her bring her dog to work with her, she was quite pleased with it.

She might even find that she liked the less stressful work. She'd know in time. The secretary had been gone for twenty minutes when Avery heard the outside door open. She was about to get up to see if she could help whoever had come in but froze in her seat when a six-foot giant of a man filled her doorway.

She was speechless as she gazed into Carl's eyes. Was she imagining this? Had she fallen asleep at her desk, and this was nothing more than a dream? This hadn't been what she'd expected at all.

"Hello, Avery. You haven't answered my calls," he said as he moved into the room.

"I couldn't talk to you," she admitted.

He came closer. "Why is that? Is it because you feel nothing for me?"

Wow. He went straight to the point. She was unable to lie to him, but she didn't want to speak the truth.

"I don't need to answer that," she said as a compromise.

He smiled. She didn't understand why he appeared pleased by that comment.

"I need to file a lawsuit."

Avery looked at him with suspicion. What in the world was he talking about? Her heart was pounding, and it was taking all of her power to fight back her tears.

"And you ended up in this law firm of all of the places in the entire United States?" she asked, her brow raised.

"I heard the firm just hired a fancy lawyer from SF with a nearly perfect record of wins. I need to do it right," he assured her as he moved closer and leaned against her desk.

The smell of him was driving her insane. After over a month of not seeing him, she'd have thought some of his appeal would've evaporated. Nope. Not the case at all. If anything, the attraction had gone nuclear. She wanted to clear off her desk and have him take her right then and there.

"That fancy lawyer was a defense attorney. I'm now a prosecutor, so I don't think I'll be of service to you," she said. She was proud of the control in her voice. Maybe he wouldn't realize how much she was hurting, how much she'd missed him.

"Well, I think you're wrong. I think you can *definitely* help me. As a matter of fact, I think you're the *only* one who can," he said, his intense gaze boring into her. "You see, there's this woman who stole something from me, and I want it back."

She narrowed her eyes. She was trying to figure out where this was going. She had no idea. She was left with no choice but to play along, because she had no doubt he wasn't going anywhere until this conversation was over.

"What was taken from you?" she asked.

He moved around the desk, then knelt in front of her so they were eye to eye. He reached out and placed his hands on her legs, and all sorts of feelings shot through her. She couldn't have spoken if her life depended on it.

"This woman took my heart, my soul, and my desire. She holds all of it in her hands. I don't want my heart back, but I'd really like for us to merge our souls. I'd really like to share our desires. I'd really like to give this a real chance. You see, it's been over a month since I've seen this woman, and I can't stop thinking about her. I wake up in the morning, and her name is on my lips. I see something cool or funny, and she's the first person I want to share it with. I lie down at night and my arms are empty without her. And then, when I manage to fall asleep, she finally comes to me in my dreams, but then she evaporates like smoke when I wake again, feeling lost."

Tears flowed down Avery's cheeks as Carl said those words. He looked her in the eyes, unafraid to be vulnerable, unafraid to risk breaking his heart.

And her walls came crashing down. She was finally able to admit she loved him. She didn't care about the hows and whys. She just cared that she loved him.

"I love you," she said. It was odd. She'd said those words to only two other people her entire life — her mother and her uncle. And now they easily rolled off of her tongue. "I love you," she said again.

The smile that lit his face was so bright it could've led a boat in through a storm on a foggy night. He pulled at her, bringing her out of her chair and straight into his lap, his arms wrapped tightly around her.

"I love you, Avery," he said. "I've missed you. And I'm more than happy you chose to come here."

She paused as he was about to kiss her, her brows furrowing. "What do you mean?" she asked.

"What do you mean, what do I mean?" he responded. He looked just as confused as she felt.

"Do you live here?" she asked. She'd assumed he'd found her, that he'd traveled to her.

"Yes, well, about an hour from here," he told her.

"Did you have anything to do with my job?"

He looked truly perplexed. "No. How would I have any influence over a law firm?" he questioned.

"How is it that we both ended up in the same place?" she asked.

He smiled again, that halo of light engulfing her. "I call it fate," he said.

Maybe he was right. He leaned in and *finally* kissed her, and she melted against him. They might've forgotten where they were if they wouldn't have felt little claws scratching at them and heard a whimper.

Carl pulled away and looked down, then he grinned as he picked Cynder up. "Who is this?"

Avery's heart grew even fuller as her sweet baby nuzzled Carl, who seemed to be enamored by her dog.

"This is Cynder. I just adopted her," she said. They'd never have a chance if he wasn't an animal lover. She hadn't known she wanted to be a pet mom until she'd made the decision, but now she knew nothing would keep her apart from her baby.

"I've always loved French bulldogs. My mom had a few when I was growing up," he said.

And just like that, Cynder and Carl were buddies.

The three of them were pressed together, sitting on the floor next to her desk, and Avery felt better than she had in a very long time.

"What happens now?" she asked.

He smiled again as he looked into her eyes, lifting his free hand and cupping her cheek.

"What happens now is the real adventure begins."

He kissed her again, and she knew for certain he was right. She was starting over with a new life, a new home, a new pet, and a new love. It might not actually get better than this right here, right now.

Maybe she'd even get a fairy-tale ending. She'd wait until later and see if a falling star lit up the sky. She could always make a wish . . . and hope all of her dreams came true.

Epilogue

The table was a sight to behold. Five men sat there — five men who inspired awe, trust . . . and fear, if you were on the wrong side of the law. Though they weren't wearing badges, they were formidable. You could look at them together, and know they weren't men you wanted to cross. Their very demeanor gave a sense of security to those who needed safety — and a sense of fear to those up to no good.

The former Special Forces men had spent the entire night staking out a group they suspected as gang members. It was early in the morning, and they were wired and hungry.

Jon Eisenhart, aka Eyes; Carl Schwartz, aka Sleep; Tyrell Rice, aka Smoke; Steve Bregon, aka Brackish; and Hendrick Meeks, aka Green, sat at the all-night diner on an off-the-beaten-path road far from the city. They had to be careful where they came together in public. They didn't want their covers, which had been so beautifully created, to be blown.

This was their first time together outside of their operation base. They'd been in Seattle for two months, and the work was tolling. It certainly wasn't for the average man. But these men weren't ordinary. They'd been trained to go for days, weeks, even months without time off. They could last that long on only hours of sleep, with little food and minimal direction. Once they got an assignment, they were ready to go. They knew how to adjust to a new situation, and they wouldn't stop until their mission was complete. They'd each proven that time and time again.

In their two months of operation, they'd already tracked a dangerous high level ringleader. He'd killed an unknown number of men, women, and children. He was soulless, making him the worst kind of enemy. He didn't care if he died — but he'd damn well take down as many as he could on his way out.

That man's niece was a waitress at this diner they'd chosen to eat at.

She was thirty-two and had no clue her family was involved in the underworld. That made her an asset. She might give them information without a clue of what she was revealing. They knew if her uncle figured out she was a potential threat to his operation, he'd eliminate her, so they had to proceed with caution. Enough innocent people had been killed — they wouldn't be the cause of another death.

Brackish grinned as she approached, her step visibly catching as she spotted them sitting there. He watched her hand flutter up to her hair as she attempted to smooth her messy bun. He was used to women having that reaction to him. With all of them sitting together, it had to be a bit intimidating.

"Good morning," she said in a breathy voice. "I can get . . . um . . . I mean, can I get you . . ." She stopped speaking as her lips clamped together and her cheeks flushed. Her chest pushed out as she sucked in a deep breath and pushed her shoulders back.

Brackish liked her. She had spunk and courage, and she wasn't going to let her nerves get the better of her.

"Sorry about that," she said with a chuckle. "It's been a long night. I'm Erin, your waitress this morning. Would you like something to drink?"

There were circles beneath her eyes, making it obvious she worked long hours. That confirmed the men's belief that she wasn't involved in her uncle's world. If she was, there was no way she'd be busting her ass night after night at this diner; she'd take a free handout from her criminal family.

Each of them had spent weeks at a time with dark circles. They knew what it was like to feel utter exhaustion — and then push their way through it. They might each have millions in their bank accounts, but they'd never be okay sitting on their asses. They believed in a strong work ethic and wouldn't be satisfied with anything other than doing their very best.

The silence had gone too long and Erin shifted on her feet as she looked down at the pad in her trembling fingers. Brackish took mercy on her . . . sort of.

"No need to apologize, beautiful. These guys are idiots. They make my brain cells shrink when I'm around them, and I stutter too," he told her with a wink as she looked at him, her blush deepening.

He knew those words would push the men into action.

"Dream on," Sleep said as the others grunted and rolled their eyes.

"We're not the only customers, and I'm starving, so let's get this show on the road," Smoke said to his tablemates. "I want a huge cup of black coffee, two eggs over easy on top of a large mound of hashbrowns, double order of bacon and sausage, wheat toast . . . and . . . hmm . . . a cinnamon roll heated with a slab of butter on top."

"Ditto," said Green.

"Um, we have pretty oversized portions. Are you sure you want a double order of anything?" Erin asked. It was more than obvious there wasn't an ounce of fat on any of the men, so Brackish was sure she was wondering how in the world at least two of them could eat that much food.

"We work hard and have to refuel," Brackish told her.

Her eyes widened a bit as she jotted on her pad. They finished their order, all of them ordering enough food for ten men. They were going to make the tired cook earn his money.

"Do you want the sweets with your coffee?" she asked.

"That would be great, sugar," Green said.

"Okay, it might take a little longer than normal for your meals so I'll get the coffee and rolls out quick." She turned and walked away.

The view from behind was even more appealing than the first sight of her. Brackish was more than impressed with the sway of her hips and the swell of her backside. Maybe it had been too long since he'd had a woman because he was thinking of some kinky things the two of them could get up to in the backroom of the diner.

"Hey, Erin," Green called out as she stepped up to the window of the kitchen.

Brackish's gaze flew to Green, and he glared, trying to stop him. Dammit, he knew better than to give a woman a look like what he'd been giving Erin. He couldn't do that around this group of men.

She looked back at their table, not quite connecting with any of their eyes. Damn, they had her flustered. Brackish liked her flustered — she was sexy as hell with color in her cheeks and her chest pushing in and out as she breathed a bit heavily.

"My buddy here wants to know if you're dating anyone," Green said, giving her his best smile.

That flush in her cheeks heated up, turning an even more appealing shade of pink. Damn, Brackish could picture her lying beneath him, her mouth open in a pant, her lips wet, her body ready . . .

Whoa, those thoughts had to stop right now! He shifted in his seat. He wasn't going to be able to walk from this place if he didn't get it under control . . . not without a very embarrassing display of how much he was turned on.

"Um . . . no, I don't have a boyfriend," she finally said before she clamped her lips together, turned away, and practically ran through the saloon style doors into the back of the diner.

"Really, Green?" Brackish hissed at the man who was quickly becoming one of his best friends. They couldn't do this job together without a tight bond forming, but . . .

"I figured I'd give you a helping hand since you were practically panting as you stripped her with your eyes. I wasn't the one being oggled, yet *I* feel violated," Green said with a laugh.

"She certainly is fine," Smoke said. All of the men turned toward the door she'd disappeared through to see if they could catch another glimpse.

"I can find my own dates, and right now we have a job to do. She's the niece," Brackish said in a hushed whisper.

"Nah, she's not a part of it. That's clear. Besides, we can have a little fun while we work. It relieves stress, and there are many good ways to relieve some tension at the end of the day," Sleep said.

"There are some good ways to relieve stress in the morning, too, so the day starts out right," Smoke added.

All of the men nodded. It had been a while for each of them . . . well, all of them except Sleep, who was smiling a hell of a lot more these days now that his woman had shown up.

Brackish knew it wouldn't help to keep protesting. They would simply become more determined to either one-up him or embarrass him, which was virtually impossible to do.

"Ignore these heathens, and go for it if you want," Eyes said.
The entire team knew Eyes was a good leader. He knew when it was time to work and when it was time to blow off steam. He also knew that all work and no play didn't do any of them any good. And they *all* respected him.

"Alright, all of your opinions are noted. Now, can we please get back to work?" Brackish asked.

"No way!" Green said. Brackish had to hold back a sigh.

"We *are* at a diner," Sleep said with a wicked grin. Brackish rolled his eyes, knowing something from the gutters was coming. "Why don't you go on back to the kitchen and check if her melons are ripe. She could check to see if your sausage is hard and salty enough. I mean, *we* all know it's expired, short, and shriveled." Sleep was leaning against the wall laughing as he finished, quite amused with himself.

Brackish sat there as each of the men made a few food analogies, the laughter growing louder as the comparisons became more and more obscene. But he refused to show a reaction.

A few of the tables near them overheard, and though they attempted to hold in their laughter, it slipped out. Brackish inwardly groaned. These men didn't need any further encouragement to continue.

Erin returned with a tray loaded with coffee and sweets and nearly dropped it when all five pairs of eyes zeroed in on her. She quickly looked back at the tray as she visibly took a deep breath.

"What's so amusing?" she asked, pulling herself together quickly this time as she began placing their coffee and plates in front of them. She leaned over Brackish to place Smoke's cinnamon roll in front of him, and Brackish got a nice view of her appealing cleavage, making his fingers itch, along with a whiff of her sweet vanilla scent that made him want to take a bite out of her instead of his roll.

"Erin," Green said, "My buddy, Ben, is trying to figure out how to ask you out, and he's so shy he can't come up with a good pick-up line, so we're trying to help him."

Brackish wanted to punch Green right in his smug mouth. Even as they were having a good time, the men were always on. Green had used his alias name, which they all had to do when meeting anyone new.

Brackish met Erin's eyes, noting the green flecks in the large blue gaze. She was stunning with a shy, sweet quality about her that made him even more attracted. He held out a hand. "I'm truly sorry about my friends, Erin. It's a pleasure to meet you."

Erin smiled, this time a genuine one that lit up her face. She took his hand and shook. He noted it was a firm handshake, impressing him even more. The spark of electricity that flowed between them was also noted. She hadn't missed it either, if pulling her fingers away and looking at them was any indication. Her smile faltered, but didn't fade away fully.

"Doesn't it say more about you that you're choosing to hang out with such men than it says about them?" she asked with a smirk and a twinkle in her eyes.

After the shock of her words, the table erupted again in a round of laughter.

"Dang, I like you," Smoke said. "I was thinking you were all shy and stuff, but you can hold your own."

"I work at a diner; all sorts of characters come through these doors. I might be thrown off kilter sometimes, but I usually recover," she told Smoke with a wink.

"Then are you gonna have mercy on our buddy and ask him out on a date?" Green asked.

Before Brackish could punch his friend, or before Erin could respond, another man in the diner spoke up — a very stupid move on his part.

"You dudes do realize there are other people in this place, right?" the man sitting at the far end of the diner, who appeared to be around forty, snapped out. "The rest of us aren't as amused by you this early in the morning, and we'd like some attention from the pretty little waitress too. Come on over here, baby doll, and I'll show you how a real man gets a woman as hot as you, and then I'll tell you exactly what I plan to do once you're sitting on my lap."

The team's reaction was like an flipping a switch. All five men's smiles fell. They turned and looked at the man, who visibly seemed to shrink.

Power.

It was all about power. Some men had it and some didn't. The man, who'd obviously been drinking too much and had a big loud mouth, would be the unfortunate one to find out what real power was if he didn't shut up.

It took less than three seconds for the five men looking at one another to nod and silently agree who'd handle the matter.

Smoke stood.

"Wait . . ." Erin began. But Eyes reached out and touched her arm, nodding. She seemed to understand without any words being spoken. She shifted, but didn't protest further.

It only took a few large strides for Smoke to reach the man's table. Towering over him at six four, Eyes knew the sight he made to the man he was facing . . . and to the other diners, whose attention was all on him.

He pulled out the chair across from the man and slowly sat, his eyes not breaking contact. Smoke wasn't riled, wasn't even annoyed. He was making a point.

"First, I apologize if my friends and I have disturbed your dining experience. That's why my friend is currently paying Erin for your meal and adding a nice tip, which I'm sure you would've forgotten. That means your meal is now over. There's a real difference between having a bit of fun and sending the message you just sent to Erin. Your presence is no longer acceptable at this diner — today, or any day moving forward."

The guy's mouth opened and closed as his eyes narrowed. He was just drunk enough to be an idiot. Smoke hoped that didn't happen. He didn't relish fighting — not that it would be a fight. But this man was no challenge; having to put him in his place was too easy. On the other hand, men like him took pleasure in attacking people weaker than they were, so it might do the guy some good to get knocked down.

Before the guy could open his mouth, Smoke leaned forward, his face a mask of power, his eyes showing he didn't know the meaning of backing down.

"I encourage you to think before you say a word. The option I gave you involves zero violence. My next option involves more pain than you've ever known possible. If you want to open door number two, it's not locked. I strongly encourage you to choose door number one."

He leaned back after speaking, appearing to be completely relaxed, as if he didn't have a care in the world — he didn't where this man was concerned. He never broke eye contact.

The man stared at Smoke for several tense seconds before glancing over to the table where the other men sat. He looked back at Smoke . . . and his shoulders slumped as his brain cells fired to life. If the man had consumed a few more tequilas and zero food, there might've been a different outcome.

Without uttering a word, he stood, keeping his head down as he walked to the door and stepped outside.

Smoke rose and went back to the table. The entire diner was silent as heads whipped from Smoke to the door, then to the table full of men, who were once again smiling. Green spoke as if the past several minutes had never happened.

"So, Erin, where are you and Ben going for your first date?" he asked. He picked up his fork and cut a large piece of cinnamon roll, popping it into his mouth and chewing before letting out a satisfied sigh. "Delicious!"

Erin's eyes were wide as she looked at each of the men. It might be disconcerting to the average person to switch emotions so quickly, but it was nothing new to any of the men at the table. As quickly as they'd gone into serious mode, they were right back to smiles and jokes.

Erin stood there, obviously unsure of what to do. But when she looked at Brackish again there was a look of intrigue and interest in her eyes. He might be taking the girl out after all. She just might be worth pursuing . . .

***

Joseph Anderson leaned back in the lounge chair, holding a glass of scotch in one hand, and a fine Partagus Series P No. 2 cigar in the other. He looked out at the water lapping against the shore as boats bobbed along the bay with their fishing poles dipping and skis jumping.

Sherman Armstrong turned to his friend, a serious look on his face. He took a sip of his own glass of scotch before speaking.

"How are you holding up, Joseph?"

Sherman had been a great friend for many years. Joseph considered Sherman's nephews his own. He'd watched those boys grow up, grieved as they'd lost their father, prayed as they'd fallen into despair, then cheered as they'd grown into fine young men. He might've had a hand in helping their uncle lead them in the right direction by finding their wives.

"It's been a rough few months," Joseph admitted. He took another pull on his fine cigar. "But Katherine is home, and she's positive. I'm driving her crazy with all of my worrying. I'm here today because she kicked me out of the house. She told me if I come home earlier than four, she's going to change the locks."

Sherman chuckled as Joseph's brow went down and his lips pursed.

"No one doubts your love for your wife, Joseph. Everyone who loves you knows you *might* also be a little overwhelming at times. I'm sure she simply needs a few minutes to herself."

"I just hate to be away from her," Joseph said. "I want to rush back home. What if something happens?"

"She's strong, Joseph. And needing a little time to process all she's been through isn't a reflection of how she feels, but a testament to who she is. She *will* lean on you, but she also needs to stand on her own two feet. We want to smother the people we love, but sometimes we do it to the point they can't breathe. You're a great man, and you'll go through this journey together."

"She's insisting I keep working on the veterans center and making me promise her we'll still live our lives normally while she goes through these treatments," Joseph said.

"How long will it take?" Sherman asked.

Joseph sighed, sipping on his drink again. "I don't know. But no matter how long it takes, we'll push through it. Katherine says if we lie down in defeat, or pause our lives, we'll regret it. She's making me promise we'll live each day as if there is no cancer, as if we're still in our twenties, thinking we're immortal. I'm not sure I can do that, but I can't refuse her anything, so I'll put a smile on my face, and I'll give it my best effort. There's nothing I won't give my wife, nothing I won't do for her."

"We all know that," Sherman said. "We've had many years together. I know our bodies are a bit older, and we might move slightly slower, but our minds are sharp, and we've got a lot of years to go."

"Yes we do, my friend," Joseph agreed.

"And it does feel pretty good to meddle again," Sherman reminded him.

Those words made Joseph smile. "Yes, getting that job for Avery was quite fun. I guess it does help to do some things that have nothing to do with sickness and grief," Joseph admitted.

"As soon as Chad told us what was happening with Carl, I was rubbing my hands together. I love life, but sometimes I get a little bored. My nephews are so happy, which is wonderful, but I have to admit I like playing cupid."

"I'm glad I was able to bring you into this project. It's coming along very nicely. I appreciate you donating to the cause," Joseph told him.

"I would've been offended if you hadn't talked to me about it. You know how much I respect the military and the resources out there that keep us safe. But I'm also very aware that if we sit back and watch as injustices happen in this world, we have to be willing to accept the consequences that occur because we did nothing. I have too many loved ones to watch this country fall into chaos. I have high hopes for this team," Sherman said.

"Me too," Joseph said. "Some fine men have stepped up to the plate. And it's only going to grow. Chad has some exceptional women he's secretly vetting, as well. I think the sky truly is the limit."

"What comes next?" Sherman asked. He sat up and looked at Joseph, his eyes bright, a youthful glow in his cheeks.

This time when Joseph smiled, it was genuine. There was a little bit of his natural sparkle lighting his eyes. He looked around, even though he already knew nobody was near. Then he leaned forward.

"Let me tell you all about it . . .

Note From Author Including Anderson World Read Order

If you enjoyed this new spin-off from Melody Anne's first series, *The Billionaire Bachelors,* then you can catch up on all of these characters you're going to see in and out of the series in the books listed below. Any of these series can be read alone, but it's also a lot of fun to read them in somewhat of an order. Each family has their own unique dynamic, and Joseph is the key character who pulls them all together. His meddling knows no bounds.

Also a side note from me . . . The Andersons originally began as a three book series when I started my writing career. I fell in love with Joseph and the Anderson dynamic. I went on to write other series, but I kept bringing Joseph along, wanting to take him with me to all of the worlds I was creating. So in came his twin brother George, who just happens to be named after one of my favorite uncles. He lived in Cordova, AK, where I spent a summer when I was sixteen, which is why I sent my couple there in *Blackmailing the Billionaire*. I loved that town. He moved to Anchorage, and I can't wait to go there again and do some fishing, which I've become addicted to.

At the end of book seven of the Andersons, I thought it was finished once again. Then a fan sent me an email saying they'd had a dream that Joseph and George were staring at a newspaper and saw a man who looked just like them. I was in love with the idea of a stolen baby plot. So in came Richard, who is another favorite uncle of mine. Richard, their triplet, was stolen at birth. Back when Katherine had her babies, fathers weren't often in the delivery room, and the doctor figured she already had two babies and wouldn't miss a third. So in came five more kids for Joseph and George to play cupid with.

At the end of that story, Joseph went on to meddle in the lives of his friends' children, so his legacy has continued to grow. I left openings in many of my books because I can never truly say those magical words *the end*. A new branch of Andersons are found in my Montlake series, *Anderson Billionaires*.

I storyboarded ideas with friends, and this newest spin-off happened: *Anderson Black*

Ops. This series is so much fun because I'm co-writing it. I have a friend who knows the world of black ops, so he's giving me strong outlines and chapters for these new men we've created in this fun new world. We have a lot of ideas for where this will all lead.

I'm getting a lot of emails asking about the order to read my books. I've created so many stories at this point even I'm a little lost on the order, but I'm going to list it as best I can by staying in the right timeframe. The newest, of course, are easiest to keep track of, but since I bring in so many other series in the middle of writing these books, it does get a bit confusing.

So here we go. And as always, I love feedback from you. After all, I can't do this job, can't write these fantastic stories, and can't live in my dream world without your support. You make the magic happen. You give me a voice to put on paper, and you make my dreams come true. If the order is at all messed up, then please let me know and we'll adjust.

I work with a fantastic team, and we're constantly changing and fixing things. It's amazing how easily we can fix things in this digital world we now have. Before the world of epublishing, if there was a mistake, it couldn't get fixed until the next set of books were printed. Now, it's just a few hits on the keyboard, and voilà, we're good to go again.

Thank you so much for your support. I hope you are well, are enjoying these stories, and are making magic happen in this crazy world we've found ourselves in in the parallel universe some call 2020.

Read Order for The Anderson Empire

Billionaire Bachelors

1. The Billionaire Wins the Game
2. The Billionaire's Dance
3. The Billionaire Falls
4. The Billionaire's Marriage Proposal
5. Blackmailing the Billionaire
6. Runaway Heiress
7. The Billionaire's Final Stand
8. Unexpected Treasure
9. Hidden Treasure
10. Holiday Treasure
11. Priceless Treasure
12. The Ultimate Treasure

Now, you can read the Tycoon Series, which Joseph's in, but only one of the books is truly relevant to the continuation of the Anderson's stories. I'll list all of the Tycoon books here, but highlight Damien's story, which will come up later on in a twist for *The Billionaire* Andersons listed below.

Billionaire Bachelors

Book One: The Tycoon's Revenge
Book Two: The Tycoon's Vacation
Book Three: The Tycoon's Proposal
13. Book Four: The Tycoon's Secret
Book Five: The lost Tycoon
Book Six: Rescue me

And here we go again, with another insert. So, Joseph next appears in my Heroes Series. We have a visit from *Dr. Spence Whitman* in this book you've just read, which is in this series. You can read this series next to know Spence's story, but you won't be lost if you don't. So I'll list the entire series here, and again highlight the story that has Spence in it, adding it to the list. All of these books can stand alone, but I do bring my characters in and out of most of my series because I can't let them go. So if you read *Her Hometown Hero*, it's a complete story, but the brothers will all be throughout it.

Heroes Series

Pre-Book: Safe in his arms (in an Anthology called *Baby it's Cold Outside*)
Book One: Her Unexpected Hero
Book Two: Who I am with you
14. Book Three: Her Hometown Hero
Book Four: Following Her
Book Five: Her Forever Hero

And now, we come to Sherman, who will play a big roll in this series. Sherman's another of those characters I seriously love! When I came up with Bobbi, Avery's mother, I knew right then and there, she was going to be a match for Sherman. By the way, Bobbi is named after my best friend's mother, who I absolutely adore! She mirrors some of her character traits too, and we'll be seeing a lot more of her. In real life she's married to Hal, who happens to be a fantastic man.

After I wrote the Bobbi character, I was telling the real Bobbi what she's saying and doing, and I might've made her blush. Hal's okay with it though. If he's gonna lose his wife, at least it's to Sherman, who happens to be a pretty great guy. We just spent a long weekend at their house in Northern Cali, and had a refreshing, fantastic time. But I was also putting them under the microscope for my upcoming stories. I use real life in my books all of the time because family events are definitely story worthy. So, Bobbi, beware because I'm gonna have fun with this character.

I list the Billionaire Aviators next, but don't number them because you don't have to read these to read all the rest, but if you want to get to know Sherman, then I'd dive on in. This series was one of my fav to write, because I love the characters, love the journey, and I was really growing in my writing at this point, getting a little more courageous with what I was doing within my fantasy worlds.

Billionaire Aviators
Book One: Turbulent Intentions
Book Two: Turbulent Desires
Book Three: Turbulent Waters
Book Four: Turbulent Intrigue

Joseph and other Andersons appear in my Undercover Billionaire world, where I started adding more suspense into my writing. Some of these characters will pop in and out of this world as well, because, like I said, I love to bring these characters into each world. So you can read this series, but again, won't be lost if you don't, so I won't number them.

On a side note. *Owen* is my *favorite* book I've ever written. I lost my dad in 2018, and it nearly killed me. I write men like Joseph, George, Sherman, and more because I'm a daddy's girl, through and through. He raised me with so much more love than I can even begin to explain, and he also taught me how to be independent and strong. He's the reason I'm an author, the reason I'm so strong, and the reason I still cry because I miss him so much.

He LOVED UFO stories, and when all of the news broke that they were releasing the government files on UFOs, my heart was breaking again, because he would've been so excited and absolutely glued to the internet. I know he's up in Heaven laughing because he has all of the answers now, but I sure would love him to be here with me so we could talk and wonder, and laugh . . . and so his arms could be wrapped around me.

My heroine loses her dad in Owen, which I'd begun writing before I lost my dad. I had to stop, and when I came back to the book, I cried my way through a lot of it. A lot of the lines she uses when she's talking about her father were things I asked and said. I was so lost for a long time after losing him. Writing Owen helped me heal. My heart will never be truly full again, but my dad loved me, and I love him, and I know he'd kick my butt if I didn't live my life with love, laughter, and triumph. He raised me to be a powerful woman, and I won't dishonor him by being anything less than that. So I'm gonna highlight Owen, not because it's needed for the Andersons, but because it's needed for my soul. ☺

Undercover Billionaires

Book One: Kian
Book Two: Arden
Book Three: Owen
Book Four: Declan

Now it gets a bit more confusing as I'm finishing out my Montlake series at the same time as we're writing *The Anderson Black Ops* series, so you get to go back and forth a bit if you want to stay exactly in the timeline. We're finally making it to the end . . . for now. But I guess I'll have to stay on top of this because I have no doubt that the Anderson world will continue to grow and grow and grow, even as I take time to visit other worlds in between. Thank you again for all you do. I hope you fall in love with these characters over and over again, just as I do each time I dive back into the Anderson Universe.

The Billionaire Andersons

15. Book One: Finn
16. Book Two: Noah

Anderson Black Ops

17. Book One: Shadows

The Billionaire Andersons

18. Book Three: Brandon (Oct 20, 2020)

Anderson Black Ops

19. Book Two (November 2020)

The Billionaire Andersons

20. Book Four: Crew (coming December 2020)
21. Book Five: Hudson (Coming Jan 2021)

Anderson Black Ops

22. Book Three (Coming Feb 2021)
23. Book Four (Coming March 2021)
24. Book Five (Coming April 2021)

Thank you again for reading my stories. I couldn't do it without you. Much love forever.

Melody Anne

Made in the USA
Monee, IL
08 September 2020